SPRING
BAMBOO

SPRING BAMBOO

A COLLECTION OF

▲　　　▲　　　▲

CONTEMPORARY

▲　　　▲　　　▲

CHINESE

▲　　　▲　　　▲

SHORT STORIES

COMPILED AND TRANSLATED BY

JEANNE TAI

WITH A FOREWORD BY BETTE BAO LORD
AND AN INTRODUCTION BY LEO OU-FAN LEE

RANDOM HOUSE

NEW YORK

Library of Congress Cataloging-in-Publication Data
Spring bamboo.
A collection of contemporary short stories by
ten writers, translated from Chinese.
1. Short stories, Chinese—Translations into
English. 2. Short stories, English—Translations
from Chinese. 3. Chinese fiction—20th century—
Translations into English. 4. English fiction—20th
century—Translations from Chinese. I. Tai, Jeanne.
PL2658.E8N56 1989 895.1'301'08 88-42672
ISBN 0-394-56582-7

Manufactured in the United States of America
24689753
First Edition

An age-old Chinese expression compares
a period of prodigious growth
to the springtime phenomenon of
bamboo sprouts shooting up after the rains.

This collection is a reflection of,
and is dedicated to,
the vibrant regeneration of literary fiction
that has been taking place in China
over the past four or five years.

FOREWORD BY BETTE BAO LORD

China, the country that invented printing, has in its long history both revered the written word and reviled it. In a land where custom dictated that paper ennobled by writing should not be disrespectfully thrown away, books that had been studied for centuries were also burned. These two seemingly contrary phenomena reveal one reality: that Chinese regard writing, be it to inspire or to incite, as a uniquely powerful weapon. No wonder the authorities have a love-hate relationship with writers. No wonder writers fear either embrace.

Recently, since Deng Xiaoping has championed reforms and the opening to the outside world, writers, like the rest of society, have benefited. Where once protagonists in stories could not betray human frailties, however insignificant, where once stories could not deviate from the dictates of party policy, however unintentionally, there is now considerable latitude in creating characters and themes.

This collection of short stories by some of China's foremost writers of this reform generation reflect above all the authors' concerns. I heartily welcome such individuality of style and substance. Without it, Chinese writings cannot hope to win international audiences. With it, the world will have the pleasure of seeing China as Chinese do.

CONTENTS

INTRODUCTION BY LEO OU-FAN LEE

At first blush, the stories included in this collection seem rather "un-Chinese": There is no trace of revolutionary ideology, no heavy-handed political propaganda, not even a stiff dose of moral didacticism—none of those things that the sophisticated Western reader finds so unpalatable, that have made literature from the People's Republic of China at best (in the delicate euphemism of a prominent American writer) an "acquired taste."

Yet those who have followed developments on the Chinese literary scene in the past several years will have no trouble recognizing in this very absence of ideology and politics one of the most distinctive attributes of the group of younger writers who have come to prominence on that scene. For, diverse as these writers are in background, concerns and writing style, they are all readily distinguishable by their refusal to embrace the uncritical ideological content (whether socialist, Maoist, Confucian, or some combination thereof) and the moralizing, exhortatory tone so characteristic of the older generation of writers.

The significance of this change can scarcely be underestimated, for what is happening here is not only the emergence of a new literary style but also a thoroughgoing attempt to break away from the decades-old tradition of realism in modern Chinese literature and, more fundamentally, to assail the sacrosanct view that artistic creativity must be used in the service of some overarching political purpose. To a Western reader these goals, especially the latter, may seem rather ordinary. In mainland China, however, that battle has just begun.

To appreciate the enormity of this undertaking, one must look back beyond the Cultural Revolution, beyond even the Chinese Communist Party's ascension to power in 1949. That event enabled the Party to establish that the only acceptable purpose of art was to serve the people and the only acceptable mode of artistic expression was socialist realism, but in fact the roots of those two precepts go back almost to the turn of the century. Growing up in the turbulent matrix of a society and a nation undergoing rapid change and almost constant turmoil, modern Chinese literature has been characterized from the beginning by a preoccupation with China's multitude of pressing political, economic, and cultural problems—a preoccupation reflected not only in the choice of subject matter by modern Chinese writers but also in how and why they wrote. Driven by an acute historical consciousness (some would call it "ideology") and a keen sense of mission, most of these writers saw the main function of creative writing, including fiction, to be the truthful depiction of the social reality of the times, in order to hasten the destruction of the ancient and decrepit order so that out of its ashes a new China could be created. It is hardly surprising, then, that realism was the dominant school in most of the arts—long before it became the official doctrine of socialist realism after 1949. Nor is it surprising that the works of modern Chinese writers so often evince, if not an overtly political message, at least a strong moralizing and didactic tendency.

With the exception of a few notable writers, this ideological stance has dominated the Chinese literary imagination ever since the May Fourth Movement of 1917–23 (the cultural watershed generally considered to mark the emergence of modern Chinese literature), culminating in its elevation by the Communist Party to the status of official dogma. At the height (or the depth) of the Cultural Revolution of 1966–76, this dogma took the extreme form of the suppression of all artistic creativity, except for a few officially sanctioned "model" operas and ballets and fiction that depicted only victorious "proletarian heroes" in their resolute battles against scoundrels of every stripe in this or that "two-line struggle."

After the Cultural Revolution ended, the first writings to appear in print focused on the effects of the violence and mass hysteria unleashed during that tumultuous period. While this so-called scar literature no doubt provided a measure of cathartic relief to a nation still emerging from psychic shock, it was of more interest as sociology than as literature.

Then, about five years ago, the first glimmerings of a new literary movement appeared. Known as the *xungen* ("searching for roots") school, the young writers identified with this movement—all of whom have come to maturity during or after the Cultural Revolution—deliberately eschewed the traditional strictures of socialist realism in order to explore what they believed to be the larger reality that lay beneath or beyond the confines of politics and ideology. The "roots" they were searching for were not so much personal and familial as they were cultural and historical. As A Cheng, author of "The Tree Stump" and one of the earliest spokesmen of this movement, has argued, the strands of Chinese culture have been so severely ruptured by the ideological campaigns of recent decades, and by the Cultural Revolution in particular, that the younger generation has been cut off from its cultural roots and must go in search of them in order to reestablish the continuity of Chinese culture and civilization.

The impulse behind this literary movement has also given rise to a much broader movement of "cultural self-reflection" *(wenhua fansi)*, a critical reexamination of all aspects of Chinese culture and history by artists and intellectuals in various fields of endeavor. In both cases the impetus has come from the cataclysmic upheavals wrought by the Cultural Revolution, which may well turn out to be as significant a cultural watershed as the May Fourth Movement, if not more so. For the Great Proletarian Cultural Revolution not only reduced the new Socialist China created in 1949 to rubble, it also left the generation that grew up idolizing Chairman Mao and accepting unquestioningly every one of his dictates utterly disillusioned by their own bitter, often devastating experiences during those years of upheaval. It is out of this acute sense of void that these writers, artists, and intellectuals feel compelled to redefine their own culture as they seek to redefine themselves, even while the Party, recognizing the heresy inherent in this critical reexamination of every facet of Chinese society, launches one futile effort after another to contain these "deviationist" tendencies. But these artists and intellectuals have disdained any direct altercation in the political arena and have instead "retreated" into the realm of culture, where through discourse and artistic expression they can engage in the creation and exploration of a reality beyond the reach of political ideology. In the process they have managed to stand on its head Mao's dictum to put "politics in command."

But these new writings, exemplified by the stories in this collection, are notable not just for the striking absence of ideology and politics, but also for their ambitious attempts to explore new idioms and to experiment with plot, characterization, and language. In searching for their roots, these young writers have rediscovered the wealth of myth and folklore—long disdained as "feudal" remnants to be eradicated—not only in the dominant Han culture but also, perhaps especially, in the minority cultures in the border regions. In part this fascination with the more exotic regions and cultures of

China stems from the critical reexamination of, and resulting dissatisfaction with, the dominant Han culture, but it is also due to the fact that many of these writers either hail from these regions (for example, Zheng Wanlong, from the Xing'an mountains in Heilongjiang province, and Zhaxi Dawa from Tibet) or spent a considerable part of their youth in these areas as a result of the movement during the Cultural Revolution to send educated young people to the countryside (for instance, A Cheng in Yunnan and Han Shaogong in the hinterlands of Hunan).

Many of these writers have also been inspired by the writings from Latin America, particularly those of Gabriel García Márquez, whose *One Hundred Years of Solitude* served almost as a model for the possibilities of combining myth with reality. For instance, in Zhaxi Dawa's "Souls Tied to the Knots on a Leather Cord," the fictional world is also a carefully wrought metaphor for the search for a mythic past, a story within a larger allegorical story. In several other works in this volume—for instance, "Clock," "The Homecoming," "Like a Banjo String," and "The Nine Palaces"—the story is set in a seemingly remote landscape, where myth and reality are so interwoven as to create a universe unconnected to a specific time and place, yet somehow strangely familiar. For these writers, it seems, this visionary landscape represents not only their own psychic universe but also a more truthful depiction of a China, at once ancient and modern, that has been rediscovered and refracted through some fresh artistic lenses.

Beyond this common preoccupation with rediscovering their cultural roots, these writers speak in remarkably different and distinctly individual voices. Certain themes do recur in these stories: a deeply felt sense of loss, a ceaseless yearning for an unattainable goal, and a bemused resignation in the face of life's vicissitudes. But there is no single formula, no standard plot and stock characters, not even a common style. While the settings and the sensibilities are authentically Chinese, the stories hold resonance for a much broader audience. For example, Li Zhongxiang of "Looking For Fun" could be Everyman trying to come to terms with an intractable world, Shaggy Hair of "The Nine Palaces" is the restless outsider striving to find a place where he can be at peace, and the crotchety old woman in "Grandma Qi" who lives only in her vivid memories of an idealized past is a character familiar to all of us.

It may be somewhat premature to comment in detail on the craftsmanship of these young writers, as these works mark only the beginning, however daring, of a new artistic endeavor. Many of them are still developing a fictional style appropriate to their new vision and imagination. Young and ambitious, unencumbered by the strictures of convention, they paint in broad strokes, playing with colors and perspectives; rarely do they cast an introspective eye on the inner matrices of the human psyche, as in Li Tuo's "Grandma Qi." Yet already one can find some fine writing marked by a fresh approach to language and imagery. In Mo Yan's "Dry Creek," for instance, not only is the eerie beauty of the countryside depicted with sensuous lyricism, but even the violence and brutality of rural life are rendered in strangely alluring imagery. In "The Homecoming," Han Shaogong has experimented with the use of archaic words and phrases, as if he wished to juxtapose their ageless purity against the mumbo jumbo of Maoist slogans and revolutionary jargon, in order to cleanse the language of its accretions of ideological rhetoric.

In "Looking For Fun," Chen Jiangong has chosen to send up political clichés, and the people who believe in them, by the use of a folksy yet flowery idiom. On the other hand, A Cheng, in "The Tree Stump," has adopted a deceptively simple style in the telling of an equally simple story about an old prizewinning singer. His whimsical tone and lucid prose, which seems to flow so effortlessly, create an indelible picture of a small town and a way of life in which the joyful appreciation of art (in the form of folk ballads) survives all politically inspired attempts to suppress or manipulate it. Then there is the rich, evocative imagery of "Clock," the dense, gritty language of "The Nine Palaces," befitting a story set in the stark Taklimakhan desert of northwest China, and the elegiac serenity of Shi Tiesheng's heartrending story, "Like a Banjo String." Even the spare prose and the matter-of-fact tone in Wang Anyi's "Lao Kang Came Back" serve to underscore the author's delineation of quiet horror.

To a Western reader, perhaps all the stories in this collection seem surprisingly simple and serene for the works of a generation so devastated by the cataclysms of the past two decades. On the other hand, after such sound and fury, it is precisely the simplicity and lyricism of these stories that provide their appeal and their power to move the reader. In any event, we may take heart in the promise embodied in these works. As the title of this collection suggests, after the winter of cultural upheaval and political repression, the sprouting of "spring bamboo"—of artistic creativity—is to be treasured. Given a chance to grow in a climate more tolerant of creative expression, some of these early shoots may yet mature into magnificent stands of literary masterworks.

SPRING
BAMBOO

CLOCK

ZHENG WANLONG

▲ ▲ ▲

▲ ▲ ▲

▲ ▲ I*do not believe this is a true story. Nor is it a legend only among the Ulubayajier tribe, of the Oroqens in the Greater Xing'an mountains. It may also be found in the Aegean civilization of faraway Europe, on Mount Ida on the island of Crete.*

He escaped. The fog churned around him, wave upon wave surging against his face. Eyes opened to their widest though nothing could be seen, he had groped his way out of the paddock on memory alone. When Mother let go of him she had stuffed something into his pocket, the red medicine of healing or perhaps bear's grease, but by the time he slid down the river bank it was nowhere to be found. The rushes down there grew so deep they seemed bottomless.

The wind was bitter, the fog dank. His wounds began to ache as if they were soaking in brine. Yesterday afternoon Father had hung him from a hitching post and thrashed him till even the whip fell apart, savagely enough to have killed him in one breath. But he had inherited Father's spine; he took it all, made not a sound. The shaman said he was possessed, that devils lurked in his body and witches flitted across his face; the shaman claimed to have seen all this even before setting foot in their bark tent. Mother could only weep. She could not bear the sight of Father—his deerskin coat stripped off, his chest all bare—whipping their son. Hiding in the tent she stabbed her palms with a knife and watched as blood flowed from the wounds. Every family in the village was burning incense and praying amidst the shaman's drums and bells. Old women knelt before the fire chanting: "Ha-la-la, give us your blessing, Bahuriya!"

All winter long the villagers had caught next to nothing on their hunts, but he had not understood how this calamity could have been all his doing. Then Father made him understand. It was only yesterday that Father had found out about him and Baidanjia of Ogda. With the whip Father told him: "If you're my son then go die in the widow's bark tent!" Father said Baidanjia's mother was a jinx, an unclean woman who had jinxed her husband's parents, then jinxed her husband too. That Baidanjia was born after the man died—she with the milk-white skin and twinkling blue eyes, she was not of Ogda stock. Wherever mother and daughter went the fires would die; wherever they lived creatures would flee. May they burn to death in heaven's fire so we may prosper again!

"You bastard, if your eyes weren't growing out of your crotch, how could Baidanjia have seduced you? And you still have the gall to be our *ulilun*'s marksman?! If it wasn't because of you, you lowlife, how come I have not been able to kill any bears all winter or catch a single marten? Look at your mother and the other women in the ulilun—not one of them pregnant. Even our sacrificial *kawawa* plant doesn't smell sweet anymore!" In the end, tired at last from flogging him, tired too of berating him, Father dropped onto the ground and tossed a knife at his feet, saying: "If you don't die in that little widow's tent, then never let me see you again."

Actually Father was not such a devout believer in the shaman, he just could not stand the shame of not capturing a bear or a marten the whole winter. Mother came and cut the rope from which he hung, buried her face in his chest and said: "Run away, Molitu, quickly! Your father really means to kill you. He has already sharpened his knife. At daybreak, in front of everyone in the ulilun, he wants to offer your blood as a sacrifice to Bainacha."

Could it be that god of the mountains Bainacha would gag him just as Father did? Would He not even listen to his explanation? Molitu wanted to tell Bainacha, wanted to tell everyone in the ulilun: Baidanjia was the most beautiful girl he had ever seen, the loveliest doe in the Tardaji mountains. Father talked that way but he had never seen her, nor had anyone else in the ulilun. Her mother had been sick all along, and Baidanjia spent the whole day at her mother's side, coming out only at night. It was at night that they had met. Night drew everything close to each other, moon and stars were right in their laps. But where are you, Bainacha?

He ran and ran, blood oozing from every wound.

He pounded along dappled trails, splashed through soggy marshes, running, running all the while. Still darkness enveloped him, just as it had swallowed the valley. On he ran, through the stretch of wind-felled timber, past the grove of camphor trees, over the ridge and down the hill—till he tumbled headlong into the inky black bushes near the fork in the river.

Above the treetops on the crest of the hill, a layer of rich dark red appeared. Molitu was startled awake by the insistent screeching of a snow owl. It was right there in the grove of camphors, calling to something. Baidanjia had once told him that she liked this bird, because whenever she heard its cries her thoughts would wander far and wide—but she had never seen one. Molitu had. It looked sinister to him, though he had heard from the old folks that the cries of the snow owl always meant the woods were empty. As empty as his heart at this moment, with nothing left to await and nothing to hope for, a heart light and empty as a leaf fluttering to the ground. Just now, however, while he was still running, he had felt as though his heart were weighed down by a rock, plunging him deeper into the darkness with every step.

Then he came to hear the wind in the woods and the river flowing between its banks, smelled the delicate fragrance of grasses beginning to yellow. Thus it was that he followed the river and walked toward Ogda, heading for that familiar white shack hidden behind the dense wooden pickets.

He was no longer thinking about anything. Keep going, Mother had told him, go try your luck. But where? He shook his head. Now twenty-four, he had never gone beyond the valley at the edge of the Tardaji mountains, had never thought of doing so. He remembered seeing a group of people a few years ago who had come from beyond the mountains. They were carrying bags and red-and-white poles and some objects that looked like living things. Instruments, that's what they called those things. But they had no horses, no guns, no dogs. This forest doesn't belong to them! So saying, Father stuffed a bullet into his Bilatanka rifle and flattened himself on the grass, silently taking aim at the outsiders, his teeth clenched tight. Son of a bitch, if they chop one tree within my sights I'll mow them down right there! A life for a life! Do you hear me, you bastard?! I don't care how much they pay, you'd better not be their guide! They are they! No matter what Father was saying he always seemed ready to take a bite out of you. By the time the outsiders disappeared from his gunsight, though, Father had fallen asleep and was snoring loudly. But not Molitu. A feeling of bleakness came over him, as if the mountains had shrunk, as if a piece was missing from the hills, from the sun, from himself.

The snow owl began to cry again. These birds guarded the moon for mountain folk. He wondered what the mountains were like at night when there was no moon. What if there were no snow owls? His thoughts drifted off, his heart—from which a piece was missing —awash with uncertainty.

As he drew near the wooden picket fence and the gate that was tightly shut, he wondered if he should call out to Baidanjia. But no sooner did his hand touch the door than it opened, and Baidanjia appeared before him as if sprung from the earth.

"You escaped?"

"Will you run away with me?"

Baidanjia nestled against his chest and began to weep, her sobs like a fawn butting softly against his heart.

"Molitu, take Baidanjia with you, she's carrying your little lamb." Inside the bark tent Baidanjia's mother was speaking. In a voice like ripping bark, this lonely and ill-fated woman cried out: "Let him come to life, Molitu, he is Ogda's heir! Now Ogda will have an heir! O heavens, may the Lord protect you both!"

Molitu began to tremble all over. Putting his hands on Baidanjia's quivering shoulders, he asked: "Is this true, my lamb?"

"No, no, he's not yours! Run away, go!" Abruptly Baidanjia pushed him away and started to run toward the house.

But with a bang the cabin door slammed shut and was barricaded from within. Baidanjia was locked out.

"Go, child! Never mind me, go, and let Ogda's seed sprout wherever you may go!"

Something in that voice told Molitu she would never open the door again, no matter how Baidanjia cried and pleaded. Ogda women never turned back.

A sudden energy surged through Molitu. He swept Baidanjia up in his arms and, after a few faltering steps, strode away from the wooden pickets.

Like ebbing waters the fog in the valley subsided. In its wake the sodden birches on the slopes seemed to be waiting quietly for something. Molitu's fur boots kept sliding on the wet grass. Suddenly, from within his arms Baidanjia's hand shot out and grabbed his ear: "Listen, the snow owl is calling again."

"Where? Where?" Molitu turned a full circle where he stood, but still he heard nothing.

"Silly, it's right here in my belly! Listen to those tiny legs thumping, thumping—he's calling for you!"

Molitu blushed. Grinning foolishly, he held Baidanjia all the more tightly as he ran straight into the woods. Like so many hands the branches tugged at his clothes and slapped at his cheeks, but it was his heart that tickled. He liked running through the woods like this, grass, rocks, trees and wind all young like him, all full of energy and life.

He found a flat open space and laid Baidanjia down. Kneeling by her side, he pressed his ears close to her belly.

"Can you hear it?"

"Hush."

It was very quiet, so quiet that their hearts began to throb and tighten. Then gradually and from far away Molitu heard something, and all of a sudden he burst out laughing.

"Ahhhh—thunder, I hear muffled thunder!"

"It's the drumbeat of the Thunder God, you silly fool!"

"Ohhhh!" Molitu straightened up, raised his arms up to the sky and began to shout: "I hear it, I hear it! It's going dong, dong, dong! . . ."

His shouts shook the leaves and made them rustle, while overhead the clouds scuttled across the sky. Watching him, Baidanjia laughed through clenched teeth as tears streamed down her cheeks.

Then suddenly a gunshot roared through the woods. Molitu turned around to look, and was shocked. They were surrounded! Father stood at the head of the crowd. In the valley far below, the bark hut that had been Baidanjia's home stood burning, flames drifting like clouds in midair.

A bluish spark shimmered among the black depths of the gun barrel, but not a glimmer brightened the old man's face. All at once Baidanjia jumped up and stood in front of the muzzle, shielding Molitu behind her.

Then a shot rang out. Slumping to the ground was someone who had just rushed up to them from the crowd.

"Mother!" But Molitu was held back by Baidanjia.

"Run, child . . ." whispered the voice from the ground.

Another shot rang out. Baidanjia fell, Molitu also. He did not know where he was wounded, only that blood covered his body.

Suddenly Baidanjia pushed Molitu aside and stood up once more, shrieking at the top of her voice as she staggered towards the muzzle: "Run, Molitu, run quickly! My horse is in the meadow beyond the ridge!"

The icy brilliance of a steel blade flashed unmistakably before Molitu's eyes. Then a heavy blow landed on his leg. He fell, got up, fell again. No longer could he see Baidanjia, nothing but a blur of flashing steel. Finally, at the muffled blast of a gun, he somehow jumped onto his feet, then wove through the woods and ran down the hill.

He found the little brown pony. As he clambered onto its back, he realized that he had a bullet in his shoulder and a wound in one leg—a grave wound, his leg feeling heavy as a wet log, his foot completely numb in the stirrup.

The crowd milled around shouting and firing their guns, but no one gave chase. Amid the clattering of his horse's hooves the pitch-black hills and birch forests faded like a nightmare. Yet the rumbling of the Thunder God followed him like moonlight and wind, up one valley and down the next. There was absolutely nothing wrong with his mind, for beyond a doubt he could hear—ever so clearly—that transparent yet mystical drumbeat resonating in the night-blue sky.

But eventually even the drumming faded away. Everything became a dizzying blur in his sight, hills and trees rushing at him like wild beasts. He fell off the horse.

Some days later he awoke to find himself in the home of a Han*, covered with a colorful quilt and lying on top of a well-heated *kang.†* On the kang across from his sat a man smoking a tobacco so aromatic it made every pore in Molitu's body puff up.

"Awake, eh? Been sleeping seven days." It was the voice of an old man, so smoky it could have been coming from the flue of the kang. His words were followed by a string of rasping coughs.

Molitu tried to speak but could not. As if through a mist, he felt the old man's hand stroking his forehead and saw the long whiskers drifting back and forth like a white cloud before his eyes. The old man seemed wiry and alert.

"Fever in the blood, also in the liver and the lungs. And a chill too. But two more doses of my medicine and you'll be good as new." Sitting on the edge of the kang, the old man relit his long-

---

*Han: the largest ethnic group in China, comprising over 93 percent of the population.
†*Kang:* a heatable brick bed.

stemmed pipe and puffed away evenly. "Your horse I've also taken care of, it's in the barn out back. It was wounded too. . . ."

What else the old man said he did not hear clearly. He felt as if his spirit were dangling idly from the rafters, swaying, fluttering, ready to take flight at any moment. In his ears there was nothing but a constant droning—the cries of the snow owl and the sounds of the distant thunder had melded together until he could no longer tell them apart.

Several days later—he didn't know how many—Molitu was still lying on the kang. But this time his eyes were wide open, and he was staring through the double glass windows at skies that seemed somewhat sloping and somewhat level, skies that looked rather lowering yet rather bright. His senses told him it was snowing, the first snow of the season. His senses also told him he was not far from Tardaji.

All of a sudden an unusual sound pierced him—a ponderous, tidy and clear-cut sound that penetrated all the way into his heart. "Ticktock, tick-tock." His whole body began to shiver involuntarily to its beat. What sound was this—as mysterious as the bells and drums of the shaman's demon dance, as enchanting as the cries of the snow owl and the muffled thunder in Baidanjia's belly? Where did it come from? How long would it go on?

He sat up with a start and stared blankly, as though in a trance. Hanging on the wall was a big wooden box (how close it seemed!), behind its shiny glass cover was a round plate (like a moon made of bronze!), on the moon's face some strange markings (just like those made by the shaman on birch bark!), around the moon two needlelike things whirling and twirling (like two goblins chasing each other!), and underneath it a bright golden thing swinging from side to side. A Living Thing! The sound was coming from right in there.

"Tick-tock, tick-tock, tick-tock . . ."

"That's a clock. A wall clock." It was the old man again, pointing at the clock in the ebony case and saying, "I've had it for many, many years. Bought it from a Russian."

"It's alive." Molitu stared fixedly at the clock.

"It follows the sun, moon, stars."

"The sun, the moon, the stars—they're all in there?"

"That's time."

"Time? What is time?"

"Time is day and night, sunup and sundown . . ."

"Who needs a clock to tell all that?"

Molitu fell back onto the kang, in his eyes a glare cold as ice. Silently he cursed: "To hell with you, lying as usual!"

"How to explain this to you? Well, we watch it to tell the passing days." The old man seemed not to mind Molitu's look at all, and with a little shake of his head, walked away chuckling.

Han folk watch it to tell the passing days? Molitu turned his gaze upon the clock again. But even as he listened in a daze to its sonorous and steady tones, he could feel his spirit gradually leaving his body and being snatched away by the clock.

To hell with them! Lies, all lies! The Hans must have a more important reason for keeping this Living Thing. Molitu never believed a word they said. When he used to trade his pelts, deer embryos and bear glands with the Hans for salt, rice, cloth and gunpowder, he had learned for himself how those mongers would blink their snakelike eyes while robbing him blind.

Through the window he looked out on the bustling little town, at the narrow and filthy street cramped by row upon row of tile-roofed houses and filled with a constant hubbub, at the tavern streamers and shop banners fluttering above the crowds. At the other end of the street stood several large chimneys, their thick dark smoke staining the sky the same shade of metallic gray.

Night came, but sleep did not come to Molitu at all as he lay on the kang, his heart brimming with desolation and with fear.

The clock on the wall continued to go "tick-tock, tick-tock," filling the whole house with its mysterious sound, while around him the four walls shut out one and all, leaving Molitu alone with this Living Thing. At times, this "tick-tock, tick-tock" seemed to be dashing against him, powerfully, persistently, just like the clip-clop of hoofbeats, or the gurgling of leaves—or perhaps it was like the cries of the snow owl and the thunderclaps in Baidanjia's belly. Other times, it was like a savage beast that had been crouching in the dark, then creeping up murderously, now pouncing on him in one fell swoop! . . . Then suddenly in the darkness he saw the clock's shimmering light, a light that shone right into his heart. This Living Thing, so mysterious, so menacing—it must be a treasure of some sort, he thought, probably even more precious than the sun, moon and stars. Why else would the Hans keep it alive?

The snow fell more and more thickly, the night turned white. The clock on the wall grew louder as well, like the rumbling of a caravan as one by one the wagons lumber out of the valley, or like the crashing of timber as tree after tree is felled. He could not understand how this Being came to have such power that heaven and earth trembled at its strokes, such force that it had even shattered his heart.

"Tick-tock, tick-tock." The clangor filled his ears. Every wound on his body began to throb with pain again, as if they were still oozing blood. His head too felt like it had been split open.

No more, no more of this awful sound! Like a frightened roe deer Molitu scampered off the kang, took off one of his gold-inlaid armlets and left it on the supper table to pay for his meals, then slipped out of the house, went to the backyard, got his horse, and ran off without looking back. As he went through the door he saw the old man standing in the dark, eyes ablaze like torches and shining right on Molitu. Neither said a word. There did not seem to be anything that could be said.

This time, though, Molitu's flight was not so carefree as the time he ran away from home, because not a day passed but the sound of the clock pursued him, now behind him, now before him; now on his body, now in his dreams; now falling from the sky, now rising from the earth; now like his shadow, or like his specter, constantly haunting him.

Clip-clop, clip-clop.

Tick-tock, tick-tock.

Eight months passed. Whatever the place, whatever the hour, Molitu could not shake off that hellish din. Alone he wandered through the woods and across the marshes, eyes sunken, his once iron-hard body now a withered stump, and on his face a clouded look—as if his eyes saw nothing and his mind were blank. His life seemed to be throbbing away right there in the fluttering of his harness straps; then again, it seemed to be dissipating under the horse's hooves and blowing away on the wind.

Finally came a day when he found himself with no road left to travel, so he returned to the Tardaji mountains. By this time their Thunder God would have already come on earth if Baidanjia were still living in Ogda. But when Molitu returned he found the wooden pickets and the shack all gone, the weeds growing tall and thick, no trace of a fire anywhere. The valley was so quiet it was as terrifying as the exodus from mother's womb into this world.

Standing there in a daze, he once again heard the cries of the snow owl and the thunder in Baidanjia's belly—but this time he heard them in the midst of the noise that had been pursuing him relentlessly. For the first time he felt a tenderness in the sound of the clock.

Then suddenly he noticed some smoke—like that from a cooking fire—appearing above the woods on the hill. It rose all the way into the sky before finally breaking up into little brown puffs.

When he went up the hill, then through the birch grove, and came at last upon that once-familiar cluster of bark tents, he was stunned. The first things he laid eyes on were the two corpses hanging from the willows on the river bank. Swaying and twisting in the wind, they were wrapped only in reeds, not even the ritual birch bark—so pitiless were their executioners—and hung not from a scaffold but only a few skimpy poles. From their head ornaments Molitu knew they were Baidanjia and her mother. On their bodies were strung the entrails of various animals, curses for one thing or another. Green and goldenly glistening flies swarmed around the willows like a fog. Even at a distance he could smell the odor coming from the flies.

The next things he saw were the men on the sandbank beneath the willows, humming "Zhe-wei Zhe-hui leng" as they skinned bears with their knives. They had certainly done well with bears after he left. Father, his face and body all splattered with blood, was working on one at least a head taller than a man. The women were tending kettles over the fire. Huge tongues of green and golden flames leapt up into midair, turning every one of those flat, blank faces a bright red.

All those red blank faces filled Molitu with disappointment—the disappointment of someone who finally found what he had been looking for, only to discover it was not at all what he had expected. Those people seemed so near to him, so familiar; yet so far away, so very alien.

The air above the river bank gradually became a universe of flies. Perhaps those green and golden flecks were not flies after all, but a horde of spirits on the sacrificial altar. Why else did their droning sound so much like wailing? In the cool clear world beneath that green and golden fog the people began to feed. Their sweat-drenched faces remained expressionless. "Ding-ding dong-dong" they clanged their wine bowls, "ba-ji ba-ji" they chomped their meat, "shi-lu shi-lu" they slurped up the broth. All energy seemed concentrated in their mouths; they seemed to neither see nor think at all. Over hill and dale the only sound was the chorus of gulping throats.

The guttural sounds, and the droning, and the "tick-tock, tick-tock" of the clock jangled together. In the midst of this cacophony the people on the riverbank all turned into stone—except for their mouths, which continued to move. These rocks, too, gave off a green and golden glow.

Molitu sank to the ground. But even there he found no trace of himself, or anything else. Nothing but the splintering sounds of the Chaos.

FIRST PUBLISHED IN SEPTEMBER 1985 IN *BEIJING WENXUE (BEIJING LITERATURE)*

THE
HOMECOMING

H A N   S H A O G O N G

▲ ▲ ▲

▲ ▲ ▲

▲ ▲ Many people have said that once in a
while, when they visit some place for the first time, they experience
a feeling of familiarity they cannot explain. Now I too know this
feeling.

I am walking. The mud path, scoured and eroded by water
running down the hillsides, stretches before me in an array of
narrow ridges and clumps of pebbles, like bones and dried-out
entrails after skin and flesh have been stripped away. In the gully
are a few sticks of rotting bamboo and a length of tattered rope,
portents that a village is close at hand. Some dark shapes stand
motionless in the ditchwater. Only when you look carefully do you
discover that they are not rocks at all but water buffalo, their heads
barely breaking the surface, their eyes fixed on me in a furtive gaze.
Mere calves, these, yet already wrinkled, bearded, already senile at
birth, senility running in their blood. Rising above the banana
grove ahead is a squat blockhouse, its portholes like cheerless eyes
staring out of smoke-darkened walls, walls black from the countless
nights congealed within them. I have heard this area used to be

infested with bandits, and that every so often there had been
pitched battles between hill folk and outlaws. No wonder there is
a blockhouse in every village. And the dwellings, in spite of their
thick walls and beady-eyed windows set way up high, look fearful
as they huddle in a tight circle.

All this seems familiar, yet strange too, like a word you've been
staring at for too long—now it looks right, now it doesn't. Damn
it, have I been here before or not? Let me take a guess: Down that
flagstone path, past the banana grove, left at the oil mill, and just
behind the blockhouse I should find an old tree—a gingko or a
camphor—long dead from a bolt of lightning.

Moments later I find I am correct—down to the last detail, including the hollow in the tree and the two youngsters in the fore-
ground playing with a small bonfire.

Nervously I try again: Behind the old tree there should be a low
barn with piles of dung in front and a rusty plow or rake leaning
against the side.

And there they all are, clear as day, seeming to come toward me
in greeting as I approach. Even the large stone pestle in its lopsided
mortar, with the leaves and muck at the bottom—even these look
familiar to me.

Actually, the mortar in my mind's eye is clean and dry. But wait
—it stopped raining only a short while ago, and water running off
the eaves would have been dripping right into the mortar. So once
again a chill rises from my heels all the way up to the back of my
neck.

No, this is impossible, I cannot have come here before. I have
never had meningitis, no mental illness, I still have my wits about
me. Maybe I saw this in a movie once, or maybe it was in a dream
that . . . Anxiously I rack my brains.

Stranger still, the hill folk all seem to know me. Just now as I was rolling up my pant legs to cross the creek, a fellow came down the slope carrying a couple of logs lashed together at one end. He watched awhile as I teetered along reaching uncertainly for the stepping stones. Then he went over to the melon stand by the side of the road, pulled out a dried branch and tossed it over to me. On his face was an odd, yellow-toothed grin.

"Back, eh?"

"Yeah, I'm back . . ."

"It's been about, what, ten years?"

"Ten years . . ."

"Let's go sit in the house. Sangui is plowing the field up yonder."

Where is his house? And who is Sangui? I am completely baffled.

As I climb up a little hill, tiled roofs and courtyards begin to rise into view. Out in the clearing several figures are swinging at something, their flails cracking away unevenly. All of them have bare feet and closely cropped hair; their faces are covered by a coat of sweat that looks like a brown glaze with ragged edges, little slick patches on their cheekbones catching the light and glistening as they move back and forth under the sun. Short floppy jackets and pants that hang loosely from the hips leave their soft bellies and navels uncovered. Not until I see one of them going over to a cradle and undoing her shirt to breast feed the baby, and notice the earrings on every one of them, do I realize that they are—well, women.

One of them looks at me wide-eyed.

"Is this not Ma . . ."

"Ma Four Eyes." Someone reminds her. The name amuses them, and they all burst out laughing.

"My name is not Ma, it is Huang . . ."

"Changed your name, have you?"

"No I haven't."

"For sure, you still love to jest. Whence have you come?"

"The county seat, of course."

" 'Truth, a rare visitor. How is Missy Liang?"

"Which Missy Liang?"

"Your missus, is not Liang her maiden name?"

"Mine is surnamed Yang."

"Sakes alive, did I remember amiss? No, that cannot be, I know she once told me we were distantly related. My husband's family is the Liang clan, from Liang's Knoll, over at Three Rivers. You know that."

What is it I know? And whatever it is, what does it have to do with me? How did I end up here when it seems I was . . . was I looking for her?

The woman throws down her flail and takes me into her house. The doorsill is very high, very heavyset, and over the years legions of young and old have stepped on it, sat on it, until a gentle depression has been worn into the middle. Yellowish rings in its wood grain spill over the sill like widening circles of moonlight forever petrified. Toddlers have to crawl across on all fours while grownups must crook their legs high in order to clamber over the threshold, their bodies leaning forward awkwardly. Indoors it is very dark. The room smells of swill and chicken droppings, but I cannot see anything except for a thin ray of light that trickles in through a high narrow window, slitting open the dank blackness. When my eyes finally adjust to the dim light I am able to make out some soot-covered beams and an equally grimy basket hanging on the wall. I sit down on a block of wood—for some reason there are no chairs in this place, only wood blocks and benches. Women old and young are crowded around the doorway chattering. The one who is breast-feeding flashes an easy smile at me while she unabash-edly pulls out one long tit, still dripping with milk, and presses the other nipple between the baby's lips. They are all saying odd things: "Xiao Qin . . ." "No, not Xiao Qin." "Then who—?" "Her name's Xiao Ling." "Oh yes, Xiao Ling—is she still teaching?" "Why didn't she come for a visit too?" "Have you both gone back to Changsha?" "Do you live in the city or the township?" "Got any youngsters yet?" "One, or two?" "Does Chen Zhihua have any youngsters?" "One, or two?" "How about Bearhead? Has he found himself a wife yet?" "Does he have any youngsters also? One, or two?" . . .

Before long I realize they have all mistaken me for a certain "Ma Four Eyes" who knows these people named Xiao Ling and Bearhead and so forth. That fellow probably looks a lot like me, maybe he also peers out at the world from behind his glasses.

Who is he? Do I need to think about him? From the women's smiling faces I presume that getting food and lodging for the night will be no problem, thank goodness. It's not so bad to be this Ma So-and-so, after all. It's not so hard to answer questions about "one, or two," to surprise or sadden the women as the case may be.

The missus from Liang's Knoll brings over a tray with four large bowls of steaming *youcha,* a sweet gruel made from fried sesame seeds and rice flour. Only later do I learn that the four bowls signify a wish for peace and prosperity all year long—one bowl for each season. At the time I am rather put off by the grubby-looking bowls, though the youcha itself smells delicious. She sets the tray down before me, then scoops some dirty baby clothes off the floor into a wooden tub and carries it all into the inner room, her words coming to me in snatches: "Long have we not had news of you, then Master Shuigen told us . . ."—a long pause, after which she returns to the outer room—"as soon as you went back they put you in prison."

I am so startled I almost scald my hand with the youcha.

"No, never! What prison?"

"A pox on that Shuigen, always running on at the mouth! My poor father-in-law was so afeared he burned plenty of incense for your sake." She covers her mouth and begins to giggle. "Aiyo! I'll be darned."

The women are all laughing. The one with a mouthful of yellow teeth adds: "He even went to pray to the buddha at Daigongling."

Nuts, now it's buddhas and incense too! What if this Ma What-sisname is really under a jinx, really rotting away in a jail somewhere? And here I sit in his place, drinking youcha and grinning stupidly.

Mistress Liang brings me another bowl. As before, one hand is clasped over the wrist of the other, as if in some kind of ritual. I am still working on my first bowl—the sesame-and-rice mush has settled onto the bottom and I don't know how to get at it politely. "He was forever fretting about you, always telling us what a kind and upstanding person you were. That coat of yours—he wore it for many winters, and after he departed I turned it into a pair of trousers. Now little Manzai is wearing it. . . ."

I try to talk about the weather.

Suddenly the room darkens. I turn around to see a black figure almost blocking the entire doorway. From the shape I can tell it belongs to a man, his upper body bare, his bulging muscles angular and hard-edged like rocks. In his hand he is carrying something—an oxhead probably, to judge from its contour. The silhouette closes in on me before I get a good look at his face. Then, dropping his load with a thud, he reaches out both of his paws and starts pumping my hand. "Aiyoyo! If it isn't Comrade Ma, hiyaya!"

I am not some hideous maggot. Why on earth is he carrying on like this?

It is not until he turns toward the fireplace and his profile is etched in light that I see the smile on his face, as well as his gaping black hole of a mouth and the tattoos on both arms.

"Comrade Ma, when did you get here?"

I want to say my name is not Ma at all, it is Huang—Huang Zhixian, as a matter of fact—and that I have not come in search of a once-familiar place in some kind of heartfelt and heroic gesture.

"Still wist"—know? recognize?—"me? The year you left we were working together on the Spiral Hill highway. I am Ai Ba."

"Ai Ba, sure I remember you," I reply shamelessly. "You were the crew leader then."

"No, I only recorded the workpoints. Wist you my wife?"

"Of course, she's famous for her youcha."

"You and I, we used to chase prey together, remember?"—Is that the same as hunting?—"That time when I wanted to make an offering to the mountain god, you said I was just being superstitious, but then you ended up with terrible sores all over your body from the poisonous *muma* weed. And then you ran right into a muntjac, but it slipped through your legs before you could spear it and—"

"Uh, yeah . . . I just missed it . . . my eyes are bad . . ."

The cavernous mouth starts to guffaw. Slowly the women get up and leave the room, swaying their ample hips as they walk away. The man who calls himself Ai Ba brings out a gourd. From this he pours me bowl after bowl of a cloudy brew that tastes sweet and fiery and bitter all at the same time—a drink made from steeping herbs and tiger bones in alcohol, I am told. Turning down the cigarettes I offer him, he shakes some tobacco onto a strip of news-paper and rolls it up into a little cone, which he lights. The paper begins to burn, brightly, and I watch with increasing apprehension while he calmly takes a drag without so much as a glance at the flame. But at last he blows it out with a casual puff, and the cigarette looks none the worse.

"Nowadays there's as much wine and meat as you want, every family's slaughtered plenty of cattle for the New Year." Wiping his mouth he adds: "That year when we were learning from Dazhai* we all had to tighten our belts instead. Remember?"

"Sure I do." I think I will talk about the excellent situation today.

"Have you beheld Delong? He's now the village chief. Yesterday he went over to Zhuomeiqiao to plant some saplings, so mayhap he'll come, mayhap not, but mayhap he will." He goes on to talk about other people and events that leave me more confused than ever: So-and-so built a new house sixteen feet high; So-and-so also built a new house, eighteen feet high; So-and-so is about to build one sixteen feet high; So-and-so is just breaking ground for his, it may be sixteen feet high or it may be eighteen. I listen intently, trying hard to catch his train of thought behind the jumble of words, but all I notice is the occasional odd usage of "wist" for "know," "behold" for "see," and so on.

My head begins to reel, and I find myself cheering just as heartily for sixteen feet as for eighteen, and just as witlessly.

"You're a good fellow, coming back to regard your old friends and all." Once more he lights his cigarette and lets it blaze for a couple of seconds—enough to set me on edge again. "I've still got those books you gave out when you were the local schoolteacher." He clomps up the stairs, and at length reappears, cobwebs in his hair, clutching in his hand a sheaf of dusty yellow papers smelling of mildew and tung oil. It turns out to be a mimeographed pamphlet, crudely printed, with splotches of ink all over the pages. The cover has been torn off, but I gather it is a reading primer: One page is devoted to the night school anthem, others contain things like

---

*Dazhai was known as a model commune during the years of the Cultural Revolution, and the entire country was exhorted to learn from its example.

basic agricultural terms, the story of the 1911 Revolution, passages from Marx's writings on peasant movements, and maps and so forth —all copied in a large, ordinary hand. It is something I could well have produced, but so what?

"Poor devil, you had a hard time too, so thin only the eyes were left in your face, but you never missed a class."

"It was nothing really."

"It snowed a lot that December, damned cold too."

"Yeah, so cold our noses almost fell off."

"And still we had to till the fields. We'd hoist our pine torches and go to work."

"Uh-huh, pine torches."

All of a sudden he turns mysterious. The glint on his cheekbone and the blackheads underneath press close to me. "I want to know something. Was it you who slew Yang the Runt?"

What Yang the Runt? Instantly my scalp constricts, my lips freeze —all I can do is shake my head repeatedly. For heaven's sake, my name is not even Ma, I have never set eyes on this Yang the Runt or whatever, so why is someone trying to incriminate me?

"They all say it was you. That guy was a snake in the grass, he had it coming to him!" Ai Ba rages. When he sees my denial, he looks as much disappointed as disbelieving.

"Any more wine?" I change the subject.

"Sure, sure, as much as you want."

"Lots of mosquitoes around here."

"They always pick on newcomers. Shall I put some rushes on the fire for you?"

The rushes begin to burn. More people come to see me, filing through the door in droves. Invariably they would ask about my health and inquire after my family. The men would smilingly accept the cigarettes I offer them and suck noisily on one end as they sit by the door or against the wall, silent for the most part. Once in a while someone would make a remark, telling me I look fatter, thinner, older, or "young faced" as ever—must be from all that easy living in the city, they would add. Then, their cigarettes finished, they would smile again and say they have to go cut a tree or lay some manure. Several little kids run over to examine my eyeglasses, only to scamper away pellmell a few moments later, screaming excitedly in a mixture of delight and fear: "Goblins! goblins! in his glasses!" Then there is the girl who hovers by the doorway chewing on a stalk of grass. She keeps staring at me as though she were possessed, and her luminous eyes seem to be swimming in tears. I have no idea what it means but it makes me very uncomfortable, so I put on an earnest look and keep my eyes fixed on Ai Ba.

In fact this kind of thing has happened to me more than once. Just now, for instance, while I was on my way to see their poppy fields I ran across a middle-aged woman. She seemed horror-stricken at the sight of me and her face darkened like a lamp that had been suddenly snuffed out. Then she lowered her head and hurried away on tiptoe. I have no idea what that was all about either.

Ai Ba says I should go and see Grandpa San as well. Actually Grandpa is not around anymore—died from a snakebite not long ago, they say—only his name still crops up in people's conversations. Over by the brick kiln is the solitary little hut where he used to live, already tilting so badly it may keel over at any minute. But the two large tung trees are still standing. And beneath them the weeds are flourishing. Standing waist high, they have closed in from all sides and sidled up the steps, their undulating blades like sharp tongues waiting to devour the little shack, waiting to devour the last bones of a clan. The wooden door is padlocked, but termites have riddled it with little black holes. Would the house have fallen into such disrepair if its owner were still around, I wonder. Can it be that the soul of a house is its human inhabitant, and when the soul is fled the carcass decomposes oh so rapidly? A rusty lantern stands upended in the undergrowth, its top and sides spattered with chalky bird droppings. Close by is a cracked earthen jug from which clouds of buzzing mosquitoes pour forth at the drop of a hat. Ai Ba says this is the pot that Grandpa San always used for pickling. He also says I used to visit Grandpa a lot just so I could have some of his pickled cucumbers. (Really?) Big pieces of plaster have fallen off the walls, but some writing can still be seen in faded outline: "Have the whole world in view."*Ai Ba tells me I painted those words on the wall. (Really?) He has plucked a handful of herbs and is now checking some birds' nests for eggs. I glance inside the window. Standing in one corner is a basket half filled with lime, and next to it is a big round disc that on closer inspection turns out to be a metal barbell, so rusted it is almost unrecognizable. I am amazed: What is this unusual piece of athletic equipment doing here? How was it brought into these remote mountains?

Perhaps I already know the answer: I gave it to Grandpa San, right? I gave it to him to beat into a hoe or a plow, but in the end he left it untouched. Right?

Up on the slope someone is calling the cows: "Ooo-mah . . . ooh-mah . . ." and from the woods across the way comes the faint tinkling of cowbells. These cattle calls are rather unusual: They sound like someone crying for mother, plaintive cries. Perhaps it was their keening that had blackened the walls of the blockhouse.

An old woman comes down the hill carrying a small bundle of twigs. Her back is bent almost double, and her thrust-out chin punches downward like a hoe with every step she takes. When she

*The slogan "Have the whole nation at heart and leave the whole world in view" was popular during the Cultural Revolution.

looks up to stare at me (or is she merely looking straight through to the tung tree behind me?) her murky pupils push right up against her eyelids. What startles me, though, are the deep lines in her otherwise expressionless face. She takes one look at Grandpa's dilapidated shack, turns around to look at the old tree near the blockhouse, and mutters enigmatically: "Tree is dead too." Then she continues onward in her oddly plodding way, the breeze flattening the few limp white hairs bobbing up and down, up and down on her head.

I am now absolutely sure. I have never been here before. As for the old woman's statement, I have no idea what it means either— an unfathomable pool.

Dinner is a grand affair: fist-sized hunks of beef and pork, all somewhat gamy and undercooked but full of pomp and swagger. They arrive in mounds piled high above the edges of the bowls, held together by loops of straw and stacked layer upon layer like bricks in a kiln—no doubt a custom dating back to the beginning of time. Only men are allowed at the table. One person does not show up, so in front of the empty seat the host places a sheet of straw paper onto which he would plunk down a piece of meat from time to time, for the enjoyment of the absent guest. During the meal I ask about their premium white rice, but they refuse to even discuss prices, they seem ready to give it to me for nothing. As for opium —well, there is a good crop of it this year, but the state pharmacy has a monopoly on the entire supply. I can say no more.

"The Runt got what he deserved." Ai Ba slurps some hot soup from a ladle, returns it to its gluey spot on the table, then glares at a bowl of meat as he taps it with his chopsticks. "Him and his fat ass and soft hands, a real good-for-nothing, but he had money enough to build himself a new house. If you ask me, I think he was up to no good."

"That's right! And how he used to torture us at those mass criticism meetings, tying us up like animals. Not a single one of us managed to escape that! I've still got two scars on my wrists to show for it. Damn that motherfucker!"

"How did he really die? Did he really run into a vampire and fall off a cliff?"

"No matter how mean you are, you still can't fight your stars. Don't be wanting a bushel when a peck is all you're meant to have. Hongsheng from Xia's Cove was the same way."

"Rats, he even ate rats. How mean can you get?"

"That sure is mean. Unheard of."

"Poor Bearhead really got smacked around by him. I saw those little cylinders—tubes of dye, no question about it. Hardly enough to paint a few dolls, let alone to dye cloth. And he claimed they were bullets."

"But Bearhead also had his own class background to blame."

I muster up all my courage to butt in: "About Yang the Runt, didn't the authorities send anyone to investigate?"

Ai Ba munches noisily on a piece of fatty meat. "Sure they did. What a load of shit! When they tried to talk to me I went looking for my chickens. Hey, Comrade Ma, you haven't even touched your wine! Come, come, have some more to eat. Here."

He presses another slab of meat into my bowl. I begin to gag and leave the table pretending to get some more rice, but as soon as I reach a dark corner I toss the meat to a dog scampering underfoot.

After dinner they insist on preparing a bath for me. I suspect this may be another local custom, and I try to appear well acquainted with the routine. The bathtub is actually a very large barrel standing in one corner of the cookhouse. It is filled with steaming hot water that seems to have been boiled with some herbs, maybe *qinghao*. Women walk about freely in front of it, the missus from Liang's

Knoll even bringing me more hot water in a gourd dipper from time to time. I am embarrassed but all I can do is crouch lower in the barrel. When she finally steps outside with a pail of slop I let out a long sigh of relief.

By now I am sweating from the heat of the bathwater, but the herbs seem to have taken the itch out of all those mosquito bites. I rub my fingers over an inch-long scar on my calf, the result of a spiking on the soccer field. But maybe that's not it, maybe it's from . . . being bitten by some guy named The Runt. Maybe it was on that morning dripping with fog, along that narrow path up the hill. He was coming toward me under his umbrella, but when he caught the look in my eyes he began to tremble. And falling to his knees he cried out that he would never do it again, never ever, that he'd had nothing to do with Er Sao's death, that he knew nothing about Grandpa San's buffalo. In the end he put up a fight, his eyes bulging till they seemed ready to pop out and his jaws clamped around my leg. Then his hands began to clutch at a lariat around his throat. But all of a sudden they flew apart, and like two crabs began to crawl and squirm and gouge the dirt. Later, who knows when, the crabs gradually calmed down and became still. . . .

I dare not think on. I am even afraid to look at my hands—would I find on them the stench of blood, and rope marks from a lariat?

I now decide with all my might: I have never been to this place, nor do I know this fellow The Runt. No. Never.

I dress quickly and return to the main room. It is alive with people and activity. An old man comes in and stamps out his glowing pine brand, says he once asked me to buy him a little dye, he still owes me two dollars for it, now he's come to pay his debt, and also to invite me to his house tomorrow for dinner and to sleep over. At this Ai Ba gets into the act, protesting that it is his turn to play host to me, he has already invited the traveling tailor to his house tomorrow, he's got plenty of meat butchered anyway, no question about it but I am going to his house tomorrow. . . .

While they are arguing I slip out the door and, stumbling a little, set out to take a look at the house "I" used to live in. According to Ai Ba it's that shack right behind the old tree, and it wasn't until year before last that they turned it into a cowshed.

Again I pass beneath the tung trees, again I see the encroaching weeds and their prey, Grandpa San's sagging grass shack. And its shadow. It is watching me silently. It coughs in the raven's cries, talks to me in the rustling of the leaves. I think I even sniff an elusive aroma of alcohol in the air.

Child, have you come back? Pull up a chair and sit down. I told you to get away, far, far away, never to come back here.

But, I miss your pickled cucumbers. I tried making them myself, but they never taste the same.

What's so good about those wretched things? I only made them back then because I felt so sorry for all of you, poor devils. You were always hungry, always scrounging around for something to eat, and while you were plowing the fields if you found some broad beans on the ridges, you'd even eat them raw.

I know, you were always looking out for us.

Sooner or later we all find ourselves far from home. I did no more than I ought.

That time when we had to gather firewood, we only brought in nine loads. You were keeping tally, and you told them we brought in ten.

I don't remember anymore.

And you were always after us to shave our heads. You would tell us that hair and whiskers are both blood-eaters, if we let them grow they'd sap the life force right out of us.

Is that so? I don't remember.

I should have come back earlier to see you. I had no idea things would be so different, that you would be gone so soon.

It was time to go. Otherwise I would have turned into an immortal. My only fondness was for a drink or two, and now I've had my fill, I will sleep soundly.

Grandpa, would you like a cigarette.

Go and make yourself some tea, Xiao Ma.

I leave that aura of wine and head for home, holding aloft the almost extinguished pine brand and thinking about the morrow's chores. From time to time I would hear the splash of a frog jumping into the ditch. But I have no pine brand in my hand now, and my home has become a cowshed that feels so unfamiliar, so unfriendly. I can barely see a thing, though the sounds of cattle chewing cud and the warm musty smell of compost gush out of the barn door. Thinking their master has come, the cattle jostle each other trying to poke their heads outside and bump against the railing in a huge clatter. As I walk away, the sounds of my footsteps echo from the mud walls of the barn, almost as if there were someone walking on the other side, perhaps even within the wall itself—someone who knows my secrets.

The hills across the valley are pitch black. In the dark they appear taller and closer, stiflingly so. Looking up at the uneven strip of starry sky far above me, I suddenly feel so close, too close to the ground, as though I have been seized by an unnamed force and am about to be pulled inexorably down, down through this crack in the earth into the depths.

Just then an enormous moon appears, and the dogs in the village bay as if in fright. I turn toward the creek, treading on the flecks of moonlight that have been sifted through the trees and now dapple the ground like the floating leaves of some aquatic plant.

There may be someone sitting on the bank, I think—probably a young woman, a leaf whistle between her lips.

There is no one by the creek. But when I walk back I see the shadow of a person underneath the old tree.

A silhouette—the perfect touch for such a beautiful night.

"Is that you, Xiao Ma?"

"Yes, it's me." How calm and confident comes the answer.

"Did you just come from the creek?"

"Who . . . who are you?"

"Simeizi."

"How you've grown! I wouldn't recognize you at all if I'd run into you somewhere else."

"You've seen the outside world, now everything seems different to you."

"How is everyone at home?"

Suddenly she falls silent. Looking at the mill, she finally answers in a rather strange voice: "My older sister, how she hated you. . . ."

"Hated . . ." I am so unnerved I glance at the path leading to the clearing and some lights, thinking of escape. "I . . . many things are hard for me to say. I told her once that . . ."

"Why did you put those ears of corn in her basket that day? Did you not know you cannot just up and put something in a maiden's basket? And she gave you one of her hairs, did you not understand that either?"

"I . . . I didn't, I didn't know any of the customs around here then. I needed some help that day, so I asked her to carry the corn for me."

My answer seems to pass muster.

"Everyone was talking about it, were you deaf too? I beheld it with my own eyes, you were teaching her acupuncture."

"She wanted to learn, she wanted to be a doctor. Actually, back then I didn't really know much about it myself. We were just fiddling around."

"You city folk are all heartless."

"Don't be like this. . . ."

"It's true! It's true!"

"I know . . . your sister was a good girl, I know that. She could really sing, and her needlework was so fine. Once we went eel fishing, and she caught one right after another. When I got sick she cried her eyes out. . . . I know all of that. But, some things you don't understand, and I can't explain. My way of life will never be easy, I will always be on the go, I . . . I've got my lifework to do."

I finally settle on the term "lifework," even though it sticks a little in my throat.

She covers her face and begins to sob. "That fellow Hu, he was so mean."

I seem to know what this means, though I continue to answer tentatively: "I heard about that. I'm going to make him pay for it."

"What's the use? What's the use?" She stamps her feet as she sobs even more bitterly. "If only you had said something back then, none of this would have happened. Now my sister has turned into a bird, she sits here day after day calling, calling for you. Can you not hear it?"

Her slender shoulders heave with each sob. I can see them clearly in the moonlight, as well as her smooth neck, even her creamy-white scalp showing through the center parting of her hair. I want so much to wipe away her tears, I yearn to hold her by the shoulders and kiss that thin line of scalp, just as I would kiss my own little sister, I want to let her tears—salty ones—cling to my lips, so I can drink them in.

But I dare not. This is a strange story, and I dare not break the spell.

There really is a bird singing in the tree: "Do not go—go—go, do not go—go—go . . ."—a lonesome cry that shoots high into the heavens like an arrow before fluttering down into the midst of those hills and forests, down into those black clouds and noiseless flashes of lightning in the distance. I smoke a cigarette as I gaze at the silent thunderbolts.

Do not go, go, go.

I leave. Before going I ask the missus from Liang's Knoll to give Simeizi a letter from me. In it I talk about her sister's wish—unfulfilled in the end—to become a doctor, and how I hope she would be able to realize her sister's ambition. Where there is a will, there is a way. Would she like to take the entrance exams for medical training? I will send her all kinds of study materials. I promise. I also tell her I will never forget her sister. Ai Ba caught that partridge in the tree, and I am going to take it home with me where it will sing in my window every day and be my constant companion.

I steal away like a fugitive, without saying goodbye to the people in the village, and without taking care of the premium white rice. Anyway, what do I want with rice or with opium? It seems they are not what I came for originally. I feel suffocated by it all—the whole village, the entire enigma that is me. I must escape. But I turn around for another look, and once more I see the old tree that lightning killed, still standing at the entrance to the village, its withered limbs outstretched like trembling fingers. The master of that hand fell in a battle long ago and turned into a mountain, but he struggles to keep his hand raised above the earth, where even now it is grasping for something.

I go to the inn in the county seat and fall asleep to the twittering of the partridge by my bed. A dream comes to me. In it I am still walking on and on along a rutted path, its skin and muscles of mud long since stripped away by runoffs from the hills, only bones and bowels left now to bear the trample of the hill folk's straw shoes. The road is endless. The calendar watch on my wrist tells me I have been walking for an hour, a day, a week . . . but still the road runs beneath my feet. Later I am to have the same dream over and over, no matter where I go.

I awake in terror, I get a drink of water, then another, and another, I go to the bathroom, once, twice—finally I make a long-distance call to a friend. I mean to ask him whether he has managed to "waste" Mangyhead Cao at cards yet, but instead I blurt out a question about how to study for entrance exams on your own.

My friend addresses me as "Huang Zhixian."

"What?"

"What do you mean 'what'?"

"What did you call me?"

"Aren't you called Huang Zhixian?"

"Did you call me Huang Zhixian?"

"Didn't I call you Huang Zhixian?"

I am stunned. My mind is blank. It is true, I am at the inn, in the corridor is a dim light swarming with bugs, underneath it a row of makeshift cots. Right beneath the telephone there is even a big round face snoring away. But . . . is there still someone in the world named Huang Zhixian? And this Huang Zhixian—is that me?

I will never be able to walk out of the enormity that is me. I am tired.

FIRST PUBLISHED IN JUNE 1985 IN *SHANGHAI WENXUE (SHANGHAI LITERATURE)*

LAO KANG
CAME BACK

WANG ANYI

▲   ▲   ▲

▲   ▲   ▲

▲   ▲   Heard Lao Kang had come back and
was living at his brother's house, that he was very sick. A bunch of
us talked about visiting him, but because of one thing or another
—we were busy, it was a long way to go, there were so many of
us—we never managed to get together and settle on a date. Now
here it was more than a month later, and still no one had gone to
see him. Besides, there had been no further news about him in the
meantime, and so gradually he slipped from our minds.

It's been twenty years since I last saw him—twenty years, that's
half a lifetime, or almost. So many things have happened, so many
changes, I really haven't had the time or any wish to look back on
it all. And then one day you turn your head, and suddenly it's as
if you've just traveled a hundred and eight thousand miles with one
snap of the fingers. I still remember clearly the things that happened
in the past, but now they seem to belong to another life, as unreal
as a dream.

Lao Kang and I had been classmates together. Back then we were
only in our early twenties, each with our own lofty ideals, our

soaring aspirations—the sky was the limit. Lao Kang's ambition was
to write a complete history of Chinese music—not a particularly
grandiose ambition, though not too modest either, but for him it
turned out to be much easier said than done. He'd always had the
reputation of being a "walking warehouse" of reference material;
by the time he was a sophomore he had already accumulated a
soapbox full of index cards. He was fond of saying that China was
the first country to chronicle its history, and that he was determined
to carry on this tradition. But all we ever saw was Lao Kang diligently and painstakingly collecting his material, we never saw him
put pen to paper and actually produce anything, not even a brief
essay for the school journal, let alone a whole book. It was rather
disappointing. During that same period, someone else with vault-
ing ambition had managed to compose a majestic and stirring piece
of music called "Cantata of the River of Happiness," which won
first prize in the choral competition at the Seventh International
Youth Festival. When asked about his project, Lao Kang would
always say: "In a little while, in a little while." But up until he was
branded "a rightist who had slipped through a loophole" in the
Anti-Rightist Campaign of 1957 and sent in internal exile to Qinghai, he had not written so much as a single word. Lao Kang and I,
while there had never been any unpleasantness between us, were
not especially close. Actually, he never had a lot of close friends
because he was such a bookworm, though as far as bookworms went
he seemed quite normal, since he never became so lost in his books
that he would do something absentminded or ridiculous and make
a fool of himself. Perhaps that was why I generally remembered
him with indifference rather than with any great emotion, though
I did feel kind of sorry for him for having been branded a rightist
so soon. His only offense had been to express, quite mildly, some
dissatisfaction with the way things were at the time, but if you

compared him with the "clique" of three dissidents who had openly presented their dissent to Xian Xinghai, his action seemed to
lack a certain air of tragic heroism. I guess that was why he never
left much of an impression. And later on, when all those people
who were even more innocent all seemed to have even worse
things happen to them, what pity I once felt for Lao Kang also
faded away.

Yet, after all, we were classmates once, and today, twenty years
later, the term "classmates" really signifies more than just having
been in school together—it also seems to encompass the memory
of those wonderful years two decades ago. Because of that, my wish
to see him was quite heartfelt.

One day I happened to be in the neighborhood on some business, not too far from their place, so after I was finished I went
directly over to his brother's home.

Lao Kang did not hail from Shanghai—he was originally from
Zhenjiang. It was his older brother who had brought him to the city
for schooling, and he used to spend his weekends with this brother
and his wife. Back in those days his brother was the first violinist
in the orchestra, but since then he had resigned from the post, and
now kept himself occupied by writing a few songs or an occasional
essay. From time to time I would run into him at a meeting or a
master class, and we would always nod and greet each other—so
we were not strangers exactly, and I even knew that he had just
moved.

Their new residence was an apartment on the twelfth floor of a
new building. I took the elevator up, made a left turn, and theirs
was the first door. There was a doorbell, which I pressed, and, when
there was no answer, pressed again. Before I had quite finished, the
door opened quietly, and a rustic woman in her sixties looked at
me inquiringly. Must be the housekeeper, I thought to myself.

"Nobody's home." Her Shanghainese had more than a touch of the provincial accent of northern Jiangsu.

"Nobody?" I was very disappointed. I had come quite some distance, and I would not soon have another chance to come this way.

"Only a sick person here," she answered.

"That's who I've come to see, the sick person," I said hastily, feeling very relieved that it was not going to be a wasted trip after all.

"Come to see the sick one?" she gave me a puzzled look before stepping aside to let me in.

It was one of those small apartments, newly built. Before moving in they must have redecorated it themselves: wallpaper, floor covering, ceramic tiles arranged in a mosaic pattern in the toilet, lamps hanging from the ceiling, a few oil paintings on the walls—it all looked rather plush, actually. Peering around as I walked down the short, narrow hallway, I noticed that the door to the south-facing room was shut. The door to the room on the north side was open, however, and I saw, next to the square table inside, a man who was sitting with his upper body hunched over the tabletop, head down, taking a nap. That must be Lao Kang, I thought to myself.

"Lao Kang," I called out.

No reply. He went on dozing.

I called him again.

Still no reply. I looked at him more closely. Somehow, he didn't seem to look quite so much like Lao Kang anymore, and I began to have my doubts. Then, turning around, I saw the old housekeeper standing behind me, watching us as she struck a studied pose, her hands folded carefully across the front of her apron.

"Is this your employer's brother?" I asked.

She answered me with a question: "Do you know him?"

I nodded.

And she said: "You call him and see." Then she walked away, and soon afterwards I heard the sound of running water in the bathroom.

I called him again, but still he did not answer. I became increasingly curious, but also uneasy. Slowly I walked around to his side, and found that he was not asleep after all. Instead, his head was bent down very low and propped on one hand, while the other hand was stiffly tracing some kind of a pattern on the tabletop. But this was a complete stranger, appallingly thin—I'd never seen anyone look so gaunt. It was as if, instead of a face, he had only this interlocking jumble of forehead and cheekbones and jawbones, all covered with a layer of skin that was almost transparent. I couldn't help feeling a chill run through me.

"Lao Kang, is that you?" I asked.

He didn't even look at me, as though he hadn't heard me at all. His fingers kept tracing something on the table.

I went up close and picked him up by the shoulders, so that we were face to face. It was only then that he gave me a blank, apathetic look.

"Do you recognize me?" I asked.

His face was expressionless. Actually there were no muscles left on his face for him to make any expressions with. On the other hand, he really had no expression.

I let go of his shoulders, and again he hunched over the table, making some pattern or other which, when I followed the strokes, appeared to be " 米 ," the character for rice.

Rather shaken, I slowly left the room. When the housekeeper, who had been washing some clothes in the bathroom, saw me come out, she asked: "Did he recognize you?"

I shook my head.

"Been like this ever since he came back from Qinghai. Still knows how to eat and sleep and go to the bathroom, though—well, you really can't say he knows how, but so long as someone takes him by the hand he can do all of that, and not make a mess of it." She seemed quite pleased about that.

"Do you know what's wrong with him?" I asked, touching my brow with my hand and feeling the thin layer of sweat.

"They say a blood vessel popped in his brain. But even that was pretty strange, because he didn't fall down, didn't run into anything, he was just sleeping quietly, and it popped."

"He must have had a stroke then."

"Well, I guess it's fate. He was all set to come back to Shanghai, had his residence permit and his job all worked out, then all of a sudden that blood vessel went a-popping on him, and he ended up like this," she prattled on as she worked energetically at her washing, scrubbing the clothes until the snowy white soap bubbles were splattering every which way.

"Are you here to take care of him?" I asked.

"I came because I felt sorry for him. I used to work over at the Long Fei building, had a real good job there, a family of four, two grownups and two kids, the older one was away at university and only came home on Saturdays. I had a real easy time. I only came because I took pity on him," she said, her hands bustling about diligently in a heap of soap bubbles.

"It can't be too busy here either."

"What do you mean, not too busy? It's just like taking care of a child; you can't leave him alone for a minute. On my old job at the Long Fei building I even had time to do the laundry for two other families. The master here said he would make up the difference in my pay. I told him I didn't come here for the money!"

I told her I must be going, but now she seemed reluctant to have me leave, and said she had forgotten to pour me some tea. Hastily I said that wouldn't be necessary and made my escape. But it wasn't until after I got out that I discovered I didn't have my bicycle key with me, and realized I must have dropped it on the table just now when I grabbed Lao Kang by the shoulders. When I went back into the room, I found him still sitting by the table, oblivious to everything, his fingers still sketching something in the shape of " ✳ ." I had no idea what it meant.

On the way home I kept thinking about Lao Kang, wondering how he ended up like this. During the twenty years that he was in Qinghai, all by himself, none of us had kept in touch with him, and now the story of how he lived, what had happened to him in those twenty years—all that was lost within his silence. Even after I got home, Lao Kang's sunken, shriveled image continued to haunt me no matter what I was doing—eating, sleeping, or playing with my children—and I became extremely restless. I kept wanting to talk about it with someone, but every time I started to, I would feel as if I could never make myself understood, and I would just remain silent. In the end I decided to visit him again, in the hope of catching his brother this time.

So one holiday I picked up some pastries and went to the Kangs' house a second time.

To my surprise, not only was Lao Kang's brother not home—at a meeting, I was told—but his sister-in-law was out as well, gone to take her child to a music lesson. Lao Kang was lying on a foldaway spring bed, taking a nap. When the housekeeper saw me she immediately shook off her drowsiness. Now that she had met me once before, she was much more gracious; she showed me to a chair right away, and then bustled about making tea as she gave me a full report: "For lunch he had a bowl and a half of rice, with ribs, green cabbage, peas, and some soup too. He sure can eat, so long as you give him the food. After lunch he went to sleep, and he'll usually sleep till three. And then he'll just sit there."

"Is he still that way—doesn't really recognize anyone?" I asked, hoping to hear that he had taken a turn for the better.

"Still like that."

"Not even his brother?"

"Well, when his brother calls him, he seems to hear something. And now when I call him, he also seems a little better."

"I guess he can still understand a few things," I said, letting out a sigh of relief.

"When I tell him it's time to eat, he knows to get his rice bowl, when I tell him it's time to sleep, he'll take off his shoes and his clothes. He's pretty easy to handle."

"You have to take good care of him."

"I sure do! My boss always tells me to buy him something good to eat, says he didn't have much to eat in Qinghai, now it's time for him to enjoy the good life. So every day I rack my brains to come up with something new. Yesterday I bought him some pig's liver, today it's spare ribs, cooked in tomato sauce."

"He likes to eat?"

"He knows what's good! Like today, the spare ribs, he had quite a few of them, because he knows they're good!"

I breathed a sigh.

"Sir"—that's what she called me—"in my opinion, to live like this, what's a person good for then? Nothing left but breathing in and out!"

I didn't know how to answer her.

"Well, when you think about it, all a person is is this breath of life, as long as you've still got it you're alive, and when it's gone, you're dead," she said, puckering her lips. Her almost hairless forehead gleamed brightly under the afternoon sun that was streaming in through the west-facing windows.

He turned over on the bed.

"Oh, he's awake," she said, getting up to help him.

With her support he sat up, then got on his feet, and, still leaning on her, walked slowly over to the table and sat down right across from me. His blank look swept over me before falling onto the tabletop. In a little while his fingers began to move, again tracing the pattern " * ."

The housekeeper told me as she folded up the cot: "There, that's how he is all the time." After she put the bed away in a closet, she walked over and helped him up, saying: "Let's go to the toilet!"

Obediently Lao Kang followed her, and soon the sound of flushing water came from the bathroom. I got up and decided to leave —I had no wish to watch while the housekeeper showed off his daily routine for my benefit. Sure enough, when I told her I was leaving, she looked very disappointed and said that I hadn't even finished my tea. But I left anyway.

I didn't want to see him again, but I was still filled with curiosity and questions: What had his life been like in those twenty years? Did he ever get married? How did he get sick all of a sudden? And, not least, what was the meaning of that " * " he kept tracing over and over? To find out about all of this I would have to ask his brother.

Then one day, as luck would have it, I ran into his brother at the arts center just before a movie. After we greeted each other, I immediately brought up the subject:

"I went to your place twice, but both times I missed you."

"So that was you! The amah told me about it, but I couldn't figure out who it was." Very cordially he invited me to go sit with him at the snack bar for a little while, and I agreed. The movie would not begin for another ten or twelve minutes at least.

"What on earth happened to him, that he ended up in this awful state?" I blurted out before we even sat down.

He was silent as he took out a cigarette and lighted up.

"He didn't get married?"

"No," he shook his head.

"Out there in Qinghai, how was he?"

He let out a puff of smoke. Then, holding the cigarette between his index and middle fingers, he toyed with the matchbox with his thumb and third finger as he said, very slowly: "At first he was doing manual labor, then later he was reassigned to the county cultural center." He mentioned the name of the county, but I had never heard of it.

"Which county was that?" I asked.

He told me the name again, but it was still unfamiliar to me—not only did it sound strange, but I couldn't even picture how the characters might be written.

"All those years, did he ever come back?"

"Once or twice. Of course he had lost quite a bit of weight, but he seemed lively enough."

"And his letters, did they come fairly often?"

"He always wrote that he was fine. Several times we sent him packages of toasted wheat flour, but he kept telling us it wasn't necessary, so we stopped. Looking back on it now, it hangs on my conscience, I feel that I didn't do right by him. We heard later that life in Qinghai was hard, very hard."

"But after all, there wasn't much you could have done for him," I tried to console him.

"After the Gang of Four was overthrown, I ran around trying to get him pardoned and sent back home. Finally I succeeded, his name was cleared, there was the Party's rehabilitation policy and all that, and he was all set to come back to Shanghai, his bags were already packed, we had even received a telegram telling us when he would arrive. We went to the station, but he wasn't on the train, so we thought something must have happened to hold him up. Then as soon as we got home from the station, we received an urgent telegram from his work unit telling us that he was critically ill. Just as we were talking about going out to Qinghai, we got another telegram saying that he was no longer in critical condition, and that in a few days they would send him back to Shangai with a personal escort. So naturally we didn't go. Afterwards I kind of regretted this decision—maybe I should have gone. Now we'll never know what kind of life he led, what it was like out there."

"Did you try to find out from the person who brought him home?"

"That was just a young kid, he'd been at their cultural center no more than a few months, and he hardly knew my brother. All he said was that my brother was a very honest and kindly person, but I didn't need him to tell me that." He smiled rather strangely, then continued: "The only things that came back with him were a tattered roll of bedding, a beat-up leather suitcase, and a few hundred yuan. That's all."

"Has he been like this ever since he came back?"

"Just the way you saw him, maybe even more dull and wooden. Now that he's been home a while he seems a little better."

"What was the illness?"

"Cerebral hemorrhage, the night before he was to board the train. Perhaps it was caused by overexcitement."

I fell silent.

He also became silent.

After some time, during which neither of us spoke, I asked: "That character ' ✳ ' that he's always writing, what does it mean?"

"We've been really puzzled by that too. Strange, isn't it, that he seems to have forgotten everything, but for no rhyme or reason he has remembered this ' ✳ .' My wife wonders if it isn't because he suffered so terribly during those years of famine, that he's managed to hang on doggedly to this symbol for rice. My kids say it must have been a girl with the family name of Mi, also written as ' ✳ ,' and they even looked it up in the *Dictionary of Family Names* to prove to us that there is such a name. I think perhaps it's neither, it's nothing at all, just a simple pattern that he began tracing unconsciously and mechanically until it's become second nature to him. It's really no more than a simple pattern made up of two X's crossed together, don't you see?" He moistened his ring finger in a little puddle of tea on the table and showed me what he meant.

Feeling rather depressed, I bummed a cigarette from him, pressed close and lighted it with his, and immediately began to choke.

"Or perhaps it really is an ideogram that means something, in which case it must be something that's carved into the very fiber of his being. What does it mean then? I don't think I really have the heart to find out." He smiled wanly.

I was still coughing.

"To get to the bottom of all this, the best thing to do would be to take a trip out there. But it's so far away, and the county he was in is so remote, I'm afraid there won't be much chance of that happening."

"All his old school friends, we haven't done enough for him all these years," I said remorsefully.

"Well, if you're going to talk about that, then I am even more guilty than you. But in those days we couldn't even fend for ourselves, let alone anyone else. You know, he and I are actually half brothers, we had the same mother. I'm afraid that my bringing him to Shanghai may have done him more harm than good."

For a while I was silent. Then, at last, I uttered the question that had been on my mind for a long time but which I had not had the courage before this to ask: "The doctor, did he say . . . how long . . . this could go on?"

"Yes, he did. He said, it could go on—for a long time." Stubbing out his cigarette, he once again fell silent.

The bell sounded in the auditorium, but neither of us stirred.

After all this I still didn't know anything about Lao Kang's experiences in those twenty years, much less have any idea what that indestructible " ✳ " represented. The only thing I knew was that within his entire being, only this " ✳ " continued to live vibrantly, vividly, and that it was only thanks to this " ✳ "'s continuing to live that he had managed to avoid perishing altogether, to hang on to a breath of life. I couldn't help remembering what that old housekeeper had said about life and living, and I came to think it quite profound and insightful, befitting someone of her advanced years.

The bell rang a second time. We both heard it, and stood up almost at the same time.

"Let's go see the movie," he said.

"Yes, the movie," I answered.

So we walked over together. Outside, the sunlight shimmered and rolled on the tree leaves like droplets of mercury.

FIRST PUBLISHED IN OCTOBER 1985 IN *CHOU XIAOYA (THE UGLY DUCKLING)*

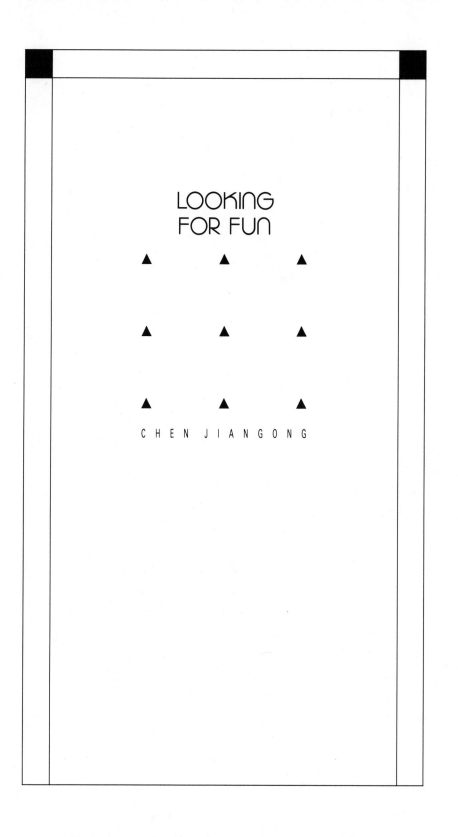

LOOKING FOR FUN

▲ ▲ ▲

▲ ▲ ▲

▲ ▲ ▲

CHEN JIANGONG

▲   ▲   ▲

▲   ▲   ▲   I

▲   ▲   Zhao-le"—that's a Beijing expression meaning "to look for fun." It also happens to be Beijingers' favorite pastime. They're fond of it, they're good at it, and this fun is not so hard to find. Keeping a pet nightingale is a kind of fun. So is flying a kite. So is nursing a bowl of wine over a clove of garlic. Even when they talk about death, for instance, Beijingers don't say, "So-and-so died," they like to say, "he's gone to hear the crickets chirp"—as though they could find some fun even in that.

Next to the Temple of Heaven is an area called Heaven's Bridge. In the old days it was a lively fairground where the common folk went to have themselves some fun. Performers had nicknames like "The Eight Oddballs," with acts to match: people like Cloud Flier with his comedy routines, and Golden Choppers with his scenic pictures and popular ditties. And Soldier Huang. The story went that this fellow had fought under Marshal Chang, who was trying to restore the overthrown Manchu monarchy. When the restoration movement fell apart Soldier Huang became just another down-and-out warrior—except he found a way to keep up the good fight.

Every day he would show up at Heaven's Bridge, pick a spot, then launch into one of his "harangues." From ancient emperors to modern rulers, from the high and mighty to the hoi polloi—no one escaped his acid tongue. And all this he did in incomparable style: phrases rhyming, voice ringing, mouth foaming, fingers jabbing. Six deep and a traffic stopper, the crowd around him would lap it all up with cheers and applause for every other word. Needless to say Soldier Huang got a big kick out of all this and would strut around like a cock of the walk. Even his listeners would feel as if they had gone from rags to riches overnight and had the whole world at their feet. Standing up at Heaven's Bridge to "harangue" or to take in the "harangues"—that was one way of having "fun."

Ever since four theater companies from the province of Anhui came to the capital and took it by storm—that would have been about two hundred years ago now—their style of performance has developed into what is known as Beijing opera, so popular it's a rare Beijinger who can't sing a few bars at least. Even pedicab drivers and street vendors would often park their wares by the roadside and toss off a song or two—*especially* pedicab drivers and street vendors and all those stuck at the bottom of the heap, who had little hope of getting out from under, let alone becoming a bigshot and going down in history. Their only thrill came when they sang a few arias and made believe they had turned into the heroes and legendary figures of their favorite operas. Even prisoners on their way to face the firing squad would often break into song. There they were, clearly branded with their crimes, all trussed up and piled onto a donkey cart, soon to depart forever for yonder banks of the Yellow Springs—and they would still manage to let loose with a couple of songs, to the cheers and ovation of bystanders. To sing at a time like this and to listen to this singing —that was another kind of "fun."

Face has always meant a lot to Beijingers, so it should come as no surprise that "emptying your pockets to buy face" was also a kind of "fun." You say you haven't got a penny to your name? Not to worry. What you would do is hang around in one of those little bars where you sat on a plank right across the top of the wine barrels. Don't think that just because the customers were mere porters and peddlers and pedicab drivers that they wouldn't know how to do things in style. Let them sit around the wine barrels and a couple of shots of rotgut later the boys would put on quite a show. This one would tell you how he once killed six men with one blow, that one would go on about the time he singlehandedly took an enemy fortress. If you were all strangers who had just met, so much the better; the tales would be even taller since you were all in the dark about each other. Anyhow by this time everyone would be pretty well plastered and the sky was the limit. You might tell someone you've been to the moon and he would answer, "Hear! hear!" Later, after you'd eaten and drunk your fill, you would get to your feet with a flourish and call for the tab. Even if you didn't own a red cent you would act like Mr. Moneybags himself. When the waiter came back with the bill you'd wave your hand airily and say: "Charge it!" Before the words were quite out of your mouth you would already have made your grand exit. Wasn't this a kind of "fun" too?

Well, all that was once upon a time. Things have changed, Beijingers are much better off now. But not everyone is living happily ever after, so "looking for fun" continues to be a popular pastime. Take those guys on the street who have deliberately stuck a foreign label on their dark glasses or their denim pants—that's their way of having some "fun" too, only they prefer to be "seen and not heard." Then there's this young fellow I know who believes in just the opposite, who likes nothing better than to strut down the street all day with his radio-cassette player blasting away, loud enough to wake the dead. If you asked him why, he'd say: "Without this thing, nobody would even give me a cross-eyed look!" You might call this a kind of "fun" too.

Anyway, old or new, these antics all seem kind of ludicrous to sophisticated folks. And in a way they're right. You say you're just a seamstress darning raggedy clothes for folks as poor as you? Well, that's your lot in life. You're never going to turn into Wang Bao-chuan the Chancellor's daughter no matter how many times you sing her song. You're a pedicab driver? Then you should know your place. Maybe it's true that you once had the famous opera star Yang Xiaolou as a customer. Maybe it's even true that you got ticked off at him and chucked him into a ditch. Sure you fixed him. He kept right on being famous opera star Yang Xiaolou, whose funeral was attended by sixty-four pallbearers and all due pomp and circumstance, while you're still a pedicab driver, lucky to have two people carry your coffin like a crate of cabbages to your final resting place! And as for those foreign labels on the sunshades, you can stick them on your forehead if you like, you'd still be a ragpicker's son who'll never set foot abroad. Life is a dud and you want to have some fun to even the score? Stuff and nonsense! Maybe that's why people who look for fun so often end up as other people's laughing-stock.

On the other hand, what's so ludicrous about this? Life may be a dud, but if you can't even have some fun then what's the point of carrying on? According to the Austrian psychiatrist Adler, it was the twin curses of psoriasis and his small size that drove Napoleon to conquer the world, to become emperor of all he surveyed. The common folk of Beijing are not quite so ambitious. All they want is to get together with their buddies and shoot the breeze or sing a few songs to drive away dull care. Is that so much to ask?

So it seems that what goes on at the Bean Street Block Office Cultural Post (just a little ways west of Winch Handle Alley), where every evening a bunch of oldtimers get together to ham it up (occasionally joined by some younger folks or old ladies who would show up to watch), now acting out a few parts from the opera *The Ferry at Xiaoyao,* now singing a few arias from *Attack on Dengzhou,* now spinning some yarns when they run out of breath, this one claiming he studied under the famous singer Gao Qingkui who had shot to stardom after appearing in *The Ferry at Xiaoyao,* that one saying he trained with Ma Lianliang, celebrated for his performance of *Attack on Dengzhou* . . . so what is going on here is a practice not only sprung from deep cultural roots but firmly based modern psychoanalytic theory as well, it seems.

II

The Bean Street Block Office takes care of the dozen-odd alleys in the neighborhood, including Winch Handle Alley. Not much else goes on at its cultural post besides these amateur songfests. The "concert hall" used to be a warehouse, so you can imagine how simple and crude everything is: not even a ceiling, only rafters sticking out overhead like so many ribs; the cement floor pockmarked with bumps and hollows; performers and audience alike sitting on benches arranged in circles that push all the way up against the walls. In the middle of the room is a clearance about the size of your palm, and part of that is taken up by a furnace, leaving room for two or three people at the most. You're all right if you sing standing still, maybe you can even strike a few poses. If two of you wanted to do that you would start bumping into each other. If you want to ham it up you'd better watch out for the furnace. It's a good thing that most of the people who've come to enjoy themselves are oldsters who don't have much left anyway in the way of posture and looks. That's why there's never been anything like a full dress performance here. At most they do a duet on the "stage"; anything more than that and some of the parts would have to be sung from the benches. But don't let appearances fool you: If you sat yourself down, closed your eyes and listened carefully, you'd hear singing that's not only tuneful but soulful as well—nothing fancy, of course, but quite respectable all the same.

Sure the oldtimers like to tell a tall story or two, but their tales usually have a few strands of truth in them. Take the one about having trained with Ma Lianliang: They probably did spend some time together as novices, only Ma made it to the top while this fellow lost his voice and ended up selling tea on the streets. But that's another story. And that one about having studied under Gao Qingkui, that's probably true too, only the guy forgot to tell you how he became addicted to opium later and ruined his career. But never mind. Most of them are at least veteran opera buffs, well versed in the matters of the opera world. One listen and they'd know which school it was, whose style of singing. Maybe you've never eaten pork, but still you know how a pig runs, don't you? So don't underestimate these old codgers. See that one over there, all bundled up in a padded overcoat, hands tucked in his sleeves and peering around like a numbskull? But when he sings, ah! what a voice—rich and clear, natural and graceful, exactly in the style of the immortal Mei Lanfang! And look at this one over here: white haired, wrinkled, bent almost double, nothing at all impressive about him—until he opens his mouth, and out comes a voice so velvety-smooth, so effortlessly beautiful, straight from the school of the great Yang Baosen. There are actually some older opera buffs who find the style of the young singers today not up to snuff, who come all the way out here just to satisfy their craving for the real thing—like it or not, the customer is always right.

So it stands to reason that it would take someone pretty special to handle these fans and fanciers of Beijing opera, someone who has sung professionally with a company, say, or at least appeared in a fair number of amateur performances. Otherwise how can you hold their attention, let alone win their respect? But that's hardly the case at the Bean Street Cultural Post: The commander-in-chief of this band of hearties is, believe it or not, a seventy-plus ex-coolie by the name of Li Zhongxiang!

Old Man Li lives at 10 Winch Handle Alley. He has a square head, a broad face, and a deep, booming voice. When he walks you can tell right away that there goes someone who used to work as a coffin carrier: small even steps, chest and stomach thrust out, hips tucked in, toes turned slightly outward. His eyes may droop at the corners and he may be getting along in years, but his complexion is always ruddy—as a result of his tippling, that's true—and he is still as cocky as a young whippersnapper. Actually, among the group of regulars there are many who can sing and act much better than Li. Some had gone through formal training, some had studied under famous coaches, there are even those who still appear professionally with various companies. As for Li, at different times he had worked as a coffin carrier, a pedicab driver, a waiter, plus quite a few other jobs, but none that had anything to do with opera. Before retirement he did work as a doorman at a theater, but that was a theater for plays. Still, from the way he's always going on about "Changhua this" and "Changhua that," you'd think he and Xiao Changhua—the opera star so famous for his clown roles—were at least bosom buddies if not blood brothers. In fact he and Xiao Changhua had had no more than a "wonton relationship." Back then he was a waiter in a snack shop and so poor he couldn't even afford the few pennies for a ticket, but his craving for opera kept gnawing at his insides. So he would pack an order of wontons in a container, march up to the door of the theater and barge right in. "Hey, where do you think you're going?" "Delivering wontons to the star." The guards actually fell for that line! After the first couple of times they didn't even bother to stop him anymore, figuring that whenever Maestro Xiao performed he had to have his order of wontons from this particular shop. Truth to tell, none of the wontons ever saw the insides of Xiao Changhua's stomach. As soon as waiter Li got inside the theater he'd hunker down in a corner somewhere and enjoy the show and the wontons at the same time. Using this trick he got to hear a good many performances by Maestro Xiao, even some by Mei Lanfang. Well, on a diet like this even an idiot could learn to sing a few snatches after a while, and today our friend Li can still do such a perfect imitation of Mr. Xiao's comic accents that he would always bring down the house. Whereupon he would say, with an air of vindication: "You know, if I hadn't been so poor back then that I couldn't even afford the props to get started, I could've turned 'pro.' I could have been a star, just like Changhua!" Of course, anyone who knew the least bit about opera could tell that Li Zhongxiang was light years away from becoming a star like Xiao Changhua.

But to these diehard fans, Li's passion for Beijing opera made him a man after their own hearts. So they went along with his conceits and good-naturedly called him "The New Changhua," even bestowing on him the title of "Chief Coach" that Mr. Xiao had held in his company's school. Li was always one to take charge anyway, with or without a title, so he was only too happy to assume "officially" the job of overseeing the activities of the cultural post.

Older residents in the Bean Street neighborhood, especially those living along Winch Handle Alley, have come to know Li inside out over the years. They remember how, back when he was just a young fellow working as a coffin carrier, he would get up at the crack of dawn, slip into his green uniform, put on his felt hat with its plume of chicken feathers, and sit on the bench outside the Eternal Peace Funeral Parlor, chatting with passersby while he waited for his assignments. Then he worked as a waiter in the Pot o' Plenty Wonton Shop, but less than a year later he got fired for always sneaking out with an order of wontons to see his "freebie" shows. After that he was reduced to hanging around the little teahouse where people who needed a day laborer would come and give him an odd job or two. Still later, he moved to 10 Winch Handle Alley and became even more of a fixture in the neighborhood.

But what the old folks remember best was the time back in the spring of '35 when the usually down-at-the-heels Li suddenly "made it." Well, maybe to say he had "made it" was stretching it a little, but to his belt-tightening and penny-pinching neighbors it sure looked that way. What they saw was a Li who no longer went hungry two meals out of three and whose clothes had fewer patches on them.

According to Li Zhongxiang himself, it all began when he met a Mr. Jiang at the little teahouse, who would show up every other day or so, grab a hold of Li and spend a few hours just chewing the fat with him. Afterward Mr. Jiang would slip him the equivalent of a day's wages. His neighbors on Winch Handle Alley were all green with envy: What's so hard about smoking some fine cigarettes and sipping choice tea—for free, you understand—meanwhile rattling away about anything and everything under the sun? At the end of it you'd get a day's wages to boot. Talk about your cushy job! Everyone told Li he had met his lucky star, a bigshot, that from then on he would have it made. Li himself didn't think so, because one day he accidentally discovered that the lining of Mr. Jiang's coat was patched together from remnants, just like his own. He would mention his puzzlement to anyone who would listen: "What a strange fellow, this Mr. Jiang—he sure doesn't have money to burn, so why is he throwing it away on just having someone to shoot the breeze with?"

It was true that Mr. Jiang was no bigwig, and Li Zhongxiang never made his fortune either. When the Marco Polo Bridge Incident* came to pass Mr. Jiang dropped from sight. As for Li, he continued to hang around the teahouse waiting for odd jobs: fixing up a shop front here, helping to bury a dead child there. His teahouse "encounter" gradually slipped from people's minds.

But after Liberation, Mr. Jiang turned out to be an honest-to-goodness bigshot. By then Li Zhongxiang had become a pedicab driver. One rainy day he was waiting for customers in front of a theater. No one seemed to want a cab, so he parked underneath the marquee to get out of the rain. Just as he was beginning to get restless, he overheard some theatergoers talking about this show that was all about a funeral parlor. That caught his ear. He thought to himself, it's time to get up-to-date and try one of these new-fangled plays, he had nothing better to do anyhow. So he bought a ticket and went inside. Not halfway through the first act and you could have knocked him down with a feather: Wasn't all this exactly like the stories he used to tell Mr. Jiang? When he asked around he discovered the playwright was none other than Mr. Jiang Tieya himself, who was now also the head of the theater company. After the show Li Zhongxiang got his pedicab and rushed backstage. Sure enough, Mr. Jiang remembered him and welcomed him with fine cigarettes and choice tea, just like in the old days. Li said: "Mr. Jiang, I don't want to push pedals anymore. You're the boss around

*Incident between Chinese and Japanese soldiers on July 7, 1937, at the Marco Polo Bridge on the outskirts of Beijing, marking the beginning of the war between China and Japan.

here, aren't you? Can't I come work for you?" Mr. Jiang asked: "What can you do?" "I've picked up a few tricks from Changhua, and I don't get stagefright either," Li answered. Mr. Jiang laughed: "That's Beijing opera. Here we do plays." But Li persisted: "I don't care what kind of show it is, I've taken a liking to your theater anyhow, because you speak up for us common folks. Just let me work as a janitor or something." And that's how Li became the doorman for this prestigious theater. The news caused a sensation on Winch Handle Alley. Those of his neighbors who had seen him in front of the theater all agreed, this time Li had really "made it." Just look at him on opening nights, all spiffed up in his spanking new tunic suit while he bustled about greeting everyone, shaking hands with those who arrived in limousines and inviting them in. He was quite an impressive sight!

Ah, but like they say, "Don't pick up the kettle that's not whistling"—in other words, let's not bring up other people's sore points. Much as Li Zhongxiang likes to run on at the mouth, to show off, have you ever heard him talk about what really happened at the theater? True, he had bought himself a nice new suit with nary a wrinkle in it, and on opening nights he would carefully put it on, then hurry to the theater, where he would stand at the entrance eagerly greeting everyone, shaking hands with those who pulled up in limousines, showing them in—"So glad you came!" "Do let us know what you think!" "This way, please!"—so that quite a few people actually mistook him for the company director or the playwright. Yes, all of that was true. But what's the big deal? He figured that he got this job thanks to Mr. Jiang and it was the least he could do to put his best foot forward for his boss. So, as with everything else he really enjoyed, he would bustle about on his job, full of enthusiasm and swagger. But soon he noticed something wrong. People in the company began to look at him in a funny way, the youngsters began pulling his leg and calling him "Director Li" or even "President Li." He didn't really mind any of that, but then even Mr. Jiang seemed to find him standing in the light. On opening nights, when he would rush excitedly to the theater in his natty new suit, all set to receive the crowds, Mr. Jiang would always find some excuse to send him away from the entrance: Would he move the flowers over there please, and see that the VIP lounge was properly set up, then . . . and so on, back and forth. Li finally got the picture: To stand at the door in fancy clothes, shaking hands and making small talk—that was only for high society, not for the likes of him! But he was also a little hurt: Just because he had been standing in the wrong place, was that any reason for them to give him such dirty looks and to snap at him? Why didn't people ever try to put themselves in others' shoes? He loved the theater, he was so proud of it. Whenever he recalled that he was one of its members he would hold his head high. . . . If I was standing in the wrong place couldn't you have come right out and said so? Others may not understand me, but at least you, Mr. Jiang, you should know me better than this! . . .

Know you how? You can't be forever wearing your heart on your sleeve, can you? And even if you did, and others got to know you, so what?!

Li was over forty when he finally got married. Less than two years later his wife died while giving birth to their son Dezhi. Years passed but he did not remarry, though to tell the truth he had his share of sexual yearnings like everyone else—especially when you remember that he could feast his eyes on pretty young actresses all day long at work. One day, while he was going about his job, he happened to hear the splashing of water mingled with women's voices laughing and chatting. The sounds came from the women's locker room upstairs, where the actresses were showering and

changing after a performance. Even Li himself didn't quite understand what came over him then: He came to a stop, turned his face
upward and stared at the open window, as if he really expected to
see something up there. Actually nothing at all could be seen from
down below. But this routine became almost like a nervous tic with
him: Whenever he passed under the women's locker room he
would compulsively slow down and gaze up at the window.
Wouldn't you know it, someone reported him to the higher-ups.
And probably because it was Mr. Jiang whom he respected the
most, Mr. Jiang it was who came to have a talk with him. In truth
Mr. Jiang himself knew that nothing could be seen from downstairs.
If Li had flatly denied ever looking up at the window that would
have been the end of the matter. Instead he said: "I was wrong. I
did try to look. But I couldn't see anything." Li thought to himself:
What's the big fuss, doesn't everyone have a few indecent thoughts
now and then? I just won't do it again, that's all. . . . But alas, my
friend, people really got to know you well this time. So what
happened but the whole bucket of shit came down on your head
and you ended up being the butt of everyone's jokes! . . . All those
lovely young things who used to call him "Uncle Li" or "Master
Li"—how sweet were their voices!—what did they do now but
wrinkle their noses at him as they passed by. The young fellows
were even more insulting: "Hey, Gramps, go buy yourself a mirror!" These were all educated folks, cultured people. Now if they
all behaved like that virtuous Liu Xiahui of old who remained cool
as a cucumber even when pretty women climbed onto his lap—
well, then, that's one thing. But these were people who made fun
of Li while they carried on with their floozies. Were they phonies
or what?!

After this Li Zhongxiang became listless and droopy. No longer
did he go on about Maestro Xiao one day and Maestro Yang the

next. Time and again friends tried to set him up with another mate. Before the incident with the women's locker room it would probably have been a simple case of "Yes" or "No." But now for some reason he made this rule for himself: He had to tell the woman about the incident, if only to test her. Of course the matches all fell through. So much the better, he thought. What if he had ended up with a dame who was a self-righteous phony—he could never put up with that!

Just before the Cultural Revolution began, he started seeing the widow Lu Guiying, who worked in the box office at the theater. He was fifty-five then and she fifty. His only thought was to find a mate, someone he could talk to, someone who'd take care of him just as he would take care of her. He and Widow Lu got along famously, but when it came time to lay his cards on the table, right away he said: "There's something I've got to tell you. I don't have a very good reputation at the theater. There was this incident . . ." "Enough already," interrupted Lu Guiying, "that's ancient history. I know all about it. Besides, we're no spring chickens, and who can honestly say they've never done anything to be ashamed of?" Before this Li Zhongxiang had been somewhat hesitant about proposing since Lu Guiying had three children from her previous marriage, but when she said those words to him his heart leaped and he thought to himself: At last! All these years no one had ever said anything like this to him, as though they were perfectly honorable, gentlemen and ladies all, while he was the only goddamn lowlife! But when those honorable folks lay in bed at night and looked deep into their hearts, could they honestly say they've never had a dirty thought in their lives? Well, why get all worked up over this anymore? At least there were still people like Lu Guiying in this world. How nice it would be to marry someone he could talk to, someone like her. . . . Alas, this match also fell through. Lu Guiying's in-laws set her own children on her to object to the marriage, and naturally quite a few nasty things were said about Li Zhong-xiang. Not wanting to hurt his feelings she told him only that her kids were almost grown, she had sweated it out so far already, why not just let it be. But by then he had heard the real story from someone else.

When the Cultural Revolution ended Li Zhongxiang was sixty-five and old enough to retire. But he was rather reluctant to say goodbye to the theater. He especially hated to part with that play about the coffin carriers, which had remained in the theater's reper-tory. Whenever someone mentioned this play his heart would skip a beat, even though he would never again get all spiffed up and stand next to Mr. Jiang greeting guests at the theater entrance. Nor would he ever mention again how back in '35 Mr. Jiang used to look for him to chew the fat with in the little teahouse. The theater had hurt his feelings. But if it hadn't been for another stupid thing he later did, something that led to his feelings being hurt again, he would have hung around a few more years just so he could watch his favorite play a few more times.

During the Cultural Revolution he had "saved" Mr. Jiang's life, although Mr. Jiang never knew anything about it. Back then Mr. Jiang had been beaten up, openly attacked in the newspapers, criti-cized on the airwaves—things seemed headed for the breaking point. One day Li Zhongxiang happened to pass by the Peace and Happiness Restaurant (in those days its name had been changed to the more revolutionary-sounding Long March Restaurant) when he saw Mr. Jiang through the plate-glass windows, sitting alone before a tableful of food and drinking away morosely. Li thought to him-self, this doesn't look good at all. Whereupon he ran back to the theater and scrawled a note, something to the effect of: "We love your plays. Please don't give up." That was about all Li could manage—you didn't get to be very literate in those literacy classes. He didn't dare put his name on the note, so he signed it only, "The Revolutionary Masses." Then he rushed back to the restaurant and asked someone to bring the note in to Mr. Jiang. After the Cultural Revolution Mr. Jiang was restored to his post, and at a rally to celebrate the revival of *The Coffin Carriers* he talked about how he had decided against suicide because of a note from an anonymous playgoer, tears streaming down his cheeks as he spoke. After the rally Li Zhongxiang deliberately went up to Mr. Jiang and shook his hand. Of course, he never breathed a word to anyone about the source of the note. On opening night of *The Coffin Carriers,* Li couldn't resist getting his suit out from the bottom of the chest and putting it on once more to go to the theater. He had long ago learned it was not his place to bustle about where Mr. Jiang was standing. But as soon as Mr. Jiang saw Li in his once-familiar outfit he said: "Master Li, we need some help backstage. Would you mind going back there to give them a hand?"

Well, it was high time that he retired. This time for sure he was going to retire.

To this day that certificate with the words "Honorable Retirement" in gold on a red background is still hanging solemnly on his wall. He still remembers the farewell party the theater gave him, still remembers how Mr. Jiang brought him back to 10 Winch Handle Alley in his own sedan. When Mr. Jiang and the other top brass of the company came in and sat down in his tiny house, he could feel the tears rolling along the wrinkles in his cheeks all the way down to the corners of his mouth, where he could taste how salty they were. Sheepishly he wiped them off before anyone noticed. He began to regret his decision: How quick he had been to feel wronged! Before Liberation he had pulled rickshaws, carried coffins, suffered all kinds of abuse and taken it all in stride. But now, now he's become a sissy, good times have spoiled him. Three square meals a day, a solid roof over his head, and he starts to fret about petty things! Couldn't he see Mr. Jiang was busy? How could he expect Mr. Jiang to think of everything, to stop and worry about his tender feelings?! Besides, was it right for him to butt in where he didn't belong? Was it right for him to want to peek into the women's locker room? . . .

But all this belongs to the past. After seeing Mr. Jiang and the others off in their car that day, Li Zhongxiang suddenly felt his days were numbered. Take it easy, live it up a bit—that was all the fun he could expect. What else could there be?

Then, lo and behold, right there on Bean Street he discovered the gang of old geezers making music and making merry! Here were people after his own heart: coffin carriers, pedicab drivers, snack peddlers, poor folks all—not a single bigwig among them, but not a single phony either. Not three days after Li Zhongxiang started coming to this place but he perked up again. At the theater he'd always had to be on his best behavior: No dirty words or they would make fun of him, no good-natured puffery even or they'd think he was laying it on too thick. After his fall from grace it became worse: He had to tiptoe around, all meek and mild, playing the fool. Anyway, the theater people were always using big words and dropping names that ended in "ski" or something like that, none of which he knew. But here at the Bean Street Block Office Cultural Post he felt right at home. So he began to sing, to gab, to bustle about with gusto, just like that fun-loving, fast-talking, opera-singing young coffin carrier of forty years ago. Sure he knew that among his new-found buddies were many fine singers and experienced performers. So what? Everyone was there for the fun of it, not to nitpick. And now they were calling him "The New Chang-hua" and "Chief Coach." That was fine with him. A chief coach takes care of business, and he was just the man for the job.

III

Hanging out with this bunch of opera buffs at the Cultural Post, Li Zhongxiang began to bubble over with energy. Meanwhile, his arrival on the scene made his new friends bubble over with enthusiasm. Li plunged right in and took charge: One day he would announce the schedule of performances, the next he'd begin to assign roles, the third day he would bring along someone to sing the old man's part, the day after that, who knows, he might find two people to try out for the part of the general. Or he would go talk to the people in the Block Office about whether they should give their "company" a name, whether they could get a few more props, and so on, and so on. His constant dickering with the office produced at least one benefit: The Cultural Post was now open every day instead of every other day. His other efforts also bore fruit: A band was pulled together, complete with gongs and drums and strings. But they were still in need of someone to play the part of the dashing young man. The "company" used to just get one of the old guys to fill in, but that left a lot to be desired. It so happens that young Guo Senlin, who lives at 26 Winch Handle Alley, not only is a graduate of an opera school but also a member of a professional opera company, and, what's more, his specialty is the role of the handsome young fellow. Time and again the guys had invited Guo to join them for a little fun, but he had always refused. Actually the fanciest part Guo Senlin had had so far was that of a spear carrier, but he thought himself too good to team up with those "crazy old fools." Leave it to Li Zhongxiang to bring him around. "I swallowed my pride and went all out," said Li. Three times he called on young Guo, now giving him the hard sell, now sweet-talking him with promises of "top billing" and "starring roles," and finally all but dragged him in. Then there's the string player they now have, Old Mr. Li, who had actually studied under the famous musician Xu Lanyuan himself. Old Mr. Li pays for a monthly bus pass out of his own pocket and spends an hour commuting each day just to play in their band—all because Li Zhongxiang had happened to meet him one day at the Heaven's Bridge bus stop, struck up a conversation, and invited him to join their fun. That's why even though Chief Coach Li would often throw his weight around at rehearsals when he hadn't the foggiest idea how to direct the performance, and everyone would then give him a hard time about how he was faking it and getting things all tangled up—in fact the guys all appreciated the many things he had done for the group.

Lately, though, while no one had actually said anything, they were all thinking to themselves: I say, old buddy, aren't you getting a bit carried away? It was fine in the beginning when Li would boost their ranks with people who knew their stuff, and the more the merrier. But he didn't stop at that, or limit himself to the Winch Handle Alley crowd. Wherever he went, whenever he saw an old man squatting in the sun in front of a store or drinking silently in a wine shop, he would strike up a conversation with him. At the first mention of worries or troubles Li would start saying how much fun it was to get together with the guys every night and sing some opera, as if the only way the man would find relief from his problems was by following Li back to the Bean Street Cultural Post. It was becoming a habit with Li Zhongxiang, a bad habit.

One day he brought along his neighbor across the way, Old Man Hao of 9 Winch Handle Alley, and solemnly announced to everyone: "My buddy here is an old hand at playing the part of a young woman." The fellows had long ago heard of Old Man Hao, of how

during the Cultural Revolution his house had been searched and his
valuables confiscated, and how later he had been compensated in
cash for all of it. They also knew his son Stinky, who was always
zooming up and down the alley on his motorcycle and making a
huge racket. But no one had ever heard of Old Man Hao's talents
on stage. In fact it was only that very day that Hao himself, under
Li Zhongxiang's enthusiastic "coaching," had found out about his
own "talent." Li was just going out the door when he saw his old
neighbor squatting in front of the wall on the other side of the alley.
"Well, well, what are we trying to hatch here?" Li joked. Old Man
Hao sighed but said nothing. Li had to press him before he would
say what was wrong. Turned out the old man was ticked off at his
new color TV set: ". . . who knows when they'll start smooching
or messing around in bed. Or else there'll be these men and women
with bare thighs that look just like carrots, bouncing all over the
place! How embarrassing to be watching this stuff with my two
kids! If I don't watch TV I might miss a good show, but if I do I
might get all this crap instead!" Right away Li Zhongxiang saw his
opening and jumped in: "Now, now, don't get your nose out of
joint about this. Why don't you come with me instead? We'll have
some good clean fun!" "Singing opera? But I don't know how."
"Don't try to be modest with me. You're a Manchu, aren't you, and
all Manchus can sing Beijing opera. You can't fool me. I'll bet you
even studied singing—you probably did the part of the young
woman. Yes, and I'll bet you looked pretty good back then. How
about singing a few lines to show your stuff?" Would you believe
it, Old Man Hao actually got all stirred up, and right then and there
belted out a song. But what on earth was our Chief Coach thinking
when he said: "You'll do fine! Just come with me and practice with
the band for a few days. In no time you'll sound just like Maestro
Mei!" Maestro Mei indeed! As soon as Old Man Hao opened his

mouth everyone burst out laughing: Wonderful! He couldn't even carry a tune in a bucket!

Once is about enough for this kind of thing, wouldn't you say? But our friend Li didn't seem to have learned from the experience at all. A few days later he was drinking in a little wine shop when he ran into another "old pal"—well no, they had never met before, but they had hit it off right away, so in a twinkling they had become fast friends—and found out his buddy was down in the dumps because he was being bossed around at home by his daughter-in-law. So of course Li pulled him into the fold right away: "Let me give you some advice. Drown your sorrows in singing instead. Why don't you come with me, I'm in charge over there. You can't sing? Never mind. Even listening can help you forget your troubles." For heaven's sake, he's just like those old men in Beijing who are always urging you to take *rendan* pills—they cure everything, you know —or those old women in Guangzhou who are forever offering you some "antirheumatism" oil. No matter what ails you, Li gives the same prescription: "Come with me, we'll sing a few!"

Time and again he did this. The Bean Street Cultural Post had been in the pink because of Li Zhongxiang; now, because of him, it was becoming red hot—too hot, in fact. Two more circles of benches had to be added in the hall: Now the open area in the middle was no longer even "palm sized." As for the performers, they no longer had to bundle up in overcoats nor tuck their hands up their sleeves, even on the coldest nights, because just to stand up there was almost to cuddle the furnace as you sang. Something else left the veteran fans not knowing whether to laugh or cry. Those new hands like Old Man Hao who had come aboard thanks to Li Zhongxiang's prodding—they all seemed to have let his words go to their heads, honestly believing that with a few days' practice they would "sound just like Maestro Mei." So they really knocked themselves out at rehearsal every night, howling out aria after aria the whole evening long. Meanwhile the real "pros" were left waiting in the wings. Worse yet, since many of the newcomers were folks with a bellyful of woes, they couldn't help but air their grievances every chance they had. After an aria from *The Wulong Courtyard* bawling out nasty women, this one would grouse about his nasty wife; after a passage from *The Four Mandarins* singing the praises of honest officials, that one would sigh and mutter: "How few there are today!" Or someone would run on and on about the injustices done to him or to a friend or to a friend's friend. *The Inn of Good Fortune* would lead to a lament on snobbery and social climbing. *Banquet at the Border* would bring on a tirade about "that good-for-nothing son of mine." From headaches to heartaches, from tight corners to loose ends—they would babble away about everything under the sun. Meanwhile some poor soul would still be trying to sing on the "stage." Things were getting out of hand, but the fellows didn't want their chief coach to lose face, so they kept their mouths shut.

It was Guo Senlin, the spear carrier all pumped up for "top billing" and "starring roles," who first reached the boiling point. He went to Old Tang Heshun, the Block Office cadre in charge of the Cultural Post, and threw a fit: "Did you ask me here to sing or to watch them butcher everything? Why don't you just butcher me instead? I'm cutting out!"

Old Man Tang is a big, tall fellow who is always hunched over, looking for all the world like a huge dried shrimp. The fellows would irreverently call him "Shrimp Head." As a lad he had been trained to sing the young female roles—you could tell from his looks even today that he must have once cut quite a smart figure onstage. But then he started to grow, and grow, and grow. You couldn't very well play the delicate heroine when you were at least half a head taller than the warrior hero, could you? So he was limited to concert singing. People who had heard him at the old Beijing Number One Teahouse before Liberation remembered him well for his fine voice and amazing breath control: He could hold on to a note forever, it seemed, and you could never tell when he inhaled between phrases. Who would have thought that only a few years later he would lose his voice? After that happened Tang decided he was never going to make it as a singer in this life, so he turned to his only other skill: He became a scribe, writing letters, petitions and the like for customers at his sidewalk stand. Not long after Liberation he went to work for the Street Committee, and because of his background was put in charge of running an opera club for the Cultural Post—back in his old profession, you might say. But his luck was no better this time around. During the Cultural Revolution he was accused of having organized a decadent capitalistic club and was given a vicious beating by the Red Guards. It's kind of funny when you realize that the characters in the operas they were singing at the club had all lived at a time when the capitalist class wasn't even on the horizon yet. But that's neither here nor there. After this our friend Mr. Tang was really through with the world of opera. If it weren't for his job he would turn tail and run at the first note from a gong or drum. The authorities solemnly promise there will be no more "mass movements," but who can say for sure? Anyway, he's finally got it figured out: It has been written in his stars that he is not to have anything to do with opera in this life; the slightest contact and he's in for it. But how to keep his distance when he is still on salary as the cadre responsible for the opera club? It would be such a pity to retire and throw all that good money away. So very reluctantly he had decided to stay on as the Cultural Post's "Shrimp Head." To fulfill his official obligations as well as to protect his own hide, he handles two items, and two items only. First, he keeps an eye on the newspapers every day to see whether they are about to "criticize" something or other. What for? In his own words: "So's we can fix up the outside." Actually it's all quite simple. On one side of the Cultural Post's front door is a board for wall posters and newspapers. Whenever Old Shrimp Head sees a slogan mentioned in the press he would clip it out and post it on the board under the heading "Notices" —you know, articles with titles like "Criticize Bourgeois Liberalism" or "Clear Away Spiritual Pollution." The space is usually chock full of clippings. Of course he knows better than anyone that no matter what is posted on the outside, inside the hall they're still singing vintage operas, the old war-horses. But he keeps at it anyway, if only to give himself a little peace of mind. Second, he would write new lyrics to old songs to keep up with "current events," whether they be the "one child per family" campaign, or a crackdown on crime, or "traffic safety month." If the District Committee decides to put on a show tomorrow, the Bean Street Block Office Cultural Post would be ready to roll. In a contest to pick the block that is "The Most Advanced in Cultural Activities," an ancient love story like *The Romance of the Western Chamber* would go over like a lead balloon, but something like *The Virtues of Vasectomy*—now there's a winner for sure!

In the beginning Tang Heshun was more than happy to let Li Zhongxiang take charge of the opera club. At the least Tang could save on tea leaves, to say nothing of time and energy. He might even have someone to take the blame in case anything went wrong. But now it seemed he had no choice but to step in. If he continued to give this fellow a free hand who knows where they'll all end up? Even if the outsiders Li brought in didn't cause a lick of trouble, how were they all going to fit into the hall?

Li Zhongxiang himself had not yet caught on to the problem.

Every evening he would sit around as usual with his old cronies and sing a little, chat a bit, hold forth on matters big and small, all the while thinking to himself that he was doing a pretty good job as chief coach. It wasn't until he heard what Tang Heshun had to say that the problem began to register. But after giving it some thought he wasn't at all convinced. Didn't everyone come here just to have some fun? If Guo Senlin really wanted to be a "star" maybe he should go somewhere else instead!

"Whoa there! You never know when to stop, do you? So they call you 'Chief Coach,' but that doesn't mean you really have an opera school under your command. Just look at the people you've dragged in: They're not exactly opera school material—more like inmates of an old folks' home!" Tang Heshun was about the same age as Li Zhongxiang and they had always been on familiar terms with each other, so now he minced no words: "Give me a break, will you? Those old geezers you brought along who can't sing worth a damn—let them go somewhere else to get their kicks!"

Old Man Tang didn't really mean it of course, but Li Zhongxiang was cut to the quick. All those fellows he had invited along, were they all to be drummed out just like that? Sure he would lose face, but that wasn't the point. What he couldn't stand was the thought of them going back to squatting in front of a store, or squabbling with their sons and bickering with their wives. For a long time he didn't say a word. Finally, his eyes drooping like a hound dog's, he said: "All right, all right, can't we at least leave things as they are? How're you going to keep some and not the others?" He thought for a while longer, then added with a sigh: "Let it be. We're all at that age now, all camels on the wagon—it's the only fun we have left."

Reckon few of the young folks in Beijing today would understand what he meant by that.

In the old days there used to be a lot of camels in Beijing—that's how this saying came about. When a camel died it was put on a wagon and carted away to the slaughterhouse, to be recycled into soup bones and other useful stuff. After a life of hard labor this ride on the wagon was the only "fun" the poor camel ever had. Some sense of humor, eh? Anyway, the saying was quite popular with folks like Li Zhongxiang. After a hard day's work carrying coffins, he would plop himself down in a wine shop somewhere, order a double shot of Burning Blade and sigh: "Camels on the wagon, that's the only fun we'll ever have!" By now it's become one of his stock phrases, so we needn't take him too seriously. Besides, to the old codgers he had recruited into the "company," their nightly music-making might well be the only fun they have left.

Tang Heshun is a sensible and sympathetic man, and he understood what was going through his friend's mind. After thinking it over for a little while, he said: "All right, let's do this: Those who're already here might as well stay, we're not going to kick people out anyway. But as for the rest of the world, why don't you leave them where they are? One more person and this place is going to burst apart at the seams!"

"It's a deal!" Li Zhongxiang waved his hands in delight. "I'll get that into my thick skull, I promise you. If I bring in one more person I'll be a donkey's ass!"

IV

An oath is a most useless thing. Take our friend Li Zhongxiang— not three days had gone by before he brought along another old crony to join his fellow buffs. What're you going to do—really make him walk on all fours? Of course he had an explanation: "But what else could I do? I can ignore the boss, even His Majesty the

Emperor himself, but this is my old buddy Wanyou who helped me out when I was desperate. I can't just watch him go to pieces."

Qiao Wanyou is ten years younger than Li Zhongxiang. He was still a child when Li was already making a living carrying coffins. When Qiao was twelve his father died and left the family destitute, so to help make ends meet he would earn a few pennies working as an extra in funeral processions, carrying a paper willow tree or holding up signs that said "Silence!" or "Make Way!" Bachelor Li had only himself to support, and every so often he would help out the Qiao family. When Wanyou's mother came down with the "swelling sickness" back in that terrible winter of '33, it was Li who pawned his clothes to buy medicine for her. When she died, again it was Li who got together a few of the guys to talk the Fellowship Pharmacy into donating a cheap coffin, then helped Wanyou bury his mother. To Li Zhongxiang all this was no more than "looking out for each other," "what friends are for." So when it comes to acts of kindness it was actually Li who had done the first good turn, even though he has forgotten all about it himself.

Long ago in Beijing there was a man who specialized in the scattering of paper money at funerals. He went by the nickname of "Hairy Patch," because of the tuft of long hairs growing out of the mole on his chin, and few if any knew his real name. As a boy Hairy Patch had also worked as an extra at funerals, but he grew tired of other people teasing him about how little money he made, so he went all out to become the best paper strewer in the whole city. It was said that when Hairy Patch scattered paper money he would have one stack under his left arm, another in the crook of his elbow, the third in his left hand; then he would wave his right hand and —swooooosh!—every last piece of paper would be whirling and swirling up, up past the top of the four-storied Sipailou, where they would dance in the air like so many snowflakes before fluttering slowly onto the ground, and no two pieces were ever found to be stuck to each other. This skill alone was enough to make him famous all over Beijing. The story went that it was he who did the honors at the funerals of the powerful warlords Yuan Shikai and Li Yuanhong. On a good day he would make a hundred silver pieces, on a bad day at least twenty, and that was not counting the clothes he would get as a member of the procession. It wasn't long before Hairy Patch had made enough money to open up his own business.

Qiao Wanyou was also determined to make good, and following in Hairy Patch's footsteps he too learned to scatter paper like magic. When Hairy Patch died Wanyou became the undisputed champ of his trade. Times had changed, though, so he didn't make as much money as his predecessor had—oh, maybe only five or six silver pieces each time—but he put it to good use. Unlike so many others, he didn't smoke, drink, gamble or whore around, and he had a good mind for business to boot. For instance, he got together a gaggle of kids to walk behind him at funerals picking up the paper money he had just scattered. Afterward they would hand it over in exchange for some candied crabapples. When he got home Qiao would carefully string up all the pieces of paper, sprinkle some water on them, then squeeze them between a couple of wooden blocks, and presto!—they were ready to be used again at the next funeral. Meanwhile he would pocket the money each customer paid him for the paper. After a few years Qiao Wanyou managed to save up a tidy little sum, found himself a wife, and bought the little compound at 10 Winch Handle Alley. That was during the days when Li Zhongxiang was hanging around the teahouse waiting for odd jobs and living from hand to mouth. As the saying goes, it never rains but it pours. Sure enough, just then the mud hovel he was living in collapsed, leaving him without even a roof over his head. As soon as Qiao Wanyou found out about this he insisted that Li move in with them. At first Li refused. Was this what it had come to? All those years of hard work and he didn't even have a place to call his own, he'd have to live off his young friend instead? How humiliating! But then where else could he go? So in the end he gave in and moved into 10 Winch Handle Alley. After much courteous yielding back and forth, Qiao Wanyou and his family took the north house and Li Zhongxiang the west. The house to the east was rented to a couple who made their living as street vendors. They have since retired and gone to live with their son, leaving the house to their daughter Lai Yufang and her husband Wang Jin.

It is now some forty years since Li Zhongxiang first moved into 10 Winch Handle Alley with Qiao Wanyou and his family. Except for the ten years or so during the Cultural Revolution when all private property was confiscated and everyone had to pay rent to the government, Li had been feeling ill at ease all along. Once or twice he had asked Qiao if he shouldn't be paying him something in the way of rent. Before Li had finished talking, the normally quiet and mild-mannered Qiao Wanyou would get all red in the face and sputter: "That's an insult!" So Li had to let the matter drop. This is what he was referring to when he said Qiao had done him a great kindness. Of course it wasn't the money he meant so much as the friendship behind it. By comparison he felt that what he had done for Qiao long ago was no more than a snap of the fingers. He had to find some way of repaying Qiao's kindness or he would never feel good about himself.

One day around noon, Li Zhongxiang was having a drink at home when Qiao Wanyou walked in without knocking—he didn't have to because after all these years they were just like family to each other.

"Where's Dezhi?"

Dezhi is Li Zhongxiang's son. Normally he would be at work at his own little tailor's stall at the market, but that day he had taken time off to have some fun.

"Has the kid got a girlfriend now?"

"It'd be about time, he's already thirty-three," Li Zhongxiang said as he poured a second bowl of wine and set out another pair of chopsticks. Once he had run into his son walking with a young woman on Bean Street. He had seen her before—she would drop by the Cultural Post from time to time—kind of pretty, not a bad figure either. But who knows whether she's actually Dezhi's girlfriend?

Now that he's getting on in years Qiao Wanyou no longer denies himself everything. Once in a while he would down a few drinks too. He is a slight, wiry man with deep-set eyes and a narrow, straight nose, and his boyish face and silver hair give him a gentle and serene look that matches his easygoing nature, so rarely found in what used to be called the "lower classes." Although a man of few words, he has never been tongue-tied around Li Zhongxiang. But today for some reason he was silent as he sipped his wine, head bowed and seemingly lost in thought.

Finally he let out a long sigh, lifted his head and looked around the room. "Yep, this is a much better arrangement. You were smart not to get married again. At least you've got your peace and quiet!"

Li Zhongxiang answered: "He who is wearing shoes always imagines how cool and comfortable it would be to go barefoot, while he who is barefoot always envies the one with shoes. To be honest with you, if it wasn't for the fun I get from my opera club every night, I might well be looking around for another mate."

Qiao Wanyou fell silent again.

"What's the matter, Wanyou? Whatever it is, two heads are

always better than one." Li couldn't stand this wishy-washy routine any longer.

"There's nothing you can do to help." Qiao smiled weakly, then added: "All right, I'll tell you. The people from the courthouse are coming tomorrow to investigate. Chuansheng and Xiulian are getting a divorce."

Xiulian is Qiao Wanyou's daughter and Chuansheng his son-in-law. The two had met while working in the same factory. After the wedding Chuansheng moved in with his wife's parents because there was no room to spare at his own parents' house.

Li Zhongxiang was furious when he heard what Qiao Wanyou said. "But it's only been six months since they got married. What is that son-of-a-bitch up to?"

"It's not his fault. If I were in his shoes I wouldn't be able to stand it either!" Qiao sighed again. "Forget it, dirty linen should be kept out of sight. To tell the truth, I don't even know what to say tomorrow to those people from the court."

Li didn't press him any more. He knew what a proud man his old friend was, and if Qiao didn't want to talk about it he certainly wasn't going to pry. But in fact Qiao had been doing a slow burn for days now and was about ready to blow his lid. Besides, while he is usually pretty reserved, a few drops of liquor would loosen his tongue immediately. A couple of bowls of the potent Beijing Daqu down the hatch and it's as if what was on his mind would turn musty if he didn't give it an airing right away. By then you would have no choice but to listen.

To begin at the beginning, it all had to do with his wife, who used to sell "watch-it food" at Heaven's Bridge. You can't find this stuff nowadays, but once upon a time it was very common. Actually it was just table scraps from restaurants—"leftovers" to some, a "hodgepodge" to others, but a "specialty of the house" for poor folks. In the same bucket you'd find big pieces of meat along with fishheads, fishbones, egg shells, peanut shells, toothpicks, cigarette butts and . . . you name it. It was served up right in the bucket too: For every five picks with your chopsticks—no matter what you fished out—you'd pay one copper, so you'd have to "watch it" as you tried to pick up only the meat. As for the proprietress, she would be busy keeping an eye on you: five passes with your sticks and she'd put a little bamboo marker next to your bowl—you can bet she was "watching it" as closely as you. Now you see how the name came about. After Liberation "watch-it food" went out of style, so Mrs. Qiao stayed home to take care of her family and to help out at the Street Committee.

The Street Committee is always trying to improve the well-being of the people, including their minds. For volunteers it can count on all the old men and old women who have nothing better to do than stand on the street corner all day talking about the importance of family planning to anyone who would listen. Or else it would hold discussions for the old folks on such serious issues as "alienation." From their discussions they might conclude that something was "entirely necessary and very timely"*, when in fact it was "entirely unnecessary and very harmful," or entirely necessary for some people—cadres, say, or intellectuals—but entirely irrelevant to old ladies. In other words, what's sauce for the goose is not always sauce for the gander. But somehow these folks never got the point. Anyway, no matter what they were doing Madam Qiao was always right there in the thick of it. Not long ago, as part of the campaign

*A phrase from *The Teachings of Chairman Mao* and a popular slogan during the Cultural Revolution.

to crack down on "criminal behavior" and arrest "bad elements," she had put on a red armband and "patrolled" the neighborhood. The young toughs hanging out in the area—up to no good, that's for sure—have maliciously dubbed her "Inspector Boundfoot." What a pity there are not more old ladies like her! Why then China would have no trouble transforming itself into a modern, civilized society—in one great leap, I dare say.

On the other hand, while it is all well and good to be so concerned with public affairs, it is something else again when you poke your nose into everyone's private affairs. Qiao Wanyou used to keep a pet nightingale. "Twenty cents a day just on birdfeed—is money burning a hole in your pocket?! You keep this up and I'll feed it twenty cents' worth of poison!" So he switched to gardening. "Listen, I'm not going to pay for all that water!" The poor guy would no more than use a toothpick but she would find something in that to nag him about for hours on end. And she has forgotten none of the tricks from her "watch-it" days, glaring so suspiciously at everything and everyone it's enough to drive you up a wall. It is only because Qiao Wanyou is such an easygoing fellow that for the longest time he hadn't bothered to argue with her. But when she began to meddle in the affairs of her daughter and son-in-law, that was absolutely the last straw.

Xiulian is the Qiaos' youngest daughter, and, as in that folk saying about youngest daughter being like mother's undershirt—in other words, closest to the heart—she was their favorite child. Needless to say Mrs. Qiao was tickled pink that Xiulian and her husband were to live with them after the marriage. But a few days before the wedding, she summoned them into her presence and very solemnly said: "So, you're getting married soon. It'd be none of my business if you're not going to be living here, but since you're going to be right under my nose I've got to tell you this: That 'thing,' it's not like your three meals a day, once a week is plenty often. If you go at it all the time it's no good for either of you. Anyway, I'm not going to let my daughter be abused, understand?" If you think that's outrageous, wait till you hear what else she pulled on them. Being normal, healthy folks and newlyweds to boot, the young couple had an understandably hearty appetite for sex, so it was only to be expected that they wouldn't always stick to the "established plan."* Unfortunately, only a wooden divider separated their "honeymoon suite" from the older couple's bedroom. Worse yet, Mother-in-law had brought her "Inspector Boundfoot" tactics right into the home. A light sleeper, she would wake up at the slightest rustle from the next room and, without pausing to find out whether it was fact or fantasy or false alarm, she'd bang on the divider and give them a thorough tongue-lashing. Can anyone in his right mind put up with this sort of thing? Never mind the two young folks, who have gone from rows to blows to divorce petitions—even someone as patient and tolerant as Qiao couldn't help but blow his top: "What the hell's wrong with you?! Sticking your nose into everyone's business, every goddamn piss and fart . . ."

The old man almost kicked the bucket when he heard her reply. In a voice loud enough for the whole neighborhood to hear, Mrs. Qiao retorted: "And why not?! Let me tell you something, you men have no idea what we women go through. Back when I first married you, I was your mother's slave by day and by night, dammit, I was your slave. You were such an animal you never let me get any sleep.

---

*Another phrase from *The Teachings of Chairman Mao* and also popular during the Cultural Revolution.

Listen, things have changed, we women have been liberated, you can't walk all over us anymore! . . ."

Qiao Wanyou kept on drinking as he spilled his guts to his old friend. By now he had had more than three bowls of wine, even though two is his usual limit, and he was beginning to slur his words and to stammer: "Y'know, s-soon as s-she opens her mouth m-my poor noggin hurts!" "What a d-d-disgrace! A goddamn d-disgrace!" In the end that was all he could say, over and over again.

Li Zhongxiang looked at the sorry figure across from him and his heart sank. He thought to himself: Of all the problems in the world, old buddy, you had to come up with something like this! If it was money you needed, I could give you three or five hundred easy. If you needed some work done you could count on me and my son, and we could even get more help. But something like this—you know how the saying goes: Even a wise man would have trouble settling a family quarrel. What am I going to do with an old married couple like you two—pack you off to get a divorce also?! Then again, all these years you've never once bellyached or asked me for anything, all these years that I've been living under your roof—what kind of a friend would I be if I can't even come up with something to cheer you up at least?! . . .

In this state of agitation, plus having had a few too many himself, Li Zhongxiang forgot all about his oath. Just like those old men in Beijing who would instinctively reach for their rendan pills at a time like this, or those old ladies in Guangzhou who would turn to their "antirheumatism oil," he didn't even hesitate before snatching away Qiao Wanyou's wine bowl and saying: "Listen, Wanyou, the ancients said: 'Each to his own.' Stop worrying and don't pay any more attention to your wife's bitching. Why don't you come with me—we'll sing a little opera and have ourselves some fun."

"Sing? Opera? Me?" Squinting his eyes Qiao Wanyou shook his head from side to side. "I . . . d-d-don't know how."

"Well then, how about doing the 'background'?"

"B-background?"

"Sure, background music—play the gongs, cymbals, strings, anything you like."

"D-don't know none o' that n-neither."

"So you'll learn! I bet you're a natural. Just look at how you learned to scatter paper money."

"Ummmm." Qiao Wanyou thought for a moment, finally sighed and said: "Why not? It sure b-beats being yelled at. All right, I'll try it."

Li Zhongxiang dug out an old *erhu** from heaven knows where, and the very next evening brought Qiao Wanyou with him to the Cultural Post. Perhaps our Chief Coach did feel a little ashamed to have broken his promise, because he also brought along a fold-up chair from home and settled his old friend—the retired champ of the paper money scatterers—in a little out-of-the-way corner.

From then on, every evening when the band played away on their erhus, *jinghus, yueqins*†, hardwood clappers and the like, providing "background" for the action on stage, you would see in a little cranny on the east side of the "concert hall" a thin-faced old man, eyes half closed and head swaying, an erhu in his lap. That was none other than our friend Qiao Wanyou.

But if you listened carefully you'd discover that the sounds of the erhu came from elsewhere. Even after he became one of the regulars and had been "sawing away" for quite some time, the most

---

Erhu: a two-stringed instrument played with a bow.
†*Jinghu, yueqin:* stringed instruments.

Qiao could manage was a very simple overture. And even then he would often miss his cue.

V

You'd be wrong if you thought our chief coach would take on anything and everything, that he would make his opera "company" open to all comers. It all depended on who the "comer" was.

The fellows, though, didn't let him get off lightly for his breach of promise.

"Hey, Chief, got any more oldtimers on Winch Handle Alley? Why don't you round them up all at once, instead of wasting time going after them one by one?"

"You know that pair of stone lions in front of Number Twenty-nine? They've been looking kind of depressed lately. Listen, Zhongxiang, why don't you bring them over for a song or two?"

Li knew they meant no harm, so sometimes he'd sass them back, sometimes he'd just laugh it off. He really couldn't blame them for having a joke at his expense. If you counted off all the old guys on Winch Handle Alley, you'd find that aside from those working as "consultants" for that travel agency set up by the unemployed youngsters in the neighborhood or as watchmen for the warehouse around the corner—to make a little extra besides their retirement pay—and except for those who couldn't move around much anymore, why, everyone else had been recruited into the "company." Well, there was that other one, Han Delai over at Number Nine, who came a couple of times and could actually sing quite well. But he really got off on the "Anti-Spiritual Pollution" campaign and started to browbeat everyone about it. The guys would have none of that, of course. Instead, they charged him with spiritually polluting the cultural post and really made a monkey out of him, so he never showed his face again. Now if they wanted to recruit anyone else from Winch Handle Alley it would have to be those two stone lions!

Then one evening out of the blue came Wang Jin, Li's neighbor across the yard in the east house.

And as fate would have it, the opera for the evening was *Qin Xianglian*, one of the classics that people never seem to tire of, perhaps because of its story about good winning out over evil: Poor scholar Chen Shimei passes the imperial examinations, climbs the ladder of success but abandons wife Qin Xianglian and their children; eventually, however, he is given the punishment he deserves by the righteous official Bao Gong.

Somewhere in the middle of all this melodrama Wang Jin walked in. Wearing a blue polyester tunic suit, a brown hat, black-framed glasses, and a dark look on his face, he sat down without a word or a nod to anyone. He was still sitting there tight lipped and buttoned up when Li Zhongxiang finally noticed him.

"Well, well, the gang from Number Ten is all here," Li whispered to Qiao Wanyou and chuckled softly. But he couldn't help feeling rather puzzled. What was a young man like Wang Jin—and well educated to boot!—doing in a place like this?

To the residents of Winch Handle Alley, Wang Jin is quite an impressive character. Even Li Zhongxiang, who has been living in the same compound with him for some twenty years now—even he was quite taken aback when, about a year ago, Wang's wife Lai Yufang very smugly announced that her husband had written a book, thick as a brick, and had been paid more than four thousand yuan for it. Sure Li Zhongxiang knew that Wang was quite an accomplished fellow, a graduate of Qinghua University and all that, but then he had been branded a "rightist" and ended up working as some sort of a technician in a factory. Someone introduced him to Lai Yufang, and not long after that he moved in with her without any kind of ceremony. For the past twenty years he had kept a low profile, going to work every day and helping out around the house afterward, lighting the fire or fetching water from the public tap down the street, or playing with their daughter. In short, there was nothing at all remarkable about his daily routine. So how did he come up with a book "thick as a brick"? Magic? Sleight of hand? But however he did it, the book itself was real enough, and so apparently were the four thousand yuan—as can be seen from the fact that his wife no longer had to work at home gluing cardboard boxes. Besides, for a while you had no choice but to hear all about their good fortune from Lai Yufang herself. See that sedan waiting in front of the compound several times a week? That was to take her husband to his lectures, she said. You know he's stopped working at the factory, don't you? That's because he has been transferred back to the university, she said, no more "nine-to-five" work for him. Then finally Lai Yufang showed everyone that book, "thick as a brick." Sure enough, right there on the cover was Wang Jin's name, and inside—why, it was so full of diagrams and charts and foreign words it made your head spin!

However, it wasn't long before Lai Yufang lost her smug look. The two of them started going at each other like cats and dogs, and the word "divorce" was thrown around more and more often. Living in the same compound and running into them every day, Li Zhongxiang couldn't help overhearing all this, but he had no idea who was in the right. On the one hand, he found that broad Lai Yufang pretty disgusting. For instance, in the summertime she would waddle around the yard in a sleeveless undershirt, her tits flopping around underneath like two flatfish. Ugh! Then there's the way she yells at her old man—like a fishwife, a spitfire, a regular shrew! Whatever, the woman is no angel. On the other hand, Li Zhongxiang would think, no matter how much of a bitch she may be, there's that ancient saying: "Forget not the friends from your humble days, cherish the wife who saw you through hard times." But this Wang Jin—no sooner is he doing a little better but he wants a divorce and a new wife—he's no saint either. In fact he's just like that scoundrel Chen Shimei in the opera! And when Li Zhongxiang thought about their daughter Yuanyuan he became absolutely furious with Wang: . . . How heartless can you get, abandoning your child just like that! So you've come here to forget your troubles, have you? Fine, maybe you'll learn a few other things while you're here, like: We may not be bigshots like you, with your book "thick as a brick" and the thousands you made from it, and the sedan taking you all over town while you parade around like a VIP, but at least we know right from wrong. We may be poor but we still have our honor! After Bao Gong finishes off Chen Shimei here, we're going to put on *The Censuring of Wang Kui* just for you! . . .

The Censuring of Wang Kui is also about an ungrateful husband, and it is perfectly understandable how Li's thoughts went from Wang Jin to Chen Shimei to Wang Kui. Then again, it's only human to make a mistake once in a while. And this time our friend Li Zhongxiang, who has always tried to give people the benefit of the doubt, forgot that there are usually two sides to a story, and that while there are cads like Wang Kui and Chen Shimei, there are also husbands who are in the right.

When the passage from *Qin Xianglian* was over Li stood right up and launched into his "censuring" of all heartless husbands:

> *Pleas and appeals you would not heed;*
> *Power and riches have turned your head.*
> *Conscience, honor—both have fled;*
> *Cursed be your name long after you're dead.*

Li Zhongxiang poured his heart and soul into the song, and whether it was because of his surprisingly moving performance, or because there were those who understood what he was driving at and wanted to help teach Wang Jin a lesson, the audience responded with loud applause and cheers.

At half past ten as usual the group broke up. A light snow was falling as Li Zhongxiang and Qiao Wanyou made their way home. A short distance ahead of them on Winch Handle Alley walked Wang Jin, a solitary and rather pitiable figure. Normally Li would still be atingle with the evening's excitement, singing and chatting away while Qiao would hum along by his side. But tonight Li felt rather ill at ease. Why were the three of them not walking together when they had gone to the same show and were now headed for the same place? Something else nagged at him even more. It all had to do with the passage from *The Censuring of Wang Kui.* Why on earth did he do it? What business was it of his anyway? If Wang Jin was in the wrong, the court or his work unit would take care of that. Most likely the poor fellow was feeling pretty low and had come to forget his troubles for a while. Why did he have to give him a hard time on top of everything else? . . .

Wang Jin reached the gate first and held it open, waiting for the other two to catch up. "Thanks," murmured Qiao Wanyou. "Not at all," said Wang Jin, locking up after they had stepped through. Li Zhongxiang was silent, but he felt even more ashamed of himself.

The next night Wang Jin showed up again at the Cultural Post and again sat glumly through the entire evening without making one sound. After the show Li Zhongxiang cleaned up in a hurry so all three of them could walk home together.

"Professor Wang, you like to sing some opera, eh?" Still feeling

a little sheepish about the night before, Li searched for some way
to break the ice.

"No, no, I can't sing at all."

"Oh, so you like listening to it then?"

"Uh, so-so."

What else could they talk about? Li couldn't think of anything.

Nevertheless, from then on every evening after dinner the three
of them would leave the compound together and walk to the Cultural Post, then come home together around half past ten. Wang
still kept to himself, answering only when spoken to, and then only
briefly. And he always wore a pained look, like he was going to the
dentist's instead of to a show.

It wasn't long before Li Zhongxiang realized that Professor
Wang was a complete ignoramus as far as opera was concerned.
A true fan has certain telltale traits: For one thing, as soon as the
gongs and drums start up he would sway and nod to their beat,
completely lost in the music whether he was singing or just listening. But Professor Wang merely sat there like a log. That alone was
enough to make Li Zhongxiang suspicious. Then one night, as he
was getting ready to go on, Li saw Wang Jin sitting there stock still,
as usual. Partly to make amends for the time when he "censured"
Professor Wang, and partly to see how much the good professor
really knew about opera, Li asked Wang if he would fill in for a
minor part. "I . . . I can't," Wang got all flustered and shook his
head vigorously.

Li persisted: "There's nothing to it, not for an old hand like you.
You don't even have to get up on stage. Just answer 'Oh!' at the
right places." Now for anyone the least bit familiar with Beijing
opera this would be child's play, but for Wang Jin it was a tall order:
He had no idea where the "right places" were. "Oh-ing" when he
should have been silent and silent when he should have "Oh-ed,"

he had them rolling in the aisles before the show was half over. To think that Li Zhongxiang had once asked him if he could sing a few passages. What a laugh! He didn't know the first thing about Beijing opera.

However, his unintentionally comic debut didn't seem to dampen Wang Jin's "enthusiasm" at all. He continued to leave the house with his two neighbors every evening and to come home with them after the show. And he continued to be tight lipped and sad eyed. By now Li Zhongxiang was thoroughly baffled: Why did Wang come along when he knew nothing about opera and seemed to care even less? Didn't he have anything better to do? Like writing another book, "thick as a brick."

Finally Li couldn't contain his curiosity any longer. As the three of them were walking home one night, he decided to get to the bottom of the matter: "Professor Wang, I hope you won't mind if I ask you a personal question."

"What is it?"

"Please don't get me wrong, I'm not trying to throw you out or anything." Li paused for a moment, then, pointing to Qiao Wanyou, he continued: "Guys like us, we've got one foot in the grave, and what's more we've got no 'culture.' We have nothing better to do than sing a little opera every night and have a good time. But you—tell me, why are you hanging out with us? I'd understand it if you were a real fan, but you don't even know enough to do a walk-on. So what gives?"

Wang Jin smiled ruefully, but said nothing.

Qiao Wanyou picked up where his friend left off: "We're over the hill and pretty useless. But you're different. Frankly, if we didn't know you could write books we wouldn't have bothered. So tell us, why are you wasting your time like this?"

At these words Wang almost broke down and cried.

As a matter of fact Wang knew three foreign languages and was an expert in computer software. The time was ripe for him to pursue his career ambitions, and he had plans to write a whole series of books, not just one or two—until the problems at home drove him to distraction. Not only was Lai Yufang ignorant and narrow minded, she was so hot tempered she'd fly off the handle over the merest trifle. Even back in the dark days when Wang Jin was living under the stigma of a "rightist" he would often think of his former girlfriend. But while he couldn't help but be attracted to beautiful and refined women—after all, he's only human—he had never even considered being unfaithful. No matter how unpleasant Lai Yufang may be, he could never forget that she had braved the times to marry him when he was still branded as a "rightist," that she had borne their daughter and taken care of the family. No, he couldn't leave her, not after all they had been through together. Now that their circumstances were improved he had plans for Yufang to take some courses, hoping that in time the distance between them would be reduced. Little did he dream that his whole world would be turned topsy-turvy by that one letter.

The letter was written by his former girlfriend. To this day he himself doesn't understand why he held on to it. Was it because it brought back so many lovely memories? Or was it because in the letter she had described her wretched family life, providing company for his own misery? Whatever the reason, there was no denying that the letter had stirred his emotions so that he couldn't bring himself to burn it. Instead he locked it away in a drawer, thinking that was the end of the matter. He neither kept the appointment she proposed nor did he ever write back. After all, he was a rational man—so rational he even considered showing the letter to Yufang before deciding against it. She didn't have the capacity to understand the matter. She would have gone on the warpath right away, charging up to the other woman's house and calling her names like "slut" and "hussy," maybe even throwing a fit and rolling on the ground in public. Why make her blood boil with this letter? Why provoke her into hurting another person? But Wang never considered what would happen if Lai Yufang ever discovered the letter herself. Then, he could talk a blue streak, explain, clarify, swear by all that he held sacred, even admit that he had been "unfaithful" in his heart—and still not convince her of his innocence. And that's exactly what happened. When she found the letter, she insisted that he go along with her to teach the woman a lesson. "Didn't you just swear you had a clear conscience? Then come with me to tell that bitch off! No? I knew you didn't have the guts! But I do. I'm going to make sure those hussies know never to mess with me. So she wants to snatch you away, eh? Well, she can just forget it!" From then on every female who called on Wang Jin, whether colleague or student, would have to suffer the lady's black looks. Sometimes she would even slam the door right in their faces. There was no reasoning with her at all. The more he tried the more insanely jealous she became. "What's the matter, did I upset one of your little darlings? You feel sorry for her, don't you? Well goddamn it, why don't you ever think about me instead?" Then she would blubber and bawl and cause a brouhaha that would set the whole neighborhood on edge. No one can put up with this kind of caterwauling day in and day out, much less a man like Wang Jin who was trying to concentrate on his career. "All right, all right, forget it! If that's how you feel, why don't we just get a divorce?" The words tumbled out of his mouth before Wang realized what he was saying. He was at his wits' end: He couldn't read, couldn't work, he couldn't produce anymore. Was he going to spend the rest of his life being raked over the coals for this one incident? But in trying to get it over with he had only made it worse. Their work units became involved, the Women's Association began to investigate. The verdict: She was the noble and long-suffering Qin Xianglian, he the contemptible Chen Shimei, of course.

"But what's the use of telling you all this? You probably wouldn't understand anyway." Smiling bitterly, Wang Jin shook his head and began puffing away on a cigarette. After some time he let out a long sigh: "Believe me, I really appreciate your concern. But where can I work on my book? At home? As soon as she sees me sitting down at my desk she'll storm right in and tear everything up, screaming at the top of her lungs, 'Go ahead! Write your goddamn book, you son of a bitch! The more you write the worse you get! I'd rather go back to the old days when we were living from hand to mouth!' If I go to my office she'll say: 'Sneaking out to see your sweetheart, eh?' Even if I do find a place to work I've lost my concentration. To be honest with you, going to the show with you two every night is just about the only thing she'll allow. 'Yes, go along with them, go hear how Bao Gong fixed Chen Shimei. That's what'll happen to all you heartless bastards!' If you don't believe me just look over at my house tomorrow evening. She'll be parked right by the window watching me as I step out the door. If I don't walk out with you two she'll run right after me and start a fight, no question about it."

Li Zhongxiang and Qiao Wanyou sighed again and again as they listened to Wang's story. When he was finished, the three of them stood wordlessly under a street light for a long while. Li's heart ached at the thought of a learned man like Professor Wang killing time every day with all these old codgers, forcing himself to listen to something he didn't understand at all. Then Li remembered how rude he had been when Professor Wang first joined them, and he could have kicked himself for it. "Professor Wang, I'm so sorry, I didn't know. That day when I sang the piece from *The Censuring of Wang Kui* I was wrong, so wrong. . . ."

"What piece?"

"You know, the one I sang the first time you came here."

"Oh, that one. What's wrong with it? I kind of liked it," said Wang Jin, looking nonplussed.

Li Zhongxiang sighed again as he became even more heartsick. Wang had not understood a word of what he was listening to that night. Just as well.

They lapsed into silence again.

After some time Li Zhongxiang suddenly spoke up: "Professor Wang, I'm just an uneducated stiff who used to carry coffins for a living, so please forgive me if I get out of line. You know me, I like to have a good time, and I like others to have fun as well. Especially those who're worried and depressed—I really want to help cheer them up if I can. But I've been thinking: There's nothing I can do to help you with your problem."

"Oh please don't say that!" Wang Jin interjected. "It makes me feel much better just to tag along with you two every day."

"Stop kidding yourself. You can't go on killing time like this. And if we let you we wouldn't be doing right by you or anyone else." Li Zhongxiang folded his arms across his chest and continued: "Let me come straight to the point: The opera club is no place for you, Professor, and I can't let you come anymore. Don't think I'm throwing you out because I don't like you or don't want to help you out—after all, we've been friends and neighbors for many, many years now. On the contrary, it's because I don't want to see you waste your time hanging around this place. Me and Wanyou here, we're not much good at anything. Even if we could talk the hind legs off a donkey and went and told everyone we met that you're no Chen Shimei, that's still not going to help you very much. If we tried to whack some sense into the dame, make her see what a great guy her old man is, it wouldn't work either. For one thing it's against the law. Besides, if she got hurt it'd not only add to your worries, it'd also cost you a pretty penny in doctor's bills! So let me make a dumb suggestion. She watches you from the window every night, right? Well, let her watch all she wants. You just come along with us as usual, but once we get out of the alley we can go our separate ways. To each his own, I always say. We trust you, we know you're not going to meet a mistress somewhere. Just find yourself a quiet spot and write another book, 'thick as a brick,' all right?"

Now it was Wang Jin's turn to ache inside.

That was how, in addition to the fun they had every evening at the Cultural Post, Li Zhongxiang and Qiao Wanyou came to enjoy another kind of "fun": escorting their pride and joy, Professor Wang, out of the compound and down the alley, so he could go to the university library to write his book, "thick as a brick."

VI

Every evening at half past six sharp, "Shrimp Head" Tang Heshun would unlock the door of the Cultural Post. Then he would either go next door to Liu Shan's to play chess or to the reading room to clip newspapers. Right on his heels would appear Li Zhongxiang in his distinctive bowlegged walk, to be followed immediately by Qiao Wanyou, carrying his battered erhu like some priceless treasure in a satchel made of blue twill. Once inside, the two old fellows would bustle around boiling water, making tea and setting out the benches, while one after another the troops would show up. Finally all would be ready—and the gongs, drums and clappers would take off! Everyone's spirits would soar, especially those with troubles of one kind or another, a disobedient son, say, or a nagging wife. For a few hours at least, their problems can all go to hell. Not even paradise on earth could hold a candle to their home away from home!

People are easily satisfied, especially someone like Li Zhongxiang. To the ancient saying, "He who is content will always find happiness," Li has added his own: "He who has fun will always be content." In other words, Li would win coming and going. At home he had a dutiful son who always made sure that there were five full bottles of Beijing Daqu stored under his bed and a carton of Hengda cigarettes lying in his drawer. Content with how things were at home, Li Zhongxiang had found happiness—just as the ancients prescribed. Moreover, every evening he would walk out of the courtyard with his old buddy Qiao Wanyou and his new friend Professor Wang, until they got to the end of the alley and went their separate ways; every evening he and Wanyou had "fun" not only from their music making but also from helping a friend in need. Having found this fun, they were quite content—that was from following Li's own prescription. And thus overflowing with happiness and contentment—not to mention a goodly amount of Beijing Daqu—Li Zhongxiang's face became even ruddier, his tales even taller, his bowlegged walk a positive swagger. To be sure, whenever he saw some old fellow his age just squatting somewhere and puffing away silently at a cigarette, he would still feel a twinge of regret, as though he had let a pearl slip through his fingers. But his hands were tied not only by his own word of honor but also by the limits of the Cultural Post. When he thought about it, though, he would realize how silly he was. So many ways to have fun under the sun: bird keeping, chess playing, tea tasting, kite flying, sauntering, exercising, shadowboxing—what's the worry?

While Li Zhongxiang was always worrying about others, he

never thought the day would come when he himself wouldn't be able to have his fun.

One evening just before Chinese New Year, the diehard opera fans showed up as usual at the Cultural Post, humming and swaying as they strolled in. But though the door was open, there was no hot water, no tea, and the benches were piled this way and that. Li Zhongxiang and Qiao Wanyou were nowhere to be seen. Surprise turned into consternation when they remembered Hu Si, who had been one of the regulars. Almost seventy he was, but his voice was still deep and resonant as a huge brass bell—perfect for the part of the general. One night he was singing away lustily with the rest of them, the next night he didn't show up, and never did again. A stroke, they later heard—gave up the ghost just like that. Ever since then, whenever one of the company was absent no one wanted to ask why.

So they all breathed a sigh of relief when Qiao Wanyou appeared in a little while. Finally, someone asked the question that was on everyone's mind: "Hey, Wanyou, where's Zhongxiang?" Usually they all called him "Chief Coach" or "The New Changhua." But not today.

Qiao Wanyou set his erhu on his lap and began to tune it. For a long time the only sound coming from him was the squeaking of strings. At last he said slowly: "He's not coming today. He doesn't feel so good."

"What's wrong?"

"Oh, not much. Headache and a fever, I think."

Qiao Wanyou didn't want to tell them what had really happened. Li Zhongxiang would be so embarrassed.

In fact the evening had started out as usual. They had hollered for Professor Wang to join them, then the three of them had left the compound together, again as usual. But after they parted company with Wang at the street corner, Li Zhongxiang's face fell. Gloomily he said to Qiao Wanyou: "You go on ahead, Wanyou. I'm not going tonight."

Qiao was completely taken aback. Rain or shine, Li had never missed a single evening. What on earth was going on?

"I don't . . . feel so good."

Alarmed, Qiao asked: "So why did you even come out? Go home and get yourself to bed right away!"

Li Zhongxiang shook his head, a mournful smile on his lips. Hemming and hawing, he finally said: "To tell you the truth, Dezhi came home when I was having dinner just now and asked me not to go anymore."

"Why not?"

"He said to me, why don't you take up something else instead? You can watch TV, listen to the radio, anything but go howling with the rest of them at the Cultural Post. He said people were laughing at us."

"Why doesn't he mind his own business?"

"Well, I guess in a way it is his business. Didn't I tell you he's got a girlfriend now? The girl lives right on Bean Street, I think it's the one in the plaid jacket who sticks her head into the Cultural Post once in a while. More than likely she's said something to him about us. I can't say as I blame them. To the young folks nowadays we're all just a bunch of old crackpots. My guess is, Dezhi doesn't want her to know his dad is the leader of this pack of old loonies. She might find us embarrassing."

"Oh no! He's not even married yet and already he's thrown his old man out the window. You should go, just to spite her! If she thinks you're embarrassing then she shouldn't marry into the family!"

Again Li Zhongxiang smiled sadly. His son had had a hard

enough life, he said. Dezhi was twenty-five before he got permission to leave the rural commune to which he had been sent during the Cultural Revolution, but right after he returned to Beijing he had come down with tuberculosis, so he had gotten off to a late start finding a job and finding a wife. Finally he was able to learn a trade at the tailoring school and had just opened up his own little stall in the market.

"He works hard every day, summertime he even works late into the evening under a street light. But at least he earns enough to keep the two of us going. You've got to admit he's a good son, he always keeps me well supplied with liquor and cigarettes. He's over thirty already and this is his first girlfriend, though he's still too timid to actually tell me about it. What he's done is to ask me very nicely not to go opera singing anymore. Well, a person's got to put himself in other people's shoes. Wouldn't you do the same for your boy? . . .

"Anyway, that's enough of that. You'd better hurry along before the guys think I've gone to hear the crickets chirp!" Waving his hands, Li Zhongxiang sent Qiao Wanyou on his way.

At the Cultural Post Li's absence put a damper on everyone's spirits. The other day the Block Office had asked them to put on a show for the New Year festivities, but now without Li Zhongxiang there was no one to whip things into shape, and the evening just dragged on. Little did the fellows suspect that their chief coach, far from lying in bed at home, was at that very moment standing like an outcast on the corner of Winch Handle Alley, drinking in every last note floating out of the Cultural Post. Just then it was Old Man Jin singing, no doubt about it. He's the one who claims to be distantly related to the famous opera star Jin Shaoshan. But listen to him:

When I am idle I look out at the mountains,
Stroll on the slopes when my spirits are low.
One day outside the fort a strange wind was blowing;
I let it pass, then grabbed its tail to see—was it friend or foe?

Ugh! Off-key, off beat—how awful can you get?! Even his words came out fuzzy, like he was sucking on something! Li Zhongxiang was dying to storm in and chew him out: You call this singing?! You may be related to Jin Shaoshan, but no one would ever know it from the way you're mewling! . . .

The longer our friend stood on the corner listening, the more pathetic he looked. There he was, itching to get in there and show them how to do it right, although often after his "demonstrations" the fellows would hoot and howl scornfully: "Stuff it! I can do better than that!" Maybe so, but not to let Li sing at all was pure torture to him—you might as well have him bound and gagged!

While Li Zhongxiang was thus loitering on the corner, he happened to spy his son Dezhi and a young woman walking down Bean Street. His pulse quickened: That's her, no doubt about it—the one in the plaid jacket, lives right next door to the Cultural Post. These two are going steady for sure. Dezhi looks real sharp tonight, from his new jacket down to his shiny leather shoes. Son, you may be meek as a mouse in front of your old man, but I bet you're as bold as the next guy right now, I bet you'd even put your arm around her waist right in public! . . .

Dezhi and the girl headed west. A shiny pair of skates peeked out of the straw basket they each carried. From the looks of it they were going to the rink in Taoran Pavilion Park.

Li Zhongxiang brightened up all of a sudden. Last night he had set it up with several of the guys that he would sing something from

A Gathering of Heroes tonight. Now was the time to sneak in and do it; besides, he had to take care of that show for Chinese New Year. He hesitated for a moment, but then he turned and went in the same direction as his son—he had to find out what time the rink closed.

In his threescore years and ten Li Zhongxiang had seen all sorts of goings-on along the frozen moat: children sledding, folks in the old days cutting out blocks of ice and hauling them to their ice-houses—but he had never seen so many smartly dressed young people, gliding around like swans on the mirror-smooth ice in the rink. Some pretty music was playing softly in the background, music that sounded kind of foreign but not too wild. The girls were all rosy cheeked and merry eyed, their silvery laughter twinkling in the air as they skated arm in arm with their young men, spinning and darting and flitting this way and that, their legs twirling and turning ever so gracefully. . . . Li Zhongxiang couldn't quite believe his eyes—he got dizzy just watching them. Completely forgetting why he had gone there in the first place, he continued to stare at the figures on the ice. Had there been places like this when he was young? Probably. But back then they were not for the likes of him, a lowly coffin carrier. Never in his whole life had he ever lived it up the way these kids are doing! The more he thought about it the more furious he got at his son: Bastard, you've got plenty of time left to enjoy yourself, but don't you know that for your father, singing some opera every night is all the fun that's left to him, just like the camel on the wagon? . . .

When he came out of Taoran Pavilion Li Zhongxiang felt a little hungry, then remembered that he hadn't had much at dinner besides a couple of drinks—his son's words had stuck in his craw and killed his appetite. Right at the entrance to the park was a newly opened snack shop, a lively little place bustling with people. Li thought to himself, well, why not go in and get an order of wontons?

The people sitting inside were all couples who had just come from the rink, their skates still sticking out of the bags stowed beneath their seats. Many of the girls were wearing colorful wool knit caps, and their pretty perfumes hung coyly in the air. Slowly sipping their beer and soft drinks, couple after couple billed and cooed to each other, paying no attention to anyone else in the wonton shop. But as soon as Li Zhongxiang stepped in the door he felt completely ill at ease. Although no one so much as glanced at him, he was sure he stuck out like a sore thumb. Turning on his heels he walked back out the door and down the steps, wondering to himself if Dezhi and his girlfriend would also be coming here in a little while. He could just see them now, rosy cheeked and sweet smelling just like everyone else. And like everyone else they would order one beer, two sodas and two bowls of wontons. They would bill and coo and gaze into each other's eyes and . . . Shame on you! You're not jealous, are you?! Then all of a sudden he thought about Lu Guiying. She had probably remarried a long time ago. . . . Why the hell did I give up so easily when she said, "Let it be"? Who cared what others thought as long as she and I were sensible about the whole thing? Why did I let other people run my life? What an ass, what a goddamn ass I was! And still am! . . .

Furiously Li Zhongxiang kicked a pebble lying in his path and sent it scudding to one side. Then he turned onto the sidewalk outside the park and started to walk home.

A short distance ahead some maintenance work was being done on the roadway. Red signal lamps marched across the asphalt, and a big cauldron sat over a blazing fire in the middle of the sidewalk. While the roadwork crew waited for the tar to melt, a large crowd had gathered around to watch a game of chess by the light of the fire. From time to time there would be whoops and cries of: "Head him off, head him off! Move the 'chariot' and head him off!" "No! No! Pull back! You've got to pull your 'horse' back!"

Li Zhongxiang wasn't particularly interested, so he merely glanced at the crowd as he passed by—and almost walked right into the tar kettle. For whom should he see among the onlookers but Professor Wang himself!

Wang Jin saw Li at the same instant. Nervously he pushed his glasses back up on his nose and opened his mouth as if to say something, but nothing came out. His face was a study in embarrassment as he came over and joined Li.

The two of them walked along very slowly. For the longest time neither said a word.

Finally, Li Zhongxiang couldn't hold it in any longer. "Well, have you been there and back, or haven't you gone yet?"

"Where?"

"Where! Where are you supposed to go every day after me and Wanyou walk you out of the alley?" It was all Li could do to keep from blowing his lid.

Wang Jin walked for a while with his head down, then pushed his glasses up again before answering: "To be honest with you, I . . . I haven't been going there for quite some time now."

"You mean, you mean . . ." Li Zhongxiang racked his brains for a more delicate way of putting it, but finally gave up. "Excuse my language. You mean you've just been jerking us off?"

Wang Jin sighed deeply. Again they walked along in silence until he said: "I did go in the beginning, but after a while I couldn't see the point of it anymore. Let me tell you what happened. They took away my position as project director—the work unit said it was because of my poor morals and bad character. So why should I bother . . ."

"Tell me the truth. Were you fooling around or not?" Li Zhongxiang had a lot of faith in the work unit.

"If I was, would I have been standing there watching a chess game?"

"Then why don't you tell them what really happened? Why don't you tell them it's not because you want to get rid of that broad, it's because you've had it up to here with her nagging and her orneriness and . . ."

"I did, but they . . . Let me tell you something: Just because you say so doesn't mean they'll believe or understand what you're saying. I'm the rotten Chen Shimei and she's the saintly Qin Xianglian—now that's a lot easier for them to understand. That opera's been around for at least a hundred years!"

Li Zhongxiang said no more. Professor Wang had a point there. Take himself for example: How many times has anyone really understood him? Bustling about in front of the theater, the pride and the pleasure he took in it—did anyone understand him then? Getting a little turned on outside the women's locker room—who else besides Lu Guiying understood that? . . . Even your own son, the one you raised from the time he was still shitting and pissing in his pants—what does he understand about the fun you get from singing a little opera every night? . . .

The night was not very cold, but a brisk wind was stirring. Little swirls of dust and litter rustled along in the gutter as the two of them walked on in silence.

Just before they reached the gate to their courtyard Li Zhongxiang spoke up again: "Well, Professor, when all is said and done there seems only one way to handle this: Look on the bright side and wait your 'turn.' That's what it all comes down to these days. Look at Stinky next door. He was riding along on his motorcycle one day when he got slapped with a big fine. Yep, you guessed it, that was back during the traffic safety campaign and it was his 'turn' to get it. When I warned my son to get a bell for his bicycle he said: 'Don't worry, all I have to do is make it through this month and I'll be all right.' Sure enough, all month long he took the back alleys to avoid the cops. Now that Traffic Safety Month is over he's home free. You're going through a rough patch at the moment, but someday it'll be a fellow's turn to make his case. Then you'll be in the clear and you can go back to writing your books. . . .''

Sometimes Li Zhongxiang made a lot of sense, other times he was full of crap, so there's no point in taking him or his blather too seriously. But he always meant well, and Professor Wang appreciated that at least. Whereupon, with a nod and a smile that looked more like a grimace, Wang opened the gate, stepped into the courtyard and disappeared inside his house.

Li Zhongxiang found his house still empty—Dezhi had not yet come home from his date. Lowering himself into a chair, Li's eyes fell on the five bottles of Beijing Daqu stacked under his bed. There was a time when the mere sight of them would have warmed the cockles of his heart, and if an old friend should drop by and happened to ask about his son, Li would have proudly shown him the bottles. But today for some reason an undescribable anger flared up inside him. Son of a gun, so you're treating me like a buddha, making me regular offerings of liquor and cigarettes to keep me happy and seal my lips, eh? To hell with that, I'm your father! Sure Professor Wang is a sadsack, but that's because he lets himself be henpecked. I'd never stand for that. I've still got what it takes to tell my own son a thing or two. . . .

Li made up his mind: As soon as Dezhi came home he would ask him to please "withdraw" his liquor and his cigarettes. . . . I'm no goddamn clay idol, I don't want any of this stuff. What I do want is to go singing every night over on Bean Street. You go tell that wench of yours it's nothing to be ashamed of. Why, back in '31, even the mayor himself sang in a production of *Qin Xianglian* at the Number One Theater over on West Willow Street, complete with costumes and makeup and everything! Your old man never got to go skating, never got to take a girl out for beer and wontons, and now at my age you want to stop me from singing too? No way! . . .

Around eleven o'clock Dezhi came home.

But not a peep came out of Li Zhongxiang.

"Dad, you didn't go . . . out tonight?" Dezhi asked as he set down the roast chicken he had brought home—probably as a special treat for his father.

"Mmmmm."

"Dad, if you get bored, why don't you watch some TV? I'll have enough saved up to buy a color set in just a couple of months." Dezhi seemed to want to do everything possible to make up for his father's loss.

Well, how could Li Zhongxiang stay angry at Dezhi? Where could he find a better son? Besides, so what if he stopped singing opera every night—it really wasn't a matter of life and death, was it?

"Dad, maybe you'd like to keep a lark instead? I'll get one for you tomorrow, and then it can learn to sing along with the one at Mr. Hao's next door. It'll sound so pretty, you'll see."

Li Zhongxiang puffed at his cigarette in silence.

"Or Dad, maybe you'd like . . . some tropical fish?"

Still no answer.

"Or Dad, maybe . . ."

"I want to go fishing!" With a roar Li Zhongxiang brought his son up short: "Go! Get your old man two fishing poles! The best kind—a hundred yuan apiece! Don't be cheap!"

VII

"Zhao-le"—that's a Beijing expression meaning "to look for fun." It also happens to be Beijingers' favorite pastime. They're fond of it, they're good at it, and this fun is not too hard to find. Keeping a pet nightingale is a kind of fun. So is flying a kite. So is nursing a bowl of wine over a clove of garlic. Even when they talk about death, for instance, Beijingers don't say "So-and-so died," they like to say, "he's gone to hear the crickets chirp"—as though they could find some fun even in that.

But I am repeating myself.

And every evening it is still the same threesome—Li Zhong-xiang, Qiao Wanyou, and Professor Wang—who walk out of 10 Winch Handle Alley together. Where are they going tonight? Besides singing opera, what other kind of fun would they find? Well, in a city as big as Beijing, with people as fond of fun and as good at finding it as Beijingers are, there is really no need to worry.

One thing is for sure. They are not going fishing, even though the fishing poles Dezhi bought continue to lie around gathering dust under the bed.

FIRST PUBLISHED IN AUGUST 1984 IN *ZHONGSHAN*

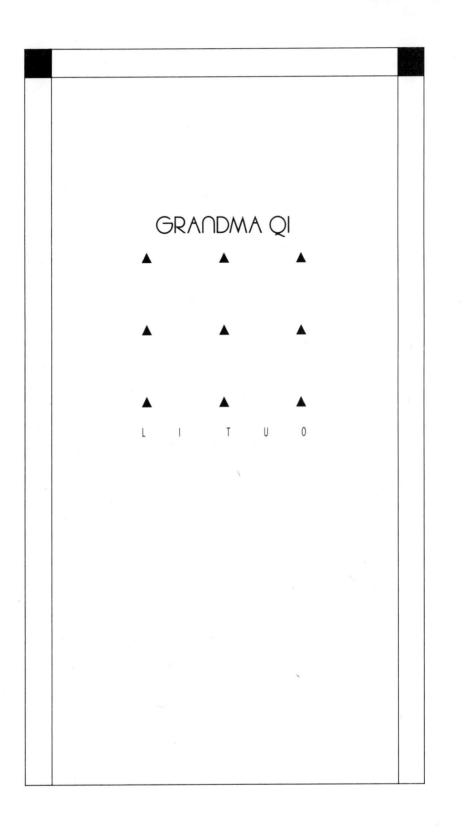

GRANDMA QI

LITUO

▲　　　▲　　　▲

▲　　　▲　　　▲

▲　　　▲　　　First came the pungent aroma of chives mixed with scallions and ginger. Must be the Changs in the north house getting ready to make dumplings—pork-and-chive dumplings. Then came the smell of burnt wheatcakes. That's probably Lil' Four, fourth daughter of the Lius to the west. The girl was forever lost in a book—must have forgotten to give the pancakes a flip. Still later came the delicious smell of fish stewing. But Grandma Qi had no idea whose house this was from, nor could she be bothered. She was too busy minding the goings-on in her own kitchen. The little cookhouse was right across the courtyard from her room, and bustling about inside was her daughter-in-law Yuhua, just home from work. With difficulty Grandma Qi managed to raise herself a little so she could look out the window. But smack on the windowsill were two pots of cactus blocking her view. Worse yet, her glaucoma had been getting so bad the last couple of years, all she could make out was a shadow here, an image there, even though she gazed long and hard in the direction of the kitchen. No telling what that woman was up to now. Just for a few moments, though, she'd had the vague feeling that Yuhua was stoking the fire. If only she weren't half deaf! Then she'd be able to figure out what was happening just by listening to the sounds from the kitchen—and she wouldn't be far off the mark. But now, now she had no way of knowing whether Yuhua was actually stoking the furnace. This filled her with alarm. Straining to peer around those two pestiferous plants, she propped herself up on her arms and tried to ease toward the edge of the bed. But her legs, still crossed together, seemed rooted to the bed and refused to budge. Undaunted, she struggled to lean forward, stretching her arms until both hands were grabbing onto the edge of the bed, then summoned up all her strength and gave it another try. But it was no good. What used to work every single time just wasn't working today. She refused to give up. Clenching her teeth, she kept tugging at the edge of the bed as if her very life depended on it, even though her heart was pounding and her breath came in short gasps. A sudden bout of coughing finally made her let go, a coughing fit that seemed to turn her inside out and in no time at all had covered her face, neck and back with large beads of sweat. She felt as though she were choking on a plug of cotton so that even her eyes were popping out of her head, and it was all she could do to gasp for air in that brief spell after one attack was over, before the next one began. She was terrified she wouldn't be able to breathe, that she would die just like that. Even so, she had no thought for anything but the kitchen. Was Yuhua puttering with the coal stove or not? What was that woman really up to? Eyes swimming in tears as well as sweat, she could no longer even see shapes and shadows, nothing but a pale shimmering blur. Just now she'd sensed that the fire had gone out in the stove and Yuhua was poking about trying to rekindle it. In that case she would have been able to smell it by now, that white smoke from the kindling just before the fire roared to life.

But at the moment there wasn't even a hint of smoke in the air. Instead it was the pleasant aroma of dumplings—pork-and-chive dumplings, freshly cooked—that came wafting over from the Changs' house. Fresh out of the pan, dumplings always smell so good.

What a sharp nose she had when she was little! She was famous for it. Back then her father used to drink—not much, really, just a jigger or so as soon as he came in the door after pulling a rickshaw all day, and then he'd go straight to bed. It was she who went to buy the liquor every day, carrying a little tin flask and shuffling along in her mother's cloth shoes, the ones that were so worn the heels had fallen off. Every day she did this, even when it snowed. How cold winters were back then! Each time it snowed there'd be half a foot on the ground, at the least ankle-deep. One New Year's Day —which year she couldn't recall now—there had been a big snowfall overnight, and in the morning nobody could open his front door. If you so much as coughed, a clump of snow would tumble off a branch. Back then things were so different. Now, heaven knows, winters aren't winters and summers aren't summers. But back then things were different. Take drinking water, for instance—now there's something you don't see anymore. Just imagine—delivered door-to-door every morning, in a creaky wagon pulled by a little donkey who knew where to stop without being told. Then there's the layer of moss covering the water wagon—how pretty it was, so green and moist and lush. And the water? Straight from a well, none of that bleaching powder nonsense. Back then even business was done differently. In the evenings the wonton peddler would come right up to your door with his little pushcart, the wontons bubbling away in the pot. She never ate any, though —couldn't afford them. But she did taste those yundou* pies. They were*

---

*Yundou: a kind of bean.

sold at night too, late at night, when the streets were almost empty. It was then that the peddler would come around with a wooden bucket on his back. "Yundooouuu—!" His voice rang like one of those Peking opera singers', his cry could be heard several alleys away. These days "home delivery" is something special, but back then everything was delivered to your door. Smash a pot or break a bowl, you could get the tinker to fix it all right on your front step. Except for the wine sellers—they never made deliveries. So every single day she'd have to carry that tin flask with the big dent in the middle to buy wine, no more than a jigger each time. Every single day she'd flop along in her mother's big shoes that no longer had any heels. Rain or shine, winter or summer, she had to bring this wine home or she'd be in for a thrashing. What a good nose she had back then. One sniff and she could tell if water had been added to the wine, and how much. Every day she'd have to go around to several shops to find the strongest drink. Once she had to go all the way to Sipailou before she found wine that didn't have too much water in it. When she got home she was spanked but good, so hard even the broom handle snapped. What a sharp nose she had back then.

She was growing more and more alarmed. Who knows, maybe it was this very panic that made the awful coughing fit go away, just like that. Quickly she wiped her tears with a sleeve and struggled to look out the window again, but the two cactus plants were still blocking her view. How many times had she told them to move those things! Her son had promised, but never did anything about it. Now suddenly a thought popped into her head: Yuhua must have been behind it all. Of course! It must have been she who stopped her husband from moving them. On purpose. That woman was so mean she was capable of anything. Time and time again Yuhua had lied to her, pretending to cook with the coal stove, but each time Grandma had managed to see through the trickery. Not for a moment could she let her guard down with this woman. Something fishy was going on right now. Dimly she could tell that the door to the cookhouse was open (she had laid down the law to her son about this: Anytime Yuhua was in there cooking the kitchen door had to stay open), and through it she could see a figure stirring about that had to be Yuhua. But what was she actually doing in there? If she had been chopping firewood for the stove, then where was the smoke? It should have begun drifting over a long time ago. All these years Grandma had been breathing in this stuff, she'd never mistake it if it was in the air. But at the moment all she could smell were the pleasant odors of cooking from the other houses, no matter how long and hard she sniffed. That's it, Yuhua must be up to her tricks again. All at once Grandma could feel her hairs standing on end. Though the coughing had stopped earlier her heart was still racing and her breath still came in gasps. Now she became worse. Her heart thumped away even more furiously and she could hardly breathe. Once again she felt like she was choking on something. She tried to shout, but a fit of coughing rattled her from head to toe, as though someone had seized her by the shoulders and was shaking her vigorously, violently. Even so, she still tried to shout, shouted inwardly, but not a sound came out.

That's what Uncle Chang said, and he never talks through his hat. There was this household with a propane stove that had somehow sprung a leak. It was in one of those apartment houses, not sure how many stories exactly, but anyway a pretty tall building. The people in that household had all gone to work, so nobody was home at the time. The leaking gas went all over the apartment, then seeped out onto the balcony, slid down to the balcony below, and snuck into the apartment downstairs like a thief in the night. Not a soul saw what was going on. But it so happened that someone was home downstairs—most likely the man of the house, who wanted a smoke, who struck a match. And the whole place went up in flames—sheets of fire hanging in the air, fire shooting up his nose and into his lungs, lungs that were filled with gas. That was how the man died, burnt alive. What's more, said Uncle Chang, it could have been much worse. If the canister itself had exploded, the whole building would have been blown sky-high. Now what kind of a person would invent such an evil, evil thing? Just the thought of it was enough to make her flesh crawl. To put a bomb in your own home and then to cook on it—how vicious can you get?!

Ever since the day she fainted she had not seen that propane stove again. They stuck it in a corner along the north wall of the cook-house so she wouldn't be able to see it at all, even when the door was wide open. At first she thought her son had wanted it out of sight, out of mind, so as not to upset her again. It was only later, after she found out that many a time Yuhua had cooked with the gas stove, that she realized she had been fooled. Yuhua would pretend to use the coal stove by setting a pan on top of it, but she wouldn't bother to light the fire. Now each day, every day, as soon as it came time to cook, Grandma Qi's heart would begin to pound and her hands, legs and eyelids would all begin to tremble. Even after the food was set down in front of her she'd still be afraid and suspicious, now even meals cooked on the coal stove would taste of gas to her. Since Yuhua had come home later than usual today she might well try her old tricks again. She had to watch that woman. What she should do is call Uncle Chang over and have him look in on Yuhua. Get him to keep an eye on her. It'd be all right, by now he should have eaten enough dumplings already. But she was coughing so hard she could barely catch her breath, never mind calling out to anyone. This coughing just wouldn't let go of her today. Out of desperation she began to pinch herself in the thighs, pinched them hard. But her legs, which were almost numb to begin with, didn't feel any pain at all, nothing—as if they weren't even connected to her. She tried slapping herself, left hand against left cheek—thwack!—right hand against right cheek—thwack!—back and forth, a dozen times and more. But even this didn't hurt much. For one thing, she was shaking so hard from the coughing, like a tree in a storm, that she had hardly any strength left in her arms. For another, her face was so slippery with sweat her hands kept sliding right off. Finally she had to stop. Again she looked over at the kitchen, again she could see nothing but Yuhua's figure flitting about. That was enough to fill her heart with dread and send a shiver through her body. All of a sudden she had an idea. A pair of scissors lay on the bed, several feet away from her. Now if she could only hurl them against the window and break the glass, Uncle Chang and the other neighbors would hear the crash and come running to see what had happened, and then she'd get her chance. But even though she bent down as far as she could the scissors remained beyond her reach. Nor could she stay in that position for long. Coughing while bent over like that, she thought she'd suffocate on the spot. She had to wait till the worst of the hacking was over before she could lean forward again and continue to stretch and grope. Once or twice her fingers brushed against the scissors, but she just couldn't get a firm grip on them. In desperation she began pinching herself in the thighs again. That gas canister kept spinning before her eyes. She seemed to hear a loud rumble, followed by bodies and blood splattering everywhere. A cold sweat broke out beneath the layer of warm perspiration that already covered her. But somehow all that desperation paid off, and at last she closed her fingers around the scissors. Just when she was about to throw them at the window, however, she began to have second thoughts. What a pity it would be to smash the glass! Almost fifty years of living in this house, and in all that time she had never broken anything, except for one goldfish bowl. That bowl must have been at least a foot wide. . . . She lifted her arm to toss the scissors, but still couldn't bring herself to let go. At that very moment a faint whiff of smoke drifted over. In an instant she had dropped the scissors and was sniffing hard. That's it all right, she knew this odor only too well. Thank goodness she had held on to the scissors. What if she had broken the glass for nothing? She'd never have forgiven herself. With the smell of smoke in her nostrils she began to relax. Somewhere a child was throwing a temper tantrum. Grandma listened. The cries were coming in through the rear window, which opened onto a narrow alley. Someone was spanking the child right under this window. She seemed to hear the little one screaming: "A donkey roll*! I want a donkey roll!"

Donkey rolls aren't all that good, they stick to your teeth and make you gag. But as a child how she too had loved them! First time she ever tasted one was when her father took her to Longfu Temple. That was also her first visit to the fair. After that she must have gone back umpteen times, but they were never as much fun as the first. Now the Longfu Temple grounds have been turned into the People's Market. She went there once, a couple of years after the change, but what a far cry it was from the hustle and bustle of the old fair. Call it a market if you like, it was no more than a department store without the big building. What's so special about that?! On the little street right opposite the main gate was her favorite place at the old Longfu Fair, a bird market where she used to hang around watching all the activity and excitement. What a lot of birds there were—mynahs, parakeets, guinea

---

*Donkey roll: a kind of sweet pastry.

*hens, love birds, peacocks, pheasants, even a kind of bird that was supposed
to have black bones (its meat was delicious, or so people said)—every kind
of bird under the sun. She'd heard tell that even tigers were sold there
sometimes, but she never saw any. Nor could you buy a donkey roll there
—for that you had to go into the fair. Inside Longfu Temple were three
streets. The one in the middle was always the busiest because that's where
most of the acts were set up. You could watch Third Treasure doing his
wrestling and acrobatics, Mr. and Mrs. Mutt in their "Family Fun" show,
Cloud Flier and his comic operas, plus storytellers, picture lantern shows
and magicians galore. Mixed in with these booths were food stalls selling
things like fermented soybean drinks, wontons, fried sausages, seasoned
millet mush, plum cakes, cotton candy, and buckwheat noodles. Further
along you'd find the face readers, fortune-tellers, and peddlers who sold those
picture cards that came inside every packet of cigarettes and were collected
by children. Beyond these was the back gate, where she once saw a beggar
sitting on the ground pounding his chest with a gray brick. His hair and
whiskers were snow white, but his body was filthy black. Next to him sat
a big black dog. People said the animal was actually sent by the chief of
beggars to watch his followers. If any of them tried to pocket some of the
money, the dog would pounce on the poor fellow and tear away at his delicate
parts. No telling if the story was true. The street on the west side of the temple
had a lot of food stalls as well. Right inside the west gate was a big stand
selling every kind of rice-flour cake you could imagine. In winter there were
bean cakes steamed in straw baskets and served piping hot; in summer there
were chilled custards, cool and refreshing; autumn meant chestnut cakes, of
course; and spring brought those little date pastries glazed in a syrup
seasoned with fresh roses. Much tastier than donkey rolls, all of them. Back
then her family lived right near Longfu Temple, and she never missed the
fair days on the ninth and tenth of every month. So as not to get a licking
at home she'd always bring her little brother along. She would buy him taffy
shaped into a monkey, or a noisemaker, or some marbles. That monkey-*

shaped taffy was the best thing for keeping a kid happy, it was so cheap and filling—but now you can't find it anymore. How many years ago that was! She wasn't afraid of dying, but oh, how she wished she could visit the fair one last time. Three nights in a row last week she dreamed that she was back at Longfu Temple with her little brother, strolling around buying a feather duster here, a goldfish there, a steam basket further along. These days people use pressure cookers instead. She heard tell those things could also explode and blow your head wide open. These new-fangled doodads in the home nowadays—why is it that all of them behave just like bombs? What is this world coming to?

She must have dozed off for a little while. Then with a start she woke up again. She was forever doing that. Night or day, she never could get a sound sleep, never any rest. No wonder she was all tuckered out. Raising herself slightly, Grandma Qi looked out the window at the kitchen again, but, just as before, couldn't make out a thing. Those two cactus plants were such a nuisance. What's more, some time ago the Lius' big black-and-white tabbycat had jumped onto the windowsill and plunked itself down right between the two flowerpots. Now she couldn't even see the kitchen door. The afternoon sun cast its slanting rays onto the tabby and the plants, and then, carrying the shadows of the cat and the cactuses, found its way onto Grandma's bed, and onto her hands, knees and feet, warming them through and through. Once more she started to doze off, but with a jerk she came to again. Right away she sniffed the air and became suspicious. What happened to that smoke? Was the kindling all burned up already? Then suddenly it hit her: Yuhua must have fooled her again! That smoke must have been another one of her tricks. The woman was a real live fox spirit, she knew exactly how to cast a spell on people. Why else would her son have insisted on buying the propane stove, come hell or high water? Yuhua must have been behind it all, it was all her doing! If it weren't for that woman there'd be peace under heaven. If it weren't for that woman, Grandma would never have ended up paralyzed from the waist down, a useless lump stuck on a bed, not quite alive and not quite dead. Without realizing it she began to grind her teeth, making all kinds of loud, crunching noises.

That day she and Uncle Chang were sitting under the trellis, sipping tea and shooting the breeze. Uncle Chang was singing her son's praises to her: "That boy of yours, heh, he's like this!" And he raised his right fist, then stuck out his thumb. At that very moment her son came into the courtyard pushing his bicycle, and there tied onto the back was a metal doohickey, kind of round and kind of long. As soon as she saw that thing she felt all her hairs standing on end. Once when she was a child she had seen a ghost. It was just getting dark when she passed by a graveyard surrounded by cypress trees, and she could see fireflies twinkling here and there among the branches and in the clumps of overgrown weeds. The ghost was standing right behind a headstone, ashen white from head to toe and not a single feature on its face, just like one of those blank tiles in a mah-jongg game. That scared the living daylights out of her. Every hair standing straight up on her head, she ran home like a wisp of smoke. Afterward she was sick for three whole days. But keeping a gas stove in the house was even more terrifying than keeping a ghost at home, it would make your hairs stand on end every single day. The ruckus that day shook all the neighbors in the alley. If she hadn't collapsed in a dead faint right then and there she would have blocked the cookhouse door for at least three days and three nights. At the time she was also coughing and wheezing so hard she couldn't get a word out. How she had wanted to give that wench a few good swings of her walking stick! But her arms refused to obey. For the rest of her life she would never forget those eyes, those ferocious eyes. She had wanted to go down on her knees before her son, right there in front of the whole neighborhood: I'm begging you on my knees! Look, everyone! See how this mother is kneeling to her son! But somehow, as soon as she saw those eyes of her daughter-in-law's she fainted dead away. Death is like a light going out. If only she had died right then.

Even though she didn't hear that crackling at the beginning, she could tell from the delicious aroma that the minced scallions had just been tossed into the hot oil and were still sizzling away in the pan. That must be Yuhua getting ready to stir fry. The smell was so close by it could only have come from their own little cookhouse. Right away Grandma relaxed. It's going to be all right now, she'd finally made it through another day. And not just her, but all dozen or so families in their courtyard, plus the people in the immediate neighborhood, fifty or sixty households in all—they too had made it through another day. Only the tabby on the windowsill was none the wiser, still fast asleep. But at last even it had had enough. It stood up and rubbed itself against the flowerpot, then, arching its back and lifting its head, let out a great big yawn before jumping off the ledge and scampering away. Now the space between the two pots was empty once more. Quickly she raised herself and stared out the window at the kitchen again, only to find the sun shining right in her face. The wider she opened her eyes, the more blinding the light, so bright and harsh that tears came to her eyes. With the back of her hand she wiped them off, but as soon as she lifted her head and looked out the window tears would gush out again. Tearing, wiping, wiping, tearing—she kept this up for a long time, although she knew in her heart that, even if the sun was not blinding her, she still would not be able to see clearly into the kitchen.

But she had to keep looking. Some time later it occurred to her to scrunch her eyes up into tiny slits and shade them with her hands. There, that's better. She could look over at the kitchen again. Now for some reason her heart began to thump and she had a feeling that something was about to go wrong. But what? She couldn't say. Nevertheless the pounding of her heart grew worse. In her mind she kept telling herself: steady there, steady does it. That seemed to work. She could see something at last. She could sense a figure like that of Yuhua's stirring about the cookhouse, though she still couldn't see what she was up to. Again she told herself: steady there, steady. And that was when she finally saw something not quite right about the kitchen. If Yuhua was actually cooking with the coal stove, then she should have been facing the south wall. Why then did she keep bustling around on the north side of the kitchen? Grandma Qi felt a sharp cramp in her chest, as if someone had gripped her heart tightly and was squeezing it for dear life. Frantically she sniffed and snorted, but she could smell nothing unusual in the air. She had long heard that gas had a special odor to it, though she could never tell what it was. She must be getting old, after all—her nose just wasn't what it used to be. No, no, she couldn't just sit there, she had to think of some way to look into the kitchen and get help if need be. She must move herself over to the edge of the bed, must try again even though she had tried just now but failed. Taking a deep breath she thrust herself forward again, stretching her arms until her fingers closed around the edge of the bed, then pulled and tugged and hauled as if her very life depended on it. This time, she thought, this time she had a chance. She held her breath. She felt that come what may she could not let go of this breath, she had to pull herself over, do what she had to do while she was still holding on to it. How was she to know that just when she could feel her legs beginning to budge, another fit of coughing would seize her like the dickens and turn her inside out again? But this time she didn't let go. Her hands gripped the edge of the bed ever more tightly. She had only one thought on her mind: She had to see what was going on in the kitchen, even if that was the last thing she ever did.

FIRST PUBLISHED IN AUGUST 1982 IN *BEIJING WENXUE (BEIJING LITERATURE)*

SOULS TIED TO THE KNOTS ON A LEATHER CORD

▲ ▲ ▲

▲ ▲ ▲

▲ ▲ ▲

Z H A X I   D A W A

▲   ▲   ▲

▲   ▲   ▲

▲   ▲   These days you don't much hear "El Condor Pasa" anymore, that Peruvian folk song with the simple yet lovely melody. But I have preserved it on my own cassette tape. Whenever I play it, I can see right before my eyes those valleys in the highlands. Flocks of sheep scampering among the jumbled rocks. Cultivated areas divided into little plots at the foot of the mountains. Scraggly crops. A mill by the side of a stream. Stone farmhouses hugging the ground. Heavily laden mountain folk. Brass bells tied around the cattle's necks. A lonely little eddy of wind. Dazzling sunshine.

This scenery does not belong to the central plateau in the Peruvian Andes but to the Pabu Naigang range in southern Tibet. I'm not sure if I once saw it in a dream or if I have actually been there. I can't remember anymore. I've been to too many places.

It was not until later, on a day when I finally got to the Pabu Naigang range, that I realized what was stored in my memory was no more than a beautiful nineteenth-century pastoral landscape by Constable.

Although this is still a peaceful mountain region, the people here are already quietly enjoying the comforts of modern life. There is a small airfield here with five helicopter flights each week to the city. Nearby is a solar energy power plant. In the little eatery right next to the gas station on the edge of the village of Jelu, a man with a big beard sits at my table, talking nonstop all the while. He is the chairman of the board of the famous Himalayan Transportation Company, the first in all of Tibet to own a fleet of tractor trailers imported from Germany. When I visit a local carpet factory, I find the technicians using a computer to produce their designs. The ground satellite station broadcasts on five frequencies, supplying viewers with a total of thirty-eight hours of television programming every day.

But no matter how strongly the modern world forces its inhabitants to break away from traditional ways of thinking, for the people of the Pabu Naigang mountain region some old mannerisms die hard. Whenever the village chief—who has a Ph.D. in agricultural science—talks to me, he will every now and then inhale loudly through his lips and make subservient ululating noises with his tongue. When people have a favor to ask, they stick out their thumb and wriggle it around while they blurt out a string of importuning clucks. When a visitor comes from the big city far away, some of the old folks still take off their hats and hold them against their chests as they step to one side, to show their heartfelt respect. Although a uniform system of measurements was established nationwide many years ago, when the people here want to describe a certain length they still extend one arm and chop at it with the flat of the other hand, across the wrist, or forearm, or elbow, all the way up to the shoulder.

The Living Buddha Sangjie Dapu was about to die. He had reached the ripe old age of ninety-eight, this twenty-third reincarnated Living Buddha of the Zhatuo Monastery. After he dies, there will be no more reincarnates to succeed him. I had met Sangjie Dapu before, and I wanted to write an article about him and his religion. When Tibetan Lamaism (and its various sects) loses the system of succession by reincarnates, and therefore no longer has religious leaders of greater or lesser importance, one of the world's most profound and mystical religions may be nearing the end of its days. To a certain extent outward form determines inner consciousness, I argued.

The Living Buddha Sangjie Dapu of Zhatuo shook his head in disagreement. His pupils were slowly dilating.

"Shambhala," his lips quavered, "the war has begun."

According to the ancient scriptures, there is a Pure Land in the north, a paradise on earth called Shambhala. It is said that the Heavenly Yogic Tantrism originated here, and that this was where Sakyamuni instructed the first king Sochad Napu, who later went on to propagate the secret doctrine of the Way of the Wheel. The scriptures also say that one day there will be a war in Shambhala, in this land surrounded by snow-capped mountains. "You command twelve celestial legions, amidst heavenly hosts you gallop onward, never looking back. You throw your lance at Halutaman's chest, at the leader of the evil gods who defy Shambhala, and all of them shall be annihilated." This is the account in "The Oath of Shambhala" extolling the last king, the Heavenly Warrior King of the Wheel. Sangjie Dapu of Zhatuo once told me about this war. He said that after hundreds of years of terrible fighting, when the monsters and devils have all been destroyed, the Tsongkaba grave in the Gandan Monastery will open by itself and the teachings of Sakyamuni will once again be propagated for a thousand years. After that there will be windstorms and fires, and finally the whole world will be inundated by a great flood. When the end comes, there will inevitably be a few lucky ones whom the gods will rescue into heaven. And then, when the world once again takes shape, religion will also be reborn.

Sangjie Dapu of Zhatuo was lying on the bed. He was hallucinating, talking to some invisible person by his side: "When you climb over the snow-covered Kalong mountains and find yourself standing among the lines of the Lotus-Born Guru's palm, do not pursue, do not seek. In prayer you will see the light, through enlightenment you will receive the Vision. Of all the crisscrossing palm lines, only one is the road of life, the one that leads to the Pure Land on earth."

It seems to me I had watched as the Lotus-Born Guru departed from this world. A chariot descended from the heavens, and in the company of two celestial maidens he climbed into the chariot and drove away into the southern skies.

"Two young people from the Kampa district, they've gone to look for the road to Shambhala," the Living Buddha mumbled.

I looked at him wearily.

"You're saying . . . in the year 1984, two Kampa people—a man and a woman—came here?" I asked.

He nodded.

"And the man got into an accident here?" I asked again.

"You know about this too," said the Living Buddha.

Songjie Dapu of Zhatuo closed his eyes and, by fits and starts, began to reminisce about the arrival of the two young people in the Pabu Naigang mountain region and what they told him of their experiences along the way. I recognized his narration: It was a story I had made up. As soon as I finished writing it I had locked it up in a box without showing it to anyone. Now he was telling it almost word for word. The time was 1984. The setting was on the road to a village called Jia in the Pabu Naigang mountains. The cast consisted of a man and a woman. The reason I didn't show this work to anyone was because at the end even I had no idea where the two protagonists were going. Now that the Living Buddha had enlightened me, I knew. There was only one difference between the two versions. At the end of my story, the characters were sitting in a wine shop when an old man showed them the way. But according to the Living Buddha of Zhatuo, it was right here in his room that he had pointed out the road for them. Even so, there was yet another coincidence: Both the old man and the Living Buddha talked about the lines on the Lotus-Born Guru's palm.

Eventually, other people came into the room and surrounded the Living Buddha. Eyes half open, he gradually entered a state of unconsciousness.

They began preparations for his funeral. The Living Buddha of Zhatuo was to be cremated. I knew that someone hoped to find his *sheli**** among the ashes as an everlasting keepsake and collectible.

When I got home, I unlocked a box labeled "The Beloved Castaways." Arranged neatly within were almost a hundred brown envelopes containing all my unpublished works, including those I didn't want published. I picked up one marked "840720," inside which was an as yet untitled short story about how two Kampa people came to Pabu Naigang. The following is what I had written:

Chiong is herding her flock of twenty-some sheep down the mountainside when she pauses on the slope halfway. She sees a tiny figure the size of an ant, way down at the bottom of the mountain, moving slowly across the dry pebbly expanses of the meandering riverbed. She can tell it is a man, and he is heading right in the

*Sheli: a fragment of bone or tooth found in the ashes after a cremation and imbued with mystical and ritual significance in Tibetan Buddhism.

direction of her home. With a crack of her whip Chiong quickly drives the sheep down the hill.

She figures it will take the man roughly until nightfall to reach her home. There is no shelter in the surrounding wilderness except for the bungalows here—several small huts built of rounded stones on top of this little hump of a hill. Right behind the living quarters are pens for the sheep. There are only two households: Chiong and her father, and a mute woman in her fifties. Father is a balladeer who sings the *Gesar,* and he is often invited to perform in villages dozens of kilometers away, sometimes farther. He would be gone for several days at least, even months at a time. Always, a messenger on horseback would ride up the hill with another horse in tow, and Father, his long-necked mandolin slung across his back, would mount the second horse. Then would come the clattering of hooves mingled with the tinkling of bells, a rhythmic duet reverberating on and on through the silence of the wilderness. Standing on top of the hill, Chiong would caress the big black dog squatting at her side and watch the two horsemen until they disappeared around the next mountain.

Chiong had grown up to this monotonous cadence of hoofbeats and horsebells. Sitting alone on a rock as she watches her sheep, she falls into a reverie, and then the ringing turns into a wordless song wafting by from some faraway valley—a song imbued with the enduring life force of the wilderness, yet tinged with a melancholy desire that seeps through the loneliness.

The mute woman works at her loom all day long making felt. Every morning she would stand at the top of the little knoll and cry out to the Bodhisatva Guanyin as she throws a handful of *tsampa** flour into the air. Then, turning to face south, she would twirl a

---

**tsampa:* roasted barley, a staple in the Tibetan diet.

grease-stained prayer wheel and intone her prayers. Once in a while Father would get up in the middle of the night and go into the woman's shack, reemerging just before daybreak, with his long fur robe tossed loosely over his head, to snuggle back into his sheep-skin cot. At dawn Chiong would get up to milk the sheep and make tea, then gulp down her breakfast of tsampa gruel. Next she would pack a day's provisions into a small sheepskin pouch and hoist it onto her back, along with a little black cooking pot. Then she would let the sheep out of the pen and drive them up the mountain with the help of her whip. Life has been nothing more than that.

Chiong prepares some food and hot tea, then stretches out on the rug to wait for the visitor. Outside the dog begins to bark. She rushes out. The moon is just rising. She grabs the dog's leash, but there is no one in sight. In a little while, though, a head pops up over the slope at her feet.

"Come up, it's all right, I'm holding onto the dog," Chiong says.

The fellow is a fine specimen of manhood.

"You must be tired, brother," Chiong says as she leads him inside the house. Under his wide-brimmed felt hat a shock of bright red tassels dangles along the side of his face. Father is away singing the *Gesar.* The banging of the loom as the mute woman works on her felt can be heard from next door. The exhausted fellow finishes his dinner, thanks Chiong and falls asleep immediately in Father's bed.

Chiong stands outside the door for a little while. The night sky is studded with countless stars. The broad valley stretching out at her feet takes on a pale shimmery glow in the moonlight, and all around her is a silence unbroken by any sounds of nature. The big black dog, confined by its chain, is turning around and around on the same spot. Chiong goes over to it, bends down and puts her arms around its neck. She begins to think about the childhood and adolescence she has spent on this lonely, desolate little hilltop, about those people—always silent and expressionless—who come to fetch her father, about the traveler sound asleep inside the house, who has come from afar and will leave for some distant place the next day. And she weeps. Falling onto the ground with her face buried in her hands, she mutely begs Father's forgiveness. Then, wiping her tears away on the dog's furry hide, she stands up and goes back into the house.

In the darkness, trembling all over like a person stricken with the ague, she crawls silently under the man's blanket.

As soon as the morning star appears in the east, Chiong rolls up her thin blanket in the flickering light of a tallow lamp. Into a cloth sack she stuffs some beef jerky, a chunk of yak butter, some coarse salt, and the leather pouch she uses for kneading tsampa. Then she heaves it all onto her back, together with the little black pot she has used for making tea every day up in the mountains with her sheep. Everything that a young woman should have with her is on her back. Finally she takes one last look around the dim little hut.

"All right," she says.

The fellow finishes his last pinch of snuff, dusts off his hands and stands up. He pats the top of her head and puts his arm around her shoulder as they duck their heads under the low doorway of the cottage. Then they set out in the direction of the west, still pitch dark at that hour. Chiong is heavily ladened with her belongings, which bang and rattle with every step she takes. She has no interest in finding out where this man will take her. It is enough to know that she is about to leave this lifeless place forever. The only thing the man carries with him is a string of sandalwood prayer beads. Striding along with his head held high, he seems full of confidence about the long journey ahead.

"Why do you have that leather cord tied around your waist?" Tabei asks. "You look like a puppy without a master at the other end of the leash."

"It's for counting the days. Can't you see the five knots on here? I've been gone from home five days already," Chiong answers.

"What's five days? I was born without a home."

And so they travel along, always on foot, she following Tabei. Sometimes they would spend the night on the threshing ground of a village or in a sheep pen, other times they would find shelter among the ruins of some temple or in a cave. And once in a while, when they are lucky, they would sleep in some farmer's outbuilding or a shepherd's tent.

Every time they enter a temple, they would stop in front of each bodhisattva statue and strike their foreheads against the altar several times, performing the ritual bow. Whenever they come across a *mani** pile, whether by the side of the road, on a riverbank, or in a mountain pass, they would never fail to add a few white pebbles on top. Along the way they also pass some people performing the long kowtow: Lying spread-eagled, these devout Buddhists would knock their heads against the ground, rise, walk up to where their foreheads had hit the earth, and once more prostrate themselves, repeating the entire sequence for every step of their journey. The thick canvas aprons they tie around themselves have been patched again and again; nevertheless these would be worn down to tatters over their chests and knees. Every protrusion on their faces would be covered with grime, and on their foreheads are swellings the size of a chicken egg, bloody and caked with mud. Their hands are sheathed in tin-sheeted wooden gauntlets, which scuff the ground

mani: a pile of stones with mystical and ritual significance in Tibetan Buddhism.

on each side of their prostrate bodies and leave behind a pair of telltale streaks. Because Tabei and Chiong are walking, they would always overtake the people doing the long kowtows.

Many are the mountains on the Tibetan Plateau, and they rise, range after range, all the way to the horizon. Human settlements are few and far between. One could walk for days without seeing another person, let alone a village. A cold wind whooshes through the canyons. The sun beats down mercilessly, and the earth is scorching hot. To look up at the blue skies for even a few moments is to feel lightheaded, to experience a sensation of levitating. The mountains, sound asleep in broad daylight, seem eternal and infinite in their serenity.

Strong and agile, Tabei climbs the mountains with ease, stepping nimbly from one teetering rock to another as he scampers upward. When he reaches a smooth boulder he would sit down to wait for Chiong, who is always far behind. They never exchange a word when they are on the move. Sometimes in the unbearable silence Chiong would burst into song, sounding like some she-animal in a canyon howling at the sky. Tabei would keep on walking without even turning to look at her. After a while Chiong would stop, and everything would again become deathly quiet. Head bowed, she would follow behind, breaking the silence only when they stop to rest.

"Has it stopped bleeding?"

"It doesn't hurt anymore."

"Let me see."

"Go catch me a few spiders. I'll mash them up and smear them over this so it'll heal faster."

"There are no spiders here."

"Go look in the cracks under the rocks."

One after another Chiong turns over half-buried rocks and stones as she hunts earnestly for spiders, and in a little while she has caught five or six. Cupping them in her hands, she brings them back to Tabei and presses them into his palm. One by one he crushes them and dabs them onto the wound in his leg.

"That dog was vicious! I ran and ran and ran and ran. The pot on my back was banging against my head the whole way and I was beginning to see stars."

"I should have pulled out my knife right at the beginning and killed it."

"That woman gave us this." Chiong mimics an obscene gesture, one of the most insulting. "I was so scared."

Tabei grabs another handful of dirt and spreads it on his wound, letting it bask in the sun.

"Where did she keep the money?"

"In the big cupboard in the wineshop. A stack of bills this thick," he motions with his hands. "I only took ten or twelve of them."

"What do you want to buy with them?"

"What do I want to buy? Listen, I'm going to make an offering to Buddha in the Tsigu Temple, down at the foot of the next mountain. I'm also going to keep some of it."

"That's good. Are you better now? It doesn't hurt anymore, does it?"

"No. Hey, my mouth is so dry smoke's coming out of it."

"Can't you see I've already set up the pot? I'm going right now to find some dry bramble."

Chewing on a stalk of dried grass, Tabei stretches out lazily on the rock, his broad-brimmed hat pulled over his eyes to shield them from the sun. Chiong gets down on her hands and knees in front of some rocks she has stacked into a hearth, her face rubbing in the dirt as she puffs away at the kindling. All of a sudden the fire roars to life. She jumps back and rubs her eyes, which are seared and stinging from the smoke. When she pulls down one of her forelocks for a look, she sees that it too has been singed.

On the peak of a lofty mountain in the distance are two tiny dark figures, one tall and one short. They are probably shepherds, but they look like eagles perched in a rocky aerie on top of the mountain. They are motionless.

Chiong sees them and waves, swinging her right arm around and around. Yonder the two people begin to stir as well, returning her greeting with the same whirling gestures. But they are too far away from Chiong for their voices to carry, not even if they shouted themselves hoarse.

"I thought we were the only ones around here," Chiong says to Tabei.

He closes his eyes. "I'm still waiting for your tea."

Suddenly Chiong remembers something. From the folds of her tunic she pulls out an object and shows it to Tabei with a triumphant flourish. It is a book she had palmed from the back pocket of a none too well-behaved young man as he murmured sweet nothings in her ear last night, in the village where they had found shelter. Tabei takes the book and examines it, but he does not understand either the language it is written in or the diagrams of machines in the book. The only thing he recognizes is the picture of a tractor on the cover.

"This thing isn't worth a straw," he says, tossing it back to her.

Chiong is crestfallen. The next time she makes tea she tears up the book and uses the pages as tinder for the fire.

As they come around a mountain at sundown, they see in the distance a village enfolded by trees. Chiong's spirits lift and she begins to sing again. Swinging her walking stick in the air, she breaks into a giddy little dance on a patch of *malan* grass nearby. Then she points the stick at Tabei and gingerly pokes him under the arms and around his middle to tickle him. Tabei grabs the stick impatiently and flings it away from him, throwing her off balance so that she totters and falls on the ground.

When they reach the village, Tabei goes off by himself to drink or to do whatever. They plan to rendezvous at the place where they would spend the night: next to the village elementary school, in the vacant building that has just been finished and is still without windows or doors. On the village common, a screen is being set up between some wooden poles for the movie about to be shown that evening.

Chiong goes into a grove of trees to gather firewood, but finds herself surrounded by a gang of children who have climbed on top of some walls nearby and are now pelting her with stones. One of the missiles hits her on the shoulder, but she does not turn around. After a while a young fellow wearing a yellow hat chases the kids away.

"They threw eight stones, and one of them hit you," Yellow Hat says as he grins at her. He thrusts his hand in front of her face to show her the electronic calculator he is holding. On its screen is the Arabic numeral "8." "Where are you from?"

Chiong stares at him.

"Do you remember how many days you've been walking?"

"No, I don't remember," Chiong says as she picks up her leather sash, "but I can find out. Come and help me count."

"Does each one of these knots mean one day?" he asks as he bends down in front of her. "How interesting . . . there, ninety-two days."

"Really?"

"Haven't you ever counted them?"

Chiong shakes her head.

"Ninety-two days, at twenty kilometers a day," he mutters, jabbing the calculator keys, "that's one thousand eight hundred and forty kilometers."

Chiong has no concept of arithmetic.

"I'm the accountant around here," the young fellow says. "Whatever problems I run into I solve them with this thing."

"What is it?" Chiong asks.

"An electronic calculator. It's a lot of fun. See here, it knows how old you are." He presses a number and shows it to Chiong.

"How old?"

"Nineteen."

"Am I nineteen?"

"You tell me."

"I don't know."

"We Tibetans never used to keep track of our age. But this thing knows. Look, that's what it says on here, nineteen."

"Doesn't look like it."

"Really? Let me see. Oh, it just takes some getting used to. The numbers on here are shaped kind of funny."

"Does it know my name?"

"Of course."

"Well, what is it?"

He punches out an eight-digit number, which fills the entire screen.

"What did I tell you? It knows."

"What's my name?"

"Can't you even read your own name? Dummy."

"How do I read it?"

"Like this." He holds it upright for her to look at.

"Does that say Chiong?"

"Of course it says Chiong, C-h-i-o-n-g."

"Hah!" she cries excitedly.

"Hah nothing, they've been doing this for years in other countries. You know, I've been thinking about this problem. In the old days we used to work from can't see in the morning to can't see at night. Well, in economic terms, the labor expended should be directly proportional to the value created." His tongue loosening, he begins to talk through his hat, sounding off about everything from the value of labor to the cash value of a workpoint to the values of commodities, with a discussion of time and arithmetic thrown in for good measure. Then he flashes another figure on his calculator. "Look, after all this calculating it comes out to be a negative number. And at the end of the year we don't even have enough to feed ourselves, we have to ask the government for surplus grain. That goes against the laws of economics. . . . Hey, why are you staring at me like that? You want to gobble me up?"

"If you have nothing to eat for dinner, you can share some of mine. As soon as I get some firewood I'll make tea."

"Damn, did you just walk out of the Middle Ages? Or are you one of those whatchamacallit extraterrestrials?"

"I came from a place very far away, and I've been walking . . ." Again she picks up the leather cord. "How many did you say just now?"

"Let me think, eighty-five days."

"I've been walking eighty-five days. No, that's not right. Just now you said ninety-two days. You tricked me!" Chiong begins to giggle.

"Oh-oh-oh! Buddha have mercy, I think I'm getting drunk," he mutters as he closes his eyes.

"Will you eat here with me? I still have some jerky."

"Young lady, how about going out with me instead? We'll go someplace with lots of happy young people, and music, beer, even disco dancing. Now get rid of those rotten twigs in your hands!"

Tabei squeezes his way out of the dark mass of people watching the movie. He is not drunk, but his head is spinning from all those brightly colored images flashing about on the screen, now close up, now far away—people, scenery, everything. They have completely worn him out. Wearily he trudges back to the vacant building. Inside, he finds the little black pot set on top of a pile of stones, all cold to the touch. Chiong's things are lying in a corner nearby. He picks up the pot and drinks a few mouthfuls of ice-cold water, then leans back against a wall to look up at the sky. He is soon lost in thought. The farther they travel, the noisier and more boisterous the villages they come across, so full of engines roaring and people singing and shouting that even the nocturnal calm of nature has been dissipated. He has no desire to travel along a road that leads to ever more frenzied and cacophonous cities. He wants to go where . . .

Lurching and swaying, Chiong stumbles in and steadies herself against the adobe wall next to the doorless portal. Even from a distance Tabei could smell the liquor on her breath, which is somewhat better smelling than his own.

"It was so much fun, they're such happy people," Chiong half sobs, half giggles. "They're as happy as the immortals. Let's leave day after tomorrow . . . no, the day after that."

"No." He never stays more than one night in the same village.

"I'm tired, I feel exhausted," Chiong shakes her head leadenly.

"What do you know about being tired? Look at those thick legs of yours, even stronger than a yak's. It's not in your nature to know what tired means."

"No, I don't mean my body." Chiong points to her heart.

"You're drunk. Go to sleep." He holds Chiong by the shoulders and presses her down onto the grimy floor. Afterwards he ties a knot for her on the leather cord.

Chiong becomes more and more tired. Whenever they stop to rest, she would lie down and refuse to get up.

"Stand up, don't lie there like a lazy cur," Tabei says.

"I don't want to go on anymore." She stretches out in the sun and squints up at him.

"What did you say?"

"You go on by yourself, I don't want to follow you anymore, walking and walking and walking all the time. Even you don't know where you're going, that's why we just wander around day after day."

But he does know which way they should go. "Woman, you don't understand anything."

"You're right, I don't understand." Chiong closes her eyes and draws herself up into a ball.

"Get on your feet!" Tabei kicks her a couple of times in the buttocks, then lifts his hand high as if ready to bring it down on her. "Otherwise I'll smack you."

"You're an ogre!" Chiong whimpers as she struggles onto her feet. Leaning on her walking stick she sets out after Tabei, who has gone on ahead.

At a seemingly opportune moment Chiong runs away. They are sleeping in a cave when she gets up in the middle of the night and slips out, taking care to bring her little black pot with her. By the light of the moon and stars she runs downhill, going back in the direction whence they came. She feels free as a bird that has just escaped from its cage. Around noon the next day, while she is resting near a cliff which drops off into a deep canyon, she sees a black speck appearing over the ridge of the next mountain, just like the one she saw that day when she was driving her flock home. Tabei has intercepted her and is now walking toward her. Trembling with anger, she grabs her pot and swings desperately at his head, ferociously enough to splatter the brains of a wild bull. Startled, Tabei manages to step aside deftly and block her arm with a counterblow. The black pot flies out of her hands and goes noisily down the side of the cliff. For quite some time they look at each other while the clattering continues to resound from the canyon. In the end Chiong has to climb down into the chasm, whimpering and sniffling the whole way. It is several hours before she reappears with the pot, which is gouged and dented all over.

"You make up for my pot," Chiong demands.

"Let me see it." He takes it from her, and together they examine it thoroughly. "Just a little crack here, I can fix it."

Tabei walks away, and a dejected Chiong follows behind.

"Aaaayyyy—" she starts to sing, so loudly she sets the whole canyon ringing.

Then one day Tabei too begins to grow tired of Chiong. He thinks to himself: "It is only because I led a virtuous life in my previous incarnation, renouncing evil and engaging in kind deeds, that I accumulated enough good karma to be born into the Middle Earth as a human being in this life, and not as some lost soul or hungry demon in the netherworld. But on the road to our final deliverance from suffering and sorrow, women and money are both extraneous things, they are stumbling blocks."

Not long after that they come to a village known as Jia. By this time the leather sash around Chiong's waist is densely braided with many little knots. To their surprise, they find the Jia villagers standing at the village gate banging gongs and drums in welcome. On each side of the entrance is an honor guard made up of members of the militia, complete with semiautomatic rifles that have been plugged with red cloth to prevent any accidents. Four villagers masquerading as yaks are dancing on the path between the guards. Greeting them at the front of the parade are the village chief and several young women, some carrying the ceremonial sashes called *hadars* and others holding silver pitchers whose spouts have been moistened with droplets of yak butter.

It turns out there has been a long drought in these parts. Not long ago a soothsayer predicted that on this very day, at sunset, two people coming from the east would arrive at the village and bring with them a propitious rainfall as wondrous as ambrosia, which would turn the parched crops into a bountiful harvest. So when Tabei and Chiong appear as presaged, the people take it as a good omen and joyfully hoist the two of them onto a tractor festooned with hadars. Then the whole jubilant procession enters the village. Men and women, young and old alike are dressed in their finest, and the five-colored prayer flags fluttering from every rooftop have been freshly changed. Somebody claims to have detected in Chiong's features, in the way she speaks and how she carries herself, the traits of the incarnated Goddess of Mercy. And so Tabei is forgotten and left to himself. But he knows Chiong is no goddess incarnate, because he has seen how hideous she looks when she is fast asleep: Her cheeks become quite jowly then, and ropey saliva oozes from the corners of her half-open mouth.

Sullenly he enters a wineshop for a drink. He is itching to start some trouble. If only someone would pick a quarrel with him, someone who doesn't like the look of his face maybe, or who just wants to give him a hard time. Then he could have a real brawl. And if the guy dares to go for a knife fight, so much the better.

But there is only an old man inside the shop, drinking by himself while flies buzz around his head. Tabei walks over and sits down across from him with a defiant look. A peasant girl wearing a colorful kerchief brings him a glass and fills it with wine.

"This stuff tastes like horse piss," he bellows after taking a swig. No one answers him.

"Well, doesn't it?" he challenges the old man.

"Now if you're talking about horse piss, I drank quite a bit of that when I was young, and, believe me, straight from the you-know-what on a stallion's underbelly."

Tabei begins to laugh with glee.

"To get my cattle back from Amilier the Archbandit, I had to chase them from Gatsar all the way into the Taklimakhan Desert."

"Who's this Amilier?"

"Hah, don't you know, she was the leader of a gang of bandits who came from Xinjiang about thirty-some years ago, a Kazakh, notorious up and down the Ali region and all through northern Tibet. One time a chieftain had all his livestock rustled overnight. Heaven knows how many yaks and sheep there were, but they were gone from the pasture just like that. When he looked out of his yurt the next morning, all he saw were countless hoofprints on the empty white plain. Even the soldiers sent by the Kesha authorities couldn't handle her."

"And then?"

"You were talking about horse piss just now. Yes, that's right, I grabbed my musket, jumped on a horse and went after my cattle. Out there in that enormous desert, it was those mouthfuls of horse piss that saved my life."

"And then?"

"And then, the leader of the bandits wanted to keep me, wanted me to stay and be her—"

"Husband?"

"—herdsman. After all, I was the chieftain's son! She was damned good-looking too. She was just like the sun, nobody dared look her right in the eye. But I escaped and came back here. Now you tell me, is there any place I haven't been other than heaven and hell?"

"The place where I am going," Tabei says.

"Where's that?" asks the old man.

"I—I don't know." For the first time Tabei feels unsure about the destination ahead. He no longer knows which road to take.

But the old man seems to understand. Pointing to a mountain behind him, he says to Tabei: "No one has ever gone there. The village of Jia used to be a stage post, and travelers came and went in all directions, but nobody ever went there. Back in 1964," he begins to reminisce, "we set up a commune here, and everyone was talking about taking the communist road. At the time few people could rightly say what communism was, we only knew it was one of the heavens. But nobody knew where it was. We'd ask travelers who came from the south, from the east, from the north, but none of them had ever seen it. That left only the Kalong mountains. So a few people sold all their belongings, slung their tsampa bags across their shoulders and set out to cross the Kalongs. They said they were going to Communism. But they never came back. After that, not a single person from the village ever headed out there again, no matter how hard the times got."

Clenching the rim of the glass between his teeth, Tabei cocks his eyes upward at the old man.

"But I know a little secret about the bottom of the snow-covered Kalong mountains," the old man says, winking at Tabei.

"Go ahead."

"Are you planning to go that way?"

"Maybe."

"Well, when you climb to the top you will hear a strange weeping, like the cries of a misbegotten child who has been abandoned. But that's alright, it's only the sound of the wind coming from a crevice in the rocks. Then after you've been climbing for seven days, you will reach the peak just at daybreak, but don't be in a hurry to go down the other side. Wait till after dark, because in broad daylight the glare off the snow will make you blind.''

''That is no secret,'' Tabei says.

''You're right, that's not a secret. What I really want to tell you is, after you've been going downhill for two days and can see the foot of the mountain, you will find countless gullies down at the bottom, some shallow, others deep, all zigzagging every which way for as far as the eye can see. Going into these gullies is like entering a labyrinth. True, this is no secret either, but don't interrupt me. Now, do you know why there are so many more gullies at the bottom of this mountain than any other place? Because these gullies are the lines on the palm of the Lotus-Born Guru's right hand. Once upon a time he fought a life-and-death duel on this spot with the demon Shivamairu. For one hundred and eight days they battled, and even though the Guru used one after another of his magic powers he could not subdue the demon. Then Shivamairu turned himself into a tiny flea, thinking that he would become invisible to his archenemy. Whereupon the Lotus-Born Guru raised his magical right hand and, thundering out a terrible curse, slapped his palm onto the earth. In one fell swoop Shivamairu was banished into the netherworld. Ever since then the ground over the spot has been marked with the lines and furrows of the Guru's palm. Any ordinary mortal who stumbles into the countless cracks and crevices would inevitably lose his way in the labyrinth. It is said there is only one way out, but there are no clues or signs marking the trail.''

Tabei stares intently at the old man.

''Well, this is only a legend, and even I don't know what lies beyond the maze,'' the old man mutters, shaking his head.

Tabei decides to go to that place. The old man then asks Tabei for a favor: Would he leave Chiong with them in the village? The old man's son has just bought a tractor. Nowadays every family wants to have one of these things. The age-old crowing of the rooster at daybreak is now drowned out by the rumbling of engines. Horse-drawn carts and donkeys are being pushed to the side of the road. Even the pure, crystal-clear water in the streams that tumble down from the snowy mountains is beginning to smell faintly of diesel. The old man runs a power-operated mill and his wife of many years farms a dozen or so hectares. Not long ago, the old man made a trip to the big city to attend something called the "Assembly of Exemplary Representatives of the Campaign to End Poverty and Achieve Prosperity," at which he was given an award as well as a prize. The newspaper even published his picture—a four-inch-square photograph, no less. Never in all the generations of their family have they ever been so well off, never in all those generations have they ever been so busy. Now they need a daughter-in-law to take care of the housework.

While the old man is talking his son comes into the shop. Trying to impress the visitor, the young man pulls out a wad of bills in various denominations and flashes it around. On his wrist is a digital watch. A sleek little cassette player hangs from his belt, a pair of earphones sits on his head, and he is bopping to the beat of music only he can hear. All the moves of a cool city dude, he has them down pat. But Tabei is not at all impressed by any of this—except for the walking tractor parked just outside the door with its engine still running. The put-put-put of the motor seems to have struck a chord in him. He gets up and walks over to the tractor.

Caressing the handlebars, Tabei says: "Alright, I'll leave Chiong with you."

The young fellow grins sheepishly—most likely he has already gotten a little something from Chiong just now.

"May I take a ride in this thing?" Tabei asks.

"Of course. Here, let me show you. You'll get the hang of it in no time.'' The young fellow gives Tabei a quick lesson in driving the tractor—how to press down on the accelerator, how to shift gears, work the clutch, how to start up and how to brake.

Slowly Tabei gets the walking tractor moving and begins to drive down the dirt road in the twilight. Chiong watches him from the side, tears of happiness streaming down her cheeks. She is about to stay behind, at last! Just then another tractor comes hurtling down the road towing a wagon behind it. It is one of those big powerful combines nicknamed ''Iron Oxen.'' Tabei doesn't know what to do. There is a shallow trench on one side, and the young fellow shouts at him to drive off the road into the ditch. Tabei jumps off the driver's seat into the middle of the road while the tractor rolls slowly into the trench, but the Iron Ox could not brake in time and its wagon knocks Tabei onto the ground. Everyone runs over and crowds around as Tabei gets back on his feet and dusts himself off. Although he has been hit in the side, he insists it is nothing, that he is fine, and they all breathe a sigh of relief.

The time has come for Tabei to leave—his first attempt to operate a machine, and he gets chewed up by it instead. He puts his arms around Chiong and touches his forehead to hers in a bow of fare-well, then sets out on the road to the Kalong mountains. That night the rains come at last, and the villagers all dance and sing for joy. By then Tabei has left the village of Jia far behind and entered the mountains. Along the way he spits out a mouthful of blood. He is hemorrhaging internally from the injury.

My story ended here.

I decided to return to Pabu Naigang and climb up over the Kalong mountains. I wanted to look for the hero of my story among the lines and furrows of the Lotus-Born Guru's palm.

It was a long way from the village of Jia across the mountains to the Place of the Palm Lines—much longer than I expected. The pack mule I had hired for the journey collapsed halfway through. It lay on the ground, foaming at the mouth, giving me one of those pitiful dying looks. I had no choice but to unload the bags it had been carrying and pile them onto my own back. Then I crumbled a few pieces of dehydrated bread and left them on the ground next to its muzzle before continuing on my way.

The first thing I heard when I climbed over the snow-covered peak of the Kalong mountains was a thunderous roar like that of a tidal wave. Down at the bottom snowdrifts rolled and billowed like clouds, while the grains of snow beneath my feet swept along like a rushing stream. But the air was as cold and still as on a windless winter's night, and I never felt even the slightest touch of a breeze over any part of my body. I began to go down the mountain without waiting for nightfall because I knew the goggles I was wearing would protect me from snow blindness. The thick blanket of snow had turned the entire mountainside into a huge glassy slope, so smooth it seemed there could not have been any rocks or hollows underneath. I began zigzagging downhill, slowly. But the heavy packs soon slithered from my shoulders until they were halfway down my back, and finally I had to stop to adjust them. Tucking in my stomach and pushing out my chest, I lifted them back onto my shoulders and was just trying to straighten up when the sudden shift in weight made me lose my balance and sent me hurtling downward. I knew I could no longer stop of my own accord, so I drew myself up into a ball and rolled down the mountain as heaven and earth spun around and around me.

Wonder of wonders, I did not end up plunging into some crevasse. When I came to I found myself lying in soft powdery snow on a patch of level ground at the bottom of the mountain. Above me the white slope had been slashed with a long trail running all the way up into the mist-enshrouded heights.

Up at the top of the mountain I had looked at my watch, and it had read 9:46. But now when I looked at it again, it read 8:03. I descended below the snow line and entered, in succession, a lichen zone, prairie, scrubland, a small thicket of trees, and finally a large forested area. When I emerged from the other side of the forest, the vegetation once again grew sparse, and the desolate landscape was dotted with rocky outcroppings and barren hillocks.

All along the way I kept looking at my watch, constantly comparing the time it showed with the time according to my own estimation. I finally came to the conclusion that after I climbed over the top of Mount Kalong, time had begun to run in reverse. That was why the calendar displays on my Seiko watch—this fully automatic, solar-powered electronic timepiece I was wearing—were all going backwards, and that was why its minute- and hour-hands were turning counterclockwise, at a speed five times normal.

The further I went, the more the scenery appeared deformed, or perhaps transformed. Before my eyes passed a parade of pipal trees with egg-shaped leaves and brown, wizened limbs, filing by slowly and methodically like a forest sprung from a moving conveyor belt. Yonder lay the ruins of an ancient temple. Ambling across a broad expanse of tableland was a huge elephant with legs as long as celestial ladders. The scene reminded me of Dali's "The Temptation of Saint Anthony." Warily I quickened my step and made a detour around all of this, careful not to cast a single look behind me. I did not stop to rest until I reached some hot springs that were giving off big clouds of vapor. But I dared not go to sleep then even though I was absolutely exhausted by that time, because I knew that once I closed my eyes I would never again wake up in this life.

Then, through the steam, I glimpsed what appeared to be relics from some long-forgotten era: gold saddles, bow and arrows, lances, suits of armor, prayer wheels, horns, even some tattered yellow banners—quite possibly the site of an ancient battle, I thought to myself. If I hadn't been so tired I would have walked over to look at them more closely. Perhaps I would have been able to verify this spot as one of the battlefields described in the epic poem *Gesar.* But at the moment I could only sit and gaze upon all of it from a distance. Prolonged exposure to the heat of the springs had caused the metal objects to become so soft they were no more than a flaccid heap of anomalous shapes, oozing amorphously into one another until they had rearranged themselves into hieroglyphs as abstruse as Mayan scripts. At first I suspected I was seeing a mirage, that my extended isolation had caused me to hallucinate about these strange transmutations. But right away I rejected this notion, because my mind was functioning logically, and my memory and analytical faculties were all quite sound. As usual the sun was journeying from east to west, and the universe, after all, still existed and turned in accordance with its own laws. Yet although day and night continued to follow one upon the other, the hands on my watch were speeding counterclockwise and the calendar displays kept reeling backward. This, I surmised, was what had confounded my biological clock and led to the sensation of disembodiment.

And then one dawn I wake up to find myself lying at the foot of an enormous red boulder, at a point where countless gullies converge and radiate outward again. It must have been the cold damp air that roused me, and my teeth chatter in the chilly wind gusting from the depths of the surrounding canyons. Hurriedly I clamber up the rocky face of a nearby ravine and look out over the top. I can see clear to the horizon. The earth all around me is carved with countless black gullies extending in every direction like the talons of some monster's claw, or like cracks in soil parched by a millenium of drought. Some of the gullies are so deep they seem bottomless. I have reached the Place of the Palm Lines. There is not a tree in sight, nor a blade of grass. Nothing but desolation. It reminds me of the last scene in a movie about nuclear war I once saw: In a wide-angled shot, the hero and the heroine are silhouetted against a background of charred earth, after the holocaust. One in the east, the other in the west, they slowly lift their heads and crawl arduously toward each other. At last the only two survivors on earth come together and embrace. Their eyes tell of the suffering they have endured. Freeze frame. They will become the new Adam and Eve.

The body of Sangjie Dapu of Zhatuo has long since been cremated. Afterward somebody probably poked around in the still-smoldering ashes and found the precious pieces of sheli. But the hero of my story is nowhere to be seen.

"Taaa—beiiii! Where—are—yooooouuu?" I shout at the top of my lungs. I am sure he could not have found his way out of this place. The sound of my voice echoes far and wide, but there is no reply.

Before long, however, I see a miracle: A black dot appears in the distance, about one or two kilometers away. Calling out the name of my protagonist, I tear along the ridges toward the tiny figure. But when I draw close enough to see clearly, I am so stunned that I stop dead in my tracks: It is Chiong! Never in a million years would I have guessed this.

"Tabei is going to die soon," Chiong sobs as she runs toward me. "Where is he?"

She takes me down into a gully nearby. Tabei is lying on the ground at the bottom, his face pale and haggard, his breathing labored. A steady trickle of water drips down a mossy crevice in the wall of the ravine and collects in a little pool on the ground. From time to time Chiong would dip one end of her sash in this puddle and squeeze drops of water into Tabei's half-open mouth.

His eyes upon my face, he says, "Prophet, I am waiting, I see the light, the Lord will enlighten me."

"He's very badly hurt, he must have water constantly," Chiong whispers into my ear.

"Why didn't you stay in Jia?" I ask her.

"Why should I stay in Jia?" she retorts. "The thought never crossed my mind. He never promised to stay in any one place. He plucked my heart and tied it onto the cord around his waist. I cannot survive away from him."

"Now don't be so sure," I said.

"All this time he's been wanting to know what that is." Chiong points to something behind me. Turning my head, I find that we are at the bottom of a deep ravine that runs in a perfectly straight line, all the way back to the gigantic red boulder where I had spent the night. It is only now that I see the snow-white " ཪྀ " carved into the heart of the sanguineous rock, but invisible to anyone looking up from the foot of the rock. " ཪྀ " is the note intoned by a lama after he has chanted the "om-ma-ni-pad-meh-hom" man-tra one hundred times. As far as I know, there can be only two reasons why it would have been carved on this boulder: Either this is a place frequented by spirits and demons, or a great hero lies buried here. By the banks of the Chumishingu River on the way from Jiangzi to Pali, there is a rock which is also carved with a " ཪྀ ," to commemorate the spot where Bunlading the Second, commander of the Tibetan army, fell in battle against the British invaders in the year 1904. But I see no point in explaining any of this to Tabei.

Not until this very moment do I discover, belatedly, the truth about my "beloved castaways": They have all been endowed with life and will. Once characters are created, their every move becomes an objective fact. In letting Tabei and Chiong come out of that numbered manila envelope, I have clearly made an irreparable mistake. And why is it that to this day I have not been able to give shape to "people of a new type"? This is yet another mistake. If someone demands to know why, in this great and heroic era, I still allow characters like Tabei and Chiong to exist, how shall I answer?

Hoping against hope, I bend down and whisper into Tabei's ear every argument I can think of that would be comprehensible to him, trying to convince him that the place he is looking for does not exist, just as Thomas More's Utopia did not exist. It doesn't exist, that's all.

But, alas, it is too late! In these final moments of his life, it is just not possible to make him give up the faith forged through the years. He turns himself over and lays his head against the ground.

"Tabei," I stammer, "you will get better. Just wait here a while, I left all my things over there, I've got some first-aid medicine in my bag and . . ."

"Hush!" Tabei stops me, his ear pressed against the cold, soggy ground. "Listen to this! Listen!"

For the longest time all I can hear is a faint murmur in the intervals between my heartbeats.

"Help me up! I want to get up there!" Tabei cries as he struggles to sit up, waving his arms about.

I have no choice but to help him onto his feet. Chiong climbs up ahead while I prop Tabei up from below, planting my feet on the rocky ledges along the wall of the ravine. To my surprise he is quite heavy. I hold him gingerly, careful to guard with one hand the spot where he has been hit by the tractor. With my other hand I grope for the rocks in the cliff face, pulling Tabei up little by little. A sharp, jagged rock cuts my hand, leaving it numb at first, then stinging as the warm blood streams out of the wound, runs along my arm and down into my sleeve. At the top of the ravine, Chiong lies on her stomach and reaches down to grab Tabei under his arms. While she tugs and pulls from above, I heave and hoist from below until we finally lift him out of the ravine onto the ground at the top.

The eastern sky is aglow with light from the sun, which is just about to appear over the horizon. Tabei takes a deep, hungry sniff of the morning air and looks around, his eyes alert and searching.

"What is it saying, Prophet? I can't understand it. Please tell me, quickly, you must have understood it, I beg of you." He turns around and prostrates himself at my feet.

His ears catch the signals long before mine do. It is not until several minutes later that Chiong and I hear a sound, a very real sound, coming from the sky. We listen intently.

"It's brass bells ringing on a temple roof!" Chiong cries excitedly.

"It's the chiming of church bells," I correct her.

"It's an avalanche! It's frightening!"

"No, this is the majestic sound of horns and drums and a multitude of voices singing," I correct her again. Chiong gives me a bewildered look.

"God is beginning to speak," Tabei proclaims solemnly.

This time I dare not correct anyone, even though the sound is the amplified voice of a man speaking in English. How can I tell Tabei that this is the grand opening ceremony of the Twenty-third Olympics being held in Los Angeles, U.S.A., and that, by means of satellites in space, television and radio networks are beaming their live coverage of this historic occasion to every corner of the earth?

I finally get a sense of time. My watch has stopped completely. From the motionless hands and calendar displays on the dial I learn that it is now 7:30 A.M., Beijing time, on the twenty-ninth day of July, in the year A.D. 1984.

"This is not a sign from God, my child. It is the sound of chimes and trumpets and a vast choir, signifying mankind's challenge to the world." It is the only thing I can think of to tell him.

I don't know if he hears me. Perhaps he already understands everything. Curling up as if he were cold, he closes his eyes and seems to go to sleep.

I lay him down on the ground again and kneel beside him, trying to straighten his tattered clothes. But I end up staining them with blood from the gash on my hand, and suddenly I am filled with remorse. It is I who have brought Tabei to this. And my other protagonists before him—how many of them, too, have I led to their deaths? It is time for some rigorous soul-searching.

"Now I am left all alone," Chiong murmurs piteously.

"You are not going to die, Chiong. You have made it through the difficult journey, and now little by little I will mold you into a new human being," I say to Chiong, lifting my eyes to look at her. Her innocent face brightens with hope.

The leather cord around her waist sways in front of my eyes. Curious to know how long it has been since she left home, I pick up one end of the cord and begin to count the knots carefully: "five . . . eight . . . twenty-five . . . fifty-seven . . . ninety-six . . ."

The last knot is number one hundred and eight, which is exactly how many prayer beads there are on the string draped around Tabei's hands.

By this time the sun has begun its majestic and stately ascent, bathing earth and sky in the same golden splendor.

I take Tabei's place. Chiong follows behind me, and we set out on the journey back. Time begins again, from the beginning.

FIRST PUBLISHED IN JANUARY 1985 IN *XIZANG WENXUE (TIBETAN LITERATURE)*

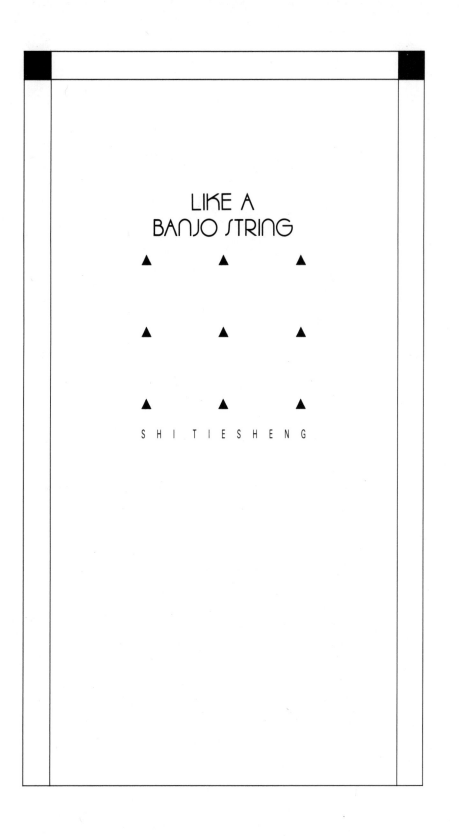

LIKE A
BANJO STRING

SHI TIESHENG

▲   ▲   ▲

▲   ▲   ▲

▲   ▲   Through the endless expanse of mountains and valleys walked two blind men, one old, one young, their grimy straw hats bobbing up and down as they hurried along, one behind the other, like two floats drifting down a wayward river. It mattered little whence they came, or where they were going. They were itinerant storytellers, their only props the three-stringed banjos they carried in their hands.

Few settlements were to be found in that vast region of rugged peaks and twisting canyons. Sometimes, at the end of a day's journey, one would see a stretch of flat, open land dotted with a handful of little villages. Every so often there would be signs of wildlife somewhere—a pair of pheasants soaring out of the underbrush, a hare, a fox, or some other small animal darting here and there, falcons circling over the canyons from time to time. Under a fierce sun, the hills lay silent and shadowless.

"Hold the banjo in your hand," cried the old blind man, his voice echoing in the hills.

"I've got it in my hand," answered the blind lad.

"Take care you don't get the banjo all sweaty, or I'll make you strum your ribs tonight!"

"I've got it in my hand."

Though they had stripped to the waist, sweat poured from their bodies and drenched the homespun doublets tied around their midriffs. Onward they pressed, feeling their way with their canes, their heels kicking up yellow clouds of bone-dry earth. It was the high season for storytelling. The days were long, and none of the village folks wanted to stay home after dinner; some even brought their bowls outdoors, eating by the side of the road or on the threshing ground. The old blind man wanted to do as much story-telling as he could this season. All summer long he had led the blind lad in a quick march through one village after another, through evening after evening of storytelling. All summer long he had grown more and more anxious and agitated. Again and again he thought to himself: This is the summer when it will happen, when the thousandth banjo string will break under his fingers during a performance. Who knows, it may even be in the village of Wild Ram's Gap just down the road.

After a day of fury the sun was just beginning to calm down, its rays softening as shadows deepened. From far and near the cicadas' chirping also became more relaxed.

"Hey, boy! Can't you walk any faster?" cried the old blind man from up ahead, neither turning around nor slowing down. The blind lad quickened his step, the big satchel slung across his hip banging and clattering as he scampered to catch up. But he was still a few rods behind.

"Even the meadowlarks are flying back to their nests!"

"What's that?" The lad ran another few steps.

"I said, even the meadowlarks are back in their nests. So hurry up!"

"Oh."

"You've been fooling around with my electric box again!"

"The hell I have!"

"You've just about worn out the earpiece."

"The hell I have!"

Chuckling to himself, the old blind man thought: Just who do you think you're fooling, boy? Aloud he said: "I can even hear ants fighting."

The blind lad stopped arguing and quietly stuffed the earpiece back into his satchel. Sullenly he trudged down the road behind the old man. The endlessly meandering, endlessly monotonous road.

After a while the young one heard a badger chomping on some crops. He began to bark with might and main, and the badger hightailed it through the fields. Feeling rather pleased with himself, he hummed a few snatches of a love song he had heard somewhere. His master the old man wouldn't let him keep a dog, for fear it would get into a fight with the villagers' dogs and make them all unwelcome. A while later the lad heard another noise: This time it was a snake, slithering close by. He bent down, found a stone and hurled it at the sound—and the leaves of the sorghum plants cackled and hissed. Feeling a little sorry for him, the old blind man stopped and waited for his apprentice.

"First there was a badger, then a snake—" the lad hastened to explain, afraid that his master would scold him again.

"We're already in the grainfields. Won't be long now." The old man passed a canteen of water to the lad.

"People in our line of business, we spend our whole lives walking," the old man went on. "You tired?"

The blind lad was silent. He knew his master hated to hear him say he was tired.

"My poor master—that would be your grandmaster—poor man,

hustled and bustled all his life, but in the end still didn't make it to a thousand strings.''

Sensing that the old man was now in a better mood, the lad asked: "What is a green lawn chair?"

"What? Oh, a long chair, I suppose."

"What about a zigzagging 'bell-vuh-deer'?"

"Bell-vuh-deer? What bell-vuh-deer?"

"A zigzagging bell-vuh-deer."

"I have no idea."

"I heard it on the box."

"You're always listening to that nonsense. But what good is it? Sure, there're lots of nice things in the world, but they don't concern the likes of you and me!"

"How come I've never heard you talk about anything that *does?*"

"Your music! Your banjo! Your dad sent you to me so you can learn to play it and become a storyteller some day."

The boy guzzled the water noisily, on purpose.

When they continued on their way, the apprentice marched ahead.

Gradually, as the shadows of the mountains lengthened across the valleys, the terrain became flatter, more open.

Just before they reached the village, the old blind man found his way to a little spring in the foothills. There in the shade was a tiny stream of water bubbling out of a crack in the rocks and collecting in a hollow no bigger than a wash basin. All around it meadow grass and sedges grew profusely. The rill trickled along for about a stone's throw and then vanished, suckled dry by the parched earth.

The old man called out to the lad to stop. "Come over here and wash yourself, wash off that stinking sweaty smell of yours."

The lad pushed aside the rushes and squatted next to the water hole. He was still thinking about that mysterious "bell-vuh-deer."

"Be sure to wash all over. I bet you look like a little beggar right now."

"Then doesn't that make you an old beggar?" the lad giggled as he stuck his hands into the water.

Even the old man chuckled as he scooped up handfuls of water and splashed them onto his face. "But we're not beggars, we have a skill."

"I think we've been here before," said the lad, cocking his head to one side as he listened to the noises around them.

"But you never pay any attention to learning your trade, your mind is always wandering. Everything I say goes in one ear and out the other."

"I'm sure we've been here before."

"Don't change the subject! Your banjo playing has a long way to go. Our lives are right here on these banjo strings, that's what my master always used to say to me."

The water from the spring was deliciously cool. The blind lad began humming that song again. The old man bristled: "Did you hear a word I just said?"

" 'Our lives are right here on these banjo strings,' your master my grandmaster said so. This I've heard about eight hundred times. Your master also left you a prescription, but you must wait until you've broken one thousand banjo strings before you can have it filled. After you take that potion you will be able to see. You must have told me that about a thousand times."

"Don't you believe it?"

The lad avoided a direct answer. Instead he asked: "How come you have to break a thousand strings before you can get that prescription filled?"

"It's the special ingredient for this prescription. Listen, wiseacre, there's a special ingredient for every prescription—that's how the medicine works."

"What's so hard about getting a thousand broken banjo strings?" the lad tittered in spite of himself.

"You think that's funny? You think you know everything, don't you? Well, here's something you didn't know: Those strings have to be broken, one by one, while you're actually playing the banjo."

The lad kept his mouth shut. He could tell his master was about to lose his temper again. It always went like this. The old man would not tolerate any doubt on this matter.

The old man also fell silent. Sitting cross-legged with his hands on his knees and his clouded eyes turned up to the sky, he seemed rather agitated, as if he was trying to recall one by one all those broken strings. How many years has he been toiling and waiting, waiting and toiling, he thought to himself. Fifty years! Fifty hard-scrabble years, over countless mountains, down endless miles of roads, in stifling heat and freezing cold, through untold sorrow and grief—through it all he had played, night after night, ever mindful that he must put his whole heart and soul into every note, or the broken strings would mean nothing. Now, at last, he was almost there. It would happen this summer, for sure. He was still hale and hearty, no grave illnesses or anything, he should have no problem living through the end of summer. "I'm so much luckier than my master," he sighed aloud. "In the end he died without being able to see, even for a little while."

"Ah-hah! I know where this place is now!" the blind lad shouted all of a sudden.

Bestirring himself, the old blind man picked up his banjo and shook it once or twice. A folded square of paper rustled against the snakeskin stretched over the sound box—there it was, the prescription, tucked right inside the banjo.

"Master, isn't this Wild Ram's Peak?" the lad asked. The old man did not answer. He could tell his apprentice was becoming fidgety again.

"Wild Ram's Gap is just up ahead, isn't it?"

"Here, boy, come over and scrub my back for me," the old man said, turning to the lad and bending his back until it was curved like a bow.

"Is it Wild Ram's Gap or not, master?"

"Yes! And what of it? Now don't you go acting up like a horny tomcat again!"

His heart thumping, the lad dutifully scrubbed his master's back. The old man could feel the energy in each stroke.

"So what if it's Wild Ram's Gap? Can you smell it like a donkey in heat?"

Afraid of being found out, the lad remained silent, trying hard not to let his excitement show.

"What's going on in that head of yours? You don't fool me one bit."

"Now what have I done?"

"Now what have you done? Don't think I've forgotten how you carried on the last time we were here, fooling around with that little hussy!" To himself the old blind man thought: Perhaps it's a mistake to bring the lad back to this place. But Wild Ram's Gap was a big village where year after year he had done good business. He can count on working here for at least half a month, maybe more. Oh, how he wished he could finish off those last strings right away!

The lad muttered something in protest, but his thoughts were already far away, his heart quickening as he remembered that girl in Wild Ram's Gap with the soft, squeaky voice.

"Take my advice, it'll do you no harm," said the old man. "You can't trust that stuff."

"What stuff?"

"None of your sass, boy. You know what I'm talking about."

"I don't think I've ever heard you talk about anything that I *can* trust." The blind lad began to titter again.

The old man paid no more attention to him. Once more he turned his bone-white eyes to the sky, where the sun was turning into a pool of blood.

The old blind man had been plying his trade for more than fifty years. In these remote, desolate mountains everyone knew him: Year in and year out, they had watched as his hair turned whiter and whiter, his back more and more bent. Still he would hie hither and yon with his three-stringed banjo slung across his back, stopping to perform wherever he found an audience willing to pay for an evening of entertainment, and, year after year, bringing gaiety and excitement into the lives of these isolated hill folks.

Almost always he would begin an evening of storytelling with a few lines like these:

> *From the time Pangu created the universe,*
> *Through the Three Kings and Five Emperors to our day,*
> *Benevolent rulers brought peace under heaven,*
> *But common folks suffered when evil kings held sway.*
> *Gather around me and their stories I will tell,*
> *My banjo playing softly the strains you love so well;*

Three thousand songs in all, each of them a treasure,
Good folks of the village, pray, what is your pleasure?

And the audience would call out their favorites: The old people always asked to hear the tale of the good son Dong Yong who sold himself into serfdom to raise money for his father's burial, the children wanted to hear the adventures of the hero Wu Erlang, the womenfolk never tired of the story of the wronged wife Qin Xiang-lian. Suddenly all his weariness and heartache would be gone, forgotten in this sweetest of all moments for the old blind man as he sipped some water leisurely and drank in the clamoring of his audience. Then, just when the hubbub from the crowd was about to boil over, he would twang the banjo hard and sing: "Tonight, for your delight, the story of Luo Cheng and his plight." Or: "Tea I'll have, tobacco too, while I sing the ballad of poor Meng Jiangnu for you." And immediately the whole courtyard would become silent—not even a peep from a sparrow or titmouse—as the old blind man plunged in and lost himself in the world of his tales.

Not only did he know the age-old stories, all thousand and one of them, but he also had a little electric box that he had bought from an outlander—for a princely sum, that's what everyone heard—so he could learn some newfangled words and write some new songs with them. Actually the hill folks didn't much care what he sang or what stories he told. They just enjoyed listening to him, especially his banjo playing. What magic lay in his fingertips! From the softest murmur to a thundering cadence, with carefree elegance or passionate abandon, his playing conjured up the sun, the moon, a whole world of its own inhabited by creatures large and small. And with his voice he could bring forth every sound on earth, from human, be it male or female, to animal, be they beasts on land or in the air, to the sound of the wind howling, of raindrops splashing. Heaven only knew what visions appeared in his mind's eye: He was blind from birth, he had never seen anything in this world.

The lad, on the other hand, did not go blind until he was three years old, though of course he had been too young to remember or understand much. When he was fourteen his father had apprenticed him to the old man, in the hope that he could one day earn a living as a storyteller and make his own way in the world. But he was really not much interested in storytelling or in playing the banjo. His father had had to beg, cajole, threaten, sweet-talk, coax and even hoax him into staying with the old man. In the end it was the electric box that did the trick. Ears glued to the box, the lad was so engrossed in what he was hearing that he didn't even notice when his father left.

This magical box never ceased to fascinate him. It spoke of faraway places and strange and fabulous things, all of which fired his imagination no end. Drawing on those dim memories of his three sighted years he would try to give color and shape to everything under the sun. Take the ocean, for example. The voice in the box said the blue sky was just like an ocean; he remembered blue skies, and so he conjured up the ocean. The box said the ocean was an endless expanse of water; he remembered the water in a pot, and so he imagined countless pots of water crowded together, all the way up to the edge of the sky. Then again, take a beautiful girl. The voice in the box said she was just like a flower in full bloom, but he really couldn't bring himself to believe that. Wildflowers were blooming all along the way as his mother's casket was being carried to that distant hilltop—he would never forget that, but he never wanted to think about it. He did, however, like to think about girls; in fact, he liked it more and more. Especially that wench with the tiny high-pitched voice in Wild Ram's Gap—whenever he thought of her ripples of excitement would wash through his heart. Yet it wasn't until one day when the voice in the box sang, "A maiden's eyes are like the sun," and he called to mind a vision of his mother walking toward him in a bright red sunset, that he at last found a fitting image for a girl.

But then there were always some things that the lad could not even begin to imagine, like a "zigzagging bell-vuh-deer."

That evening, as he and his master were performing in Wild Ram's Gap, he again heard the girl's small squeaky voice whispering and giggling from somewhere nearby. They were right at the climax of the story:

> *Luo Cheng galloped back for another bout,*
> *His lance spinning like a long, silver cloud;*
> *Su Lieh the Bold rallied his troops once more,*
> *And, broadsword blazing, rushed to the fore.*
> *Like tigers battling to be lord of the jungle,*
> *Or dragons thrashing for treasure beneath the sea,*
> *Full seven days and seven nights they struggled,*
> *With nary a bite to eat, nor a drop of tea.*

In his clear, sonorous voice the old man was breathing life into every word, while under his nimble fingers music came pouring out of the banjo, like cascading raindrops or a blustering squall. But the lad, wayward and restive as a colt, had long since lost his place and was in a complete muddle.

There was a little temple on Wild Ram's Peak, about two miles from the village. The stone walls surrounding the courtyard had fallen in, and the two or three ramshackle little buildings huddled inside seemed to be on their last legs as well. Only the middle hall provided some shelter from the elements, perhaps because it still housed a shrine inside, although the three clay statues on the altar had long ago lost their worldly trappings and reverted to the yellow earth out of which they had first taken shape, so that one could not even tell whether they had once been Buddhist or Taoist figures. Outside, a luxuriant growth of weeds and climbing plants had sprung up all over the courtyard and beyond, covering the rooftops and parapets and bringing a breath of life to the dilapidated temple. The old blind man always stayed here whenever he came to Wild Ram's Gap, and why not?—there was no rent to pay, and no neighbors to hassle with.

It was quite late when master and apprentice finished their performance and returned to the temple. The old man went into the main hall to unpack their bags and get set up for the night, while the lad bustled about trying to light a fire in the courtyard, under the eaves of the side hall. The stone hearth they built last year was still standing, and with a little fixing up was ready to be used again. The lad got down on his hands and knees to blow on the sparks, but the kindling was damp, and the smoke choked him until he was spinning around the courtyard coughing and gasping for air.

The reproachful voice of the old man shot out of the big hall: "When will you ever get anything right!"

"But the firewood's damp."

"That's not what I'm talking about. I'm talking about your banjo playing. What on earth do you think you were doing tonight?"

The lad knew better than to pick up the thread of this conversation. Filling his lungs with a few deep breaths, he bent down in front of the stove again, puffed up his cheeks and began to blow with all his might.

"If you don't want to be a storyteller, let's send word to your father right away so he can take you home. I won't put up with this nonsense, you mooning away all the time like an animal in heat. Go do that at home."

Coughing and gasping again, the lad jumped back from the hearth and darted to the other side of the yard, all the while panting and wheezing and muttering under his breath.

"What's that you said?"

"I was cursing the fire."

"Well, no wonder, the way you were blowing on it."

"So how're you supposed to blow?"

The old man snorted: "How, you ask?" He paused, then said: "Just pretend you're blowing on that wench's cheeks!"

Again the lad held his tongue and stooped next to the hearth to resume his huffing and puffing. To himself he thought: "Really, I wonder what Lanxiuer's cheeks are like."

The old man spoke again. "I bet if those were the wench's cheeks you're blowing on, you wouldn't need any lessons on how to do it right!"

The lad began to giggle, and that brought on another coughing fit.

"What's so funny?"

"I was just thinking, did you ever blow on a girl's cheeks?"

It was the old man's turn to be speechless. The lad had collapsed onto the floor, helpless with laughter.

"Go to hell," the old man finally said, a smile on his lips. Then his face darkened, and he fell silent once more.

With a whoosh the fire roared to life. The lad went to fetch more wood, still thinking about the girl called Lanxiuer. Earlier that evening, right after the performance, Lanxiuer had pushed her way through the crowd to talk to him. Standing in front of him, she whispered: "Ai! What did you promise me last time?" But the old man was right by his side, and he didn't dare say a word. The crowd milled around some more, and after a while it deposited her next to him again. "Hey, you mean I gave you that boiled egg for nothing?" Her voice was much louder than before. At that moment his master was chatting with some old men from the village. Quickly he said to her: "Shhhh, I haven't forgotten." Lanxiuer lowered her voice once more: "You said you would let me listen to the electric box but you haven't kept your promise yet." "Shhhh, I haven't forgotten." Luckily for him the crowd was still milling around noisily.

All this time the main hall had been silent. Now it began to fill with the sound of the old man's banjo—he had just put on a new string. Their first show in Wild Ram's Gap and right away he had broken another string—one would have thought he would be in good spirits. But the sounds coming out of his banjo were morose, desultory.

As he listened to the music, the lad gradually realized that something was wrong. Standing in the courtyard he shouted: "Master, the water's boiling."

No reply. The notes came gushing out now, faster and faster.

The lad brought a basin of hot water into the hall and set it down in front of the old man. Putting on a playful tone, he said: "Master, don't tell me you're trying to break another string tonight?"

The old man did not even hear the boy. He was completely lost in his own thoughts. Memories came crowding into his mind, and the music became restless, agitated, like those storms in the wilderness every year, like the streams running down the valleys day and night, like footsteps rushing helter-skelter, here, there, everywhere. The boy began to be afraid. It had been quite a while since the last time this happened, but he knew that once his master started behaving like this he would soon come down with headaches, chest pains, aches all over his body, and it would be months before the old man could get out of bed again.

"Master, why don't you wash your feet first?"

The banjo did not stop.

"Master, come and wash your feet." There was a tremor in the lad's voice.

The banjo went on.

"Master!"

Abruptly the banjo stopped. The old man let out a long sigh. The lad breathed in relief. While the old man washed up, the boy sat dutifully at his side.

"Go to bed," the old man said. "It's been a long day."

"What about you?"

"You go on ahead, I've got to give my feet a good soak. When one gets old, everything breaks down." The old man tried to make light of it all.

"I'll wait for you."

Night had fallen over the hills. Everything was quiet except for a breeze rustling through the grasses by the stone fence and the melancholy hoots of a nightowl faraway. From time to time came the barking of a dog down in Wild Ram's Gap, and then the crying of a child frightened by the noise. The moon rose, pouring its silvery light through the crumbling window lattices into the hall, onto the two blind men and the three clay statues.

"Don't bother to wait up for me, it's getting late."

"Don't you worry about me, I'm going to be just fine," the old man added.

"Do you hear me, boy?"

The lad, being just a lad, had dozed off. The old man pushed him gently to get him in bed. He mumbled drowsily, snuggled down and was soon fast asleep. Reaching over to pull a coverlet over him, the old man felt the boy's growing muscles and realized that the lad had reached the age when he would start thinking about that stuff. There was a painful period lying ahead for the boy, there's no getting around that. Well, some things you just have to learn for yourself.

The old man picked up the banjo again and held it in his lap. Running his fingers over the strings, each one of them stretched taut, he said to himself feelingly, over and over again: "Another string broken, another string broken." Then he shook the sound box once more and listened to the paper inside scratching softly against the snakeskin. This was the only thing that could make him forget all his troubles, all his unhappiness. It was a life's worth of hopes and dreams.

The lad had a happy dream, but he woke up with a start. Was it cockcrow already? He jumped out of bed and listened, and heard to his relief that the old man was still sound asleep. Feeling around for the big satchel, he found it at last and stealthily took out the electric box. Then he tiptoed silently out the door.

It wasn't until he had walked some distance in the direction of Wild Ram's Gap that he realized something was amiss. The crowing of the rooster had gradually faded away, but still there were no sounds of people stirring in the village. Quite bewildered, he stopped in his tracks, trying to figure out whether that was the first cockcrow he had heard. Then inspiration struck, and he turned on the electric box. But that too was silent. Well then, it must still be the middle of the night. He knew that because he had listened to the box late at night before, and it had made absolutely no sound. For him the electric box was also a timepiece: All he had to do was turn it on, and he could tell the time of day from the program coming out of the box.

When the lad got back to the temple, the old man happened to be turning over in his sleep.

"What were you doing?"

"Taking a leak," the lad answered.

All morning long his master made him practice on his banjo. The lad had to wait until after the midday meal before he spied his chance to slip out of the temple and sneak into the village. The sun was so hot and fierce even the chickens had dozed off under the trees, and pigs lolled in the shade by the walls, talking in their sleep. The village was very quiet.

Standing on a millstone, the lad climbed up the wall outside the compound where Lanxiuer lived and called out softly: "Lanxiuer! Lanxiuer!"

The sound of snoring rumbled out of the house like thunder.

The lad hesitated for a few moments, then raised his voice a little: "Lanxiuer! Lanxiuer!"

Some dogs began to bark. The snoring stopped, and a deep, muffled voice asked: "Who's there?"

The boy didn't dare reply. Instead, he ducked his head below the top of the wall. The person inside the house smacked his lips noisily for a while, and then the snoring started up again.

The lad let out a long sigh, stepped off the millstone and began to walk away dejectedly. Then from over his shoulder he heard the sound of a gate creaking open, followed by a string of light little footsteps running up behind him.

"Guess who!" squealed a tiny high-pitched voice as a pair of soft little hands covered the lad's eyes—how silly that was! Lanxiuer wasn't quite fifteen yet, still a child really.

"Lanxiuer!"

"Did you bring the electric box?"

The lad opened his tunic to show the box hanging around his waist. "Hush!" he said, "not here. Let's find a place where no one else goes, and we'll listen to it there."

"How come?"

"Otherwise, next thing you know there'll be a big crowd of people and everyone will want to have a listen."

"So?"

"So they'll use up the batteries."

After a few turns here, a zigzag there, they finally came to the little spring in the foothills. Suddenly the lad remembered something, and he asked Lanxiuer: "Have you ever seen a zigzagging bell-vuh-deer?"

"A what?"

"A zigzagging bell-vuh-deer."

"A zigzagging bell-vuh-deer?"

"Know what it is?"

"Do you?"

"Of course. Also a green lawn chair. That's a long chair, you know."

"Everybody knows that."

"Then what about a zigzagging bell-vuh-deer?"

Lanxiuer shook her head and began to feel in awe of the boy. With a solemn flourish the lad turned on the electric box. A lively song floated out and wafted through the ravines.

What a wonderful spot it was, cool and quiet and out of the way.

"This song is called 'Higher and Higher,' " the lad explained, humming along.

He knew the next one as well. "That's 'A Bolt Out of the Blue,' " he told Lanxiuer. She was embarrassed by her own ignorance.

"This song is also called 'The Monk Misses His Missus.' "

Lanxiuer began to giggle. "You're pulling my leg!"

"You don't believe me?"

"No I don't."

"That's up to you. All I can tell you is, this box talks about all kinds of strange things." Swirling his hands around in the delightfully cool water of the spring, the lad thought for a moment and said: "Do you know what kissing is?"

"Do I know what?"

It was the boy's turn to giggle. He laughed and laughed, but said nothing. Lanxiuer realized that must have been a bad word. She blushed and didn't ask him about it again.

When the music stopped, a woman's voice came on and said: "Next we will hear a program on hygiene."

"On what?" Lanxiuer didn't quite catch the word.

"On hygiene."

"What's that?"

"Hmmmm, do you have any lice on your head?"

"Hey! Stop that!"

The lad drew his hand back in a hurry and hastened to explain: "I was only trying to find out, because if you have lice, then that's not good hygiene."

"Of course I don't, not me." Lanxiuer's scalp began to tingle, and she scratched her head. "Hey! Let's see about you!" In a flash she had caught the boy's head between her hands and jerked it close to her face. "Here, watch me catch a few big ones!"

At that very moment the voice of the old man came booming from halfway up the hill. "Hey, boy! You come back here right away! It's time to make dinner, and after that we still have a show to do!" He had been standing there listening for quite some time.

Twilight had begun to settle over Wild Ram's Gap. From down

in the village came the sounds of animals bleating and braying and barking, and of children crying. Wisps of smoke rose from the chimneys. But up on Wild Ram's Peak a ribbon of light from the dying sun still lingered, and the little temple stood silently in the fading glow.

His rear end sticking up in the air, the lad was down on his hands and knees again, puffing on the sparks to get the fire going. The old man sat on the floor close by, washing rice in a pot. By listening as he rinsed he could pick out the pieces of sand and grit in the rice.

"The wood's pretty dry today," the lad ventured.

"Unh."

"Are we still having boiled rice tonight?"

"Unh."

The lad was feeling alert and peppy that evening, and he wanted very much just to shoot the breeze with his master for a while. But he knew the old man was still angry with him, and he decided to keep his mouth shut so as not to catch hell again. The two of them went about their own chores silently, and then made dinner together, still without exchanging a word. By that time daylight had vanished from the peak as well.

Filling a bowl with rice, the lad brought it to the old man and said, timidly: "Here you are, master." He had never sounded more docile.

The old man finally broke his silence: "Look here, boy, will you listen to what I have to say?"

"Hmmmph," the lad mumbled, all the while shoveling rice into his mouth.

"If you don't want to listen, I'll just shut up."

"Who says I don't want to listen? I said 'Uh-huh.' "

"I've been through a lot in my life. I know more about things than you."

The lad continued to wolf down his dinner in silence.

"I've been through that stuff."

"What stuff?"

"There you go sassing me again!" The old man slapped his chopsticks against the top of the stove.

"Lanxiuer just wanted to listen to the electric box. That's all we did, just listen to the electric box."

"What else?"

"Nothing else."

"Nothing?"

"Then I asked her whether she had ever seen a zigzagging bell-vuh-deer."

"That's not what I mean!"

"And then, and then," the lad stammered, not quite so self-assured anymore, "somehow we started talking about head lice. . . ."

"And then?"

"That's it. Honest!"

They went back to eating their dinner, again in silence. In the three years they had been together, the old man had always found his apprentice to be an honest lad. He knew he could count on the boy's truthfulness and good nature.

"Take my advice, I guarantee you'll be glad you did. From now on stay away from that wench."

"Lanxiuer's not a bad sort."

"I know she's not, but it's better that you keep your distance from her. Years ago your grandmaster said the same thing to me, but I didn't believe him either. . . ."

"Grandmaster? He said that about Lanxiuer?"

"What Lanxiuer, she wasn't even born then. And neither were you . . ." A shadow fell across the old man's features and once again he turned his face up to the darkened sky, his bone-white eyes roaming from side to side in their sockets.

After a long time the lad finally said to his master, trying to cheer him up: "I bet you'll break another string tonight."

That evening master and apprentice gave another performance in Wild Ram's Gap:

> *When we saw Luo Cheng last,*
> *Our hero had been fading fast.*
> *His soul from his body had fled,*
> *And taken refuge among the dead.*
> *But, good people, do not fret,*
> *My tale is not over yet.*
> *For lo and behold!*
> *The story shall be told—*
> *Luo Cheng's soul has arisen,*
> *Out of its infernal prison.*
> *Borne by a swirling gust it flew,*
> *Away from the minions of the doomed,*
> *Till the walls of Chang'an loomed,*
> *And still the eerie whirlwind blew. . . .*

But even the old man was playing erratically that evening, never mind his young apprentice. The lad was thinking about the touch of those soft little hands over his eyes, about how it felt when Lanxiuer grabbed his head and pulled it close to her face. As for the old man, he too was lost in his memories—so many many memories. . . .

That night the old blind man tossed and turned sleeplessly. Countless memories screamed in his ears, and still more swarmed through his heart. Something was about to explode inside him, it seemed. His head was spinning, his chest felt tight, his whole body throbbed with pain. "Oh, no! I'm going to be sick," he thought. He sat up and told himself, sternly: "Don't you dare get sick, or you can forget about breaking all those strings by the end of the year." He felt around and found his banjo again. If only he could thrum and strum away, play to his heart's content for a little while, perhaps the grief inside him would ease, and the memories ringing in his ears would at last leave him alone. But then he might wake the lad, who was sleeping so peacefully nearby.

And so with a mighty effort he took hold of his thoughts and turned them once again to the prescription and the banjo strings: Only a few left now, only a few more, and then he can have the prescription filled, and then he can see this world—the mountains he had climbed time after time, the roads he had traveled day in and day out, the sun that had by turns warmed him and burned him all these years, the blue skies and the moon and the stars he had dreamed about so many times . . . and then? Suddenly he felt a hollowness inside, a deep, heavy hollowness. Was that all? Was there nothing else? Somehow, in all those years of waiting and longing, he had vaguely thought there would be much else besides. . . .

The night wind roamed through the hills.

The owl was hooting mournfully again.

And suddenly he realized, as if for the first time, that he had grown quite old, no more than a few years left at the most, and what he had lost was gone forever. Seventy years' worth of grief and hardship, and all for this one look at the world before he died— was that worth it? he asked himself.

The lad was laughing in his sleep, saying: "That's a long chair, Lanxiuer. . . ."

The old blind man sat there silently. Equally silent were the three inscrutable clay figures in the hall.

By the time the first rooster crowed the old man had made up his mind: As soon as it got light, he and the lad would leave Wild Ram's Gap. Otherwise it would get to be too much for the lad, and for him as well. Lanxiuer was not a bad girl, but the old blind man could see better than anyone else how this whole thing would end. When the rooster crowed a second time, the old man began packing.

But the lad woke up with a tummy ache and a high fever. The old man had no choice but to postpone their departure.

In the following days, whether he was making a fire, washing rice, fetching firewood, or digging for herbs and brewing medicine for the lad, the old man kept telling himself, over and over: "It's worth it, of course it's worth it." Only by repeatedly reassuring himself could he find the strength to go on, it seemed. "I must see it before I go." "If not, what then? Just die like this?" "Besides, there are only a few strings left to go." These were the reasons he gave himself. He calmed down again, and continued to perform every evening in Wild Ram's Gap.

Well, what a stroke of luck this was for the lad! Now every evening, after the old man had gone into the village, Lanxiuer would prance softly into the temple like a little kitten. She came to listen to the box, and sometimes she would even bring the lad a boiled egg, on the condition that she be allowed to switch the box on herself. "Which way do I turn it?" "To the right." "It won't move." "To the right, silly, don't you even know which side is your right?" Then a click—whatever it was would come on, and whatever it was they would be all ears.

Several days passed. The old man broke three more strings.

One evening, the old man was performing as usual for the villagers of Wild Ram's Gap:

> *Of Luo Cheng's reincarnation you have heard.*
> *The rest of his story must now be deferred.*
> *Tonight I'll tell you the tale of Li Shimin,*
> *Who was Luo Cheng's master, the great Emperor Qin.*
> *When word of Luo Cheng's death reached Shimin's ears,*
> *How the emperor paled, and his eyes filled with tears:*
> *'O Luo Cheng, Luo Cheng, my general so brave,*
> *Now that you're dead, there're none left but knaves.'*

But the real action that evening was to be found up on Wild Ram's Peak. The little temple was filled with the sounds of children crying, grownups yelling, cannons roaring and trumpets blaring—it was the electric box, of course, its volume turned up all the way. Moonlight washed over the main hall and found the lad lying on his back, munching on an egg, Lanxiuer sitting beside him. They were both listening with bated breath, sometimes letting out peals of laughter, sometimes frowning in complete bafflement.

"Where did your master get this box?"

"He bought it from an outlander."

"Have you been to the outland?" asked Lanxiuer.

"No. But someday I'll go there, and then I'll take a ride on a train."

"A train?"

"You don't even know about trains? What a dummy."

"Oh I know, I know, it's got smoke coming out of it, right?"

After a while Lanxiuer spoke again. "Maybe I'll have to go to the outland soon." There was a note of apprehensiveness in her voice.

"Oh really?" The lad sat bolt upright. "Then you can see what a zigzagging bell-vuh-deer really looks like."

"I wonder if everyone there has an electric box."

"Who knows? Hey, did you hear what I said? Listen, it's called a zig-zag-ging-bell-vuh-deer, and it's right down there in the out-land."

But Lanxiuer was preoccupied with something else. As if thinking aloud, she mumbled: "That's it, I'll have to ask them for an electric box."

"Ask for one?" The boy started to guffaw, held his breath, then burst out laughing again. "Why don't you just ask for two, or three, or six? You must think you're Mighty Woman herself. Do you know how much one of these things costs? They could sell you and still it wouldn't be enough."

Lanxiuer was already feeling heartsick, and this was the last straw. "Damn you, you blind rat!" she shrieked, grabbing the lad's ears and twisting with all her might.

They started to tussle right in the hall, and there was nothing the three clay statues could do to stop them. Wrestling each other to the ground, they continued to grapple, their bodies locked together, arms and legs all atangle. But as they rolled and thrashed about, first one on top, then the other, the curses soon dissolved into laughter. And the box played on.

After a while they stopped to catch their breath. Hearts pounding, they lay face to face, panting and gasping for air. Neither of them spoke, yet neither of them pulled away. Lanxiuer's breath grazed the lad's cheek, and he felt a sudden urge. Remembering what his master had said to him that night when he was puffing away at the fire, he began to blow softly on Lanxiuer's cheeks. She did not turn away.

"Hey," the lad whispered, "have you found out what kissing is?"

"What is it?" she answered, just as softly.

The lad whispered something into her ear. Lanxiuer didn't say anything, but before the evening was over they had found out for themselves just how good it felt. . . .

That evening the old blind man broke the last two strings. Both of them. Together. He hadn't expected that. He half ran, half stumbled up the hill and into the little temple. The lad jumped up in fright: "What happened, master?"

The old man sat there, gasping and wheezing, unable to speak. The lad was full of misgiving. Could it be that his master had discovered what he and Lanxiuer had been up to?

Not until this moment did the old man finally believe: It was all worth it! The sorrows and troubles of a lifetime—they were all worth it. Just one look, one good look around, and everything would have been worthwhile.

"Listen, boy, I'm going to get that potion tomorrow."

"Tomorrow?"

"Tomorrow."

"You broke another string?"

"Two. I broke both of them."

The old man unwound the two strings and took them off the banjo. He rolled them between his hands for a little while and then tied them into a bunch with the other nine hundred and ninety-eight.

"Leaving tomorrow?"

"As soon as it gets light."

The lad's heart went cold.

The old man began to peel off the snakeskin covering the banjo's sound box.

"But I'm still feeling sick," the lad protested in a small voice.

"Oh yes, I've thought it over. Why don't you stay here for the time being? I'll be back within ten days."

The lad couldn't believe his ears.

"Can you manage by yourself?" the old man asked.

"Oh sure!" the lad replied quickly.

The old man had long since forgotten about Lanxiuer. "Now listen: Food, water, firewood, everything you need is here. And when you're feeling better, you should try to do some storytelling by yourself. Alright?"

"Alright." The lad was beginning to feel rather ashamed of himself.

The snakeskin was finally stripped off. From inside the sound box the old man pulled out a neatly folded square of paper. Then all of a sudden he remembered that he had been only twenty years old when the prescription was sealed inside the banjo. And an icy feeling shuddered through his body from head to toe.

The lad took the piece of paper and turned it over in his hands a few times. Even he grew solemn and respectful.

"Your poor grandmaster, what a shame it was!"

"How many strings did he break?"

"He could have broken a thousand strings, but he remembered wrong and thought it was only eight hundred. Otherwise he could have done it for sure."

The old blind man set out on his journey before the crack of dawn. He said he would be back in no more than ten days.

By the time the old man returned it was winter.

Snow was falling thick and fast from gray skies overhanging the whitened mountains. Not a sound, not a sign of life broke through the silent wilderness—until the old man's grimy straw hat fluttered into view, all the more conspicuous against the white stillness of the surrounding hills. Step by halting step, he hobbled up Wild Ram's Peak to the little temple on top. Inside the courtyard, withered grasses shivered and rustled. A fox, caught by surprise, scampered around and darted away.

The lad had been gone for days, the villagers told the old man.

"But I told him to wait here till I came back."

"He just upped and left, don't know why."

"Did he say where he was going? Did he leave a message?"

"He said you shouldn't bother looking for him."

"How long ago did he leave?"

The villagers thought for a spell, and everyone agreed it was the day that Lanxiuer was sent to the outland as a bride. Right away the old man understood everything.

They urged him to stay in the village. Where was he going in all that ice and snow? Why not stay in Wild Ram's Gap and help while away the winter with his storytelling. The old man pointed to something slung across his back. They looked and saw a stripped, stringless banjo. Then they noticed the old man's sunken cheeks, his labored breathing, his hoarse whisper. It was as if he had become a totally different person.

The old man told them he must go and find his apprentice.

All this time the lad had been on his mind. Had it not been for this, the old man would never have made it back to Wild Ram's Gap. The prescription that he had so carefully preserved for fifty years turned out to be a piece of blank paper. At first he refused to believe it. But when he asked any number of learned and trustworthy people to read it for him, they all told him the same thing: It really was no more than a blank square of paper. The old man slumped onto the steps in front of the medicine shop and sat there for what he thought was just a little while. It turned out to have been several days and nights. During that whole time his bonelike eyes were turned questioningly to the heavens. Meanwhile his face had also turned the color of bone. Some people thought he had lost his mind, and they talked to him soothingly, trying to comfort him. The old man smiled bitterly to himself: He was already seventy years old, what's the use of going mad now? No, it was just that he had no wish to budge anymore. In one fell swoop the only thing that had inspired him to walk on, to keep singing and playing, to keep on living—suddenly that thing had vanished, gone beyond recall. And now he was like a banjo string that could no longer be pulled taut, that could no longer make beautiful music, or any music at all.

Somehow the old man found his way to a little inn. He ended up staying there for a long, long time. But he no longer sang or played on his banjo. Instead, he just lay on the kang day after day, feeling the life ebbing from his body, watching as everything inside him flickered and began to die out. Until one day, when he had used up all the money he had, when he suddenly remembered his young apprentice. He knew that his own death was not far off, but the poor child was still waiting for him to return.

A blanket of snow, white and pure, covered the vast open plains and the mountains far and near.

A solitary black speck shuffled into sight, its back bent like an arch.

The old man was still searching for his apprentice. He knew only too well what the lad was going through.

For the sake of the boy he tried to brace himself, to pull himself together. But it was no use. That piece of blank paper kept haunting him, he could not banish it from his mind. Now there was nothing left to strive for, no goal beckoning to him up ahead.

As he walked along, he began to remember fondly those days gone by. All that hustling and bustling about, rushing up hill and down dale to get to the next town to put on the next show, even all the worrying and fretting and grieving—how full of zest all that had been, how full of joy! Back then there had been something to tighten his heartstrings with, to keep them taut and in tune, even if it was only an illusion. Then he remembered the scene just before his own master died. Taking the prescription that he himself had not been able to make use of, the dying man sealed it inside the sound box and gave the banjo back to his apprentice. "Master, don't die yet! Just live a few more years and you'll be able to see." When he said this he was still a child. For a long time his master did not answer. Finally he said: "Remember, life is like a banjo string. It must be taut before you can play it well. And when you have played it well, that is all that matters. . . ."

Deep in the mountains, the old man finally came upon his apprentice.

The lad had fallen to the ground. Lying motionless in the snow, he was waiting for death to take him away. The old man knew how deep and genuine was his grief.

The lad was too weak to move, let alone put up a fight. The old man managed to drag him into a cave. Then he found some wood and started a fire.

Gradually the lad began to sob. The old man relaxed then. He would let the boy cry to his heart's content. As long as the boy could still cry, there was hope for him yet. As long as he could still cry, a time would come when he would have cried his fill.

For days the lad wept and mourned. The old man said nothing, but kept a careful watch by his side. The only creatures that stirred were some wild animals—hares, pheasants, wild sheep, foxes and falcons—frightened by the firelight and the weeping.

At last the lad spoke: "Oh why, why are we blind!"

"Because we are," the old man answered.

Some time later the lad spoke again: "But I want to open my eyes and look around, master, I want to see! Even if it's only for a little while."

"You really want to do that?"

"I do, I really do!"

The old man stirred the fire until it burned even more briskly.

The snow had stopped. In a lead-gray sky the sun glinted like a small shiny mirror. A falcon was gliding smoothly in the air.

"Then play your banjo," the old man said. "Play it, string after string, with your whole heart and soul!"

"Oh master, did you get the potion?" the lad asked, as if awakening from a dream.

"Remember, each string must be played till it breaks."

"Can you see now, master? Can you see?"

Struggling to sit up, the lad reached out his hand to feel his master's eyes. The old man caught his hand and held it.

"Remember, you must play—till they break—twelve hundred strings."

"Twelve hundred?"

"Give me your banjo so I can seal this prescription inside for you." Now, at long last, the old man understood what his own master had tried to tell him back then, what he had meant when he said: "Our lives are right here on these banjo strings."

"How come it's twelve hundred, master?"

"That's what it's supposed to be, twelve hundred. I didn't play enough. I thought it was only a thousand." To himself the old blind man thought: Twelve hundred? There was no way the lad could break that many strings, no matter how long and hard he played! And in the end all that mattered was to keep those strings forever taut and humming, forever alive with music and commotion—no need at all to see the blank, empty paper. . . .

It was a remote and desolate place. Mountains rose one after the other, as far as the eye could see. From time to time there would be signs of wildlife somewhere—a pair of pheasants soaring out of the underbrush, a hare, a fox, or some other small animal darting here and there, falcons circling over the canyons.

Now let us return to the beginning.

Through the endless expanse of mountains and valleys walk two blind men, one old, one young, their grimy straw hats bobbing up and down as they hurry along, one behind the other, like two floats drifting down a wayward river. It matters little whence they came, or where they are going, it matters naught who they are. . . .

FIRST PUBLISHED IN FEBRUARY 1985 IN *XIANDAIREN (THE CONTEMPORARY)*

DRY RIVER

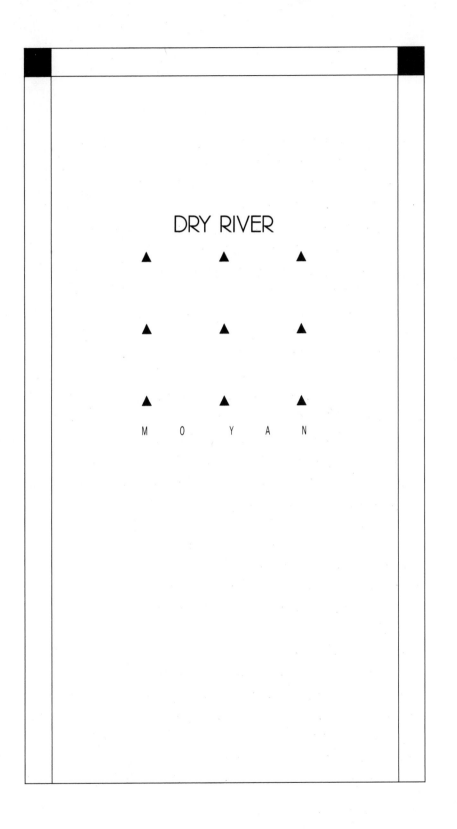

M   O   Y   A   N

▲   ▲   ▲

▲   ▲   ▲

▲   ▲   When the immense watery crimson moon
rose over the dusky fields to the east, the smoke and mist enveloping the village grew heavier and appeared to take on the bright melancholy red of the moon. The sun had just set, leaving behind on the horizon a big long swath of purple. A few stunted stars momentarily gave off a pale gleam between the sun and the moon. An eerie atmosphere shimmered through the village. Dogs did not bark, cats did not cry, geese and ducks were all mute. While the moon was rising, the sun setting and the stars dying, a child crept out from a half-open wooden door. Once out of the door he dissolved into a gray wraith-like shadow and began to float. Softly, gently, he wafted down the riverbank behind the village. Along the bank withered grasses and browned leaves fallen from willow trees gasped and sighed. He moved very slowly, through the quiet crackling of dried reeds snapping, of dead leaves crumbling, then hopped up to the top of the bank. There he squatted, a tiny figure within the huge shadow enshrouding him—until tomorrow morning, when, like a frog curled up among sweet-potato vines on the

riverbed, he would sleep for all eternity, while people from the village would be crowded around in clumps watching him, most not aware of his age, only a few knowing his name. At that time his parents would be staring blankly, their eyes like those of fishes, unable to answer accurately the villagers' questions about the boy. He was a scrawny, swarthy, large-mouthed, snub-nosed, springy-eyed child who never knew a day of sickness. His skill at climbing trees was superb. Tomorrow morning, he would be greeting the rising sun with his buttocks, his face buried deep within the blue-black melon sprouts. A horde of people, their faces bleak like the desert, would be looking at those buttocks that were just a shade paler than the rest of his body. This bottom of his would be covered with scars and bruises, and with sunshine as well. The people would gaze upon it as if looking at a beautiful and radiant face, as if looking at me myself.

He squatted on the riverbank, his hands tucked between the bends in his legs, his chin resting on his sharp, bony knees. He could feel his heart scampering around like a water rat inside his body, now up in his throat, now down in his belly, now out in his limbs, as if there were umpteen ratholes leading every which way in his body so that his water rat-like heart could move and slide around freely and easily. The moon continued to rise, still moist and watery. A cloud of vapor, not quite smoke and not quite mist, ballooned outward from the village and rose straight up until it overhung all the houses underneath. The big white poplar in the center of the village stuck its top into the hazy vapor, its tall and straight trunk like an umbrella stem, while the vapor was like the canopy of an umbrella, or a bamboo hat, or the baldachin on an imperial carriage, or a poisonous mushroom. All the other trees in the village cringed and cowered, none daring to stand taller than the white poplar, which thrust itself arrogantly into the sky. On the fork of a branch about twenty meters from the ground was a jumbled pile of twigs. Magpies and crows nested among these twigs, chattering and arguing the whole day long, and if the moon was bright, continuing their screeching and cawing by the light of the moon.

Perhaps, when he was squatting on the riverbank, enfolded by a pall of shadowy darkness, a sound like a sob had gurgled out of his parched throat. Perhaps he was reminiscing about the events just past. Back then he had been wearing a big loose tunic, his feet bare as he stood under the white poplar. In front of the tree were the only five tile-roofed houses in the whole village. Inside the house was a very pretty little girl, her pitch-black eyes like two of the black stones in a game of *go*. The girl said to him: "Xiaohu,* can you climb up this tree?"

He stared blankly at the girl. His mouth cracked open in a grin, his short stubby nose broke out in wrinkles.

"You can't, I say you can't climb up to the top!"

He bit his thick lips.

"Can you climb up and get me a branch? I want that one there, do you see it? The one that's straight and smooth, I'll whittle it into a gun, and then you and me can play with it together. You'll be the spy, and I'll be the P.L.A. soldier."

He shook his head vigorously.

"I know you can't! You're not a little tiger, you're a little old sow!" cried the girl angrily. "From now on I won't play with you anymore."

He looked at the girl with his black eyes, very brightly, his mouth cracked open as if about to cry. Rubbing his feet back and forth on the ground, he finally said, in a dull voice: "Yes, I can."

---

*Xiaohu: the name means "little tiger."

"You really can?" the girl asked in amazement and delight.

He nodded vigorously. Then he took off the big tunic and exposed his black-green belly, saying: "You keep a lookout for me, my folks won't let me climb trees."

The girl took the garment, nodding her head loyally.

With both legs he gripped the trunk. His feet were covered with a thick layer of calluses, and they held on tightly to the silver-gray trunk, never slipping in the least. As he climbed up the tree he reminded one of a cat, his movements nimble and quick, with a certain natural grace. The girl held on to his clothes, face upturned, watching the poplar bend slowly, slowly toward her. Vaguely, she also seemed to see the bare-backed, barefooted boy weighing down the poplar until its trunk was curved like a bow, as if at any moment it would catapult him away. The girl shivered and trembled under the tree. Then she saw the tree suddenly straighten up again. In the gradually lengthening rays of a late autumn sun, the gleaming white branches gathered their upturned fingers and soughingly strummed and plucked the pale blue air. In the icily clear sky, skeins of fine wispy sprigs danced and fluttered, and the few leaves still left on the treetop—though they looked withered, their dark blue coloring remained unfaded—now whispered and rustled to the undulation of the branches. The girl was dazzled by the wondrous movements of the white poplar. She thought she saw, glistening on the back of the boy who was climbing ever higher—she thought she saw, on that blackfish-like spine, a gleaming aura like the wings of a crow.

"Come back down, Xiaohu, quickly, the tree's going to fall!" the girl cried to the boy up on the tree. The boy had already climbed up into the poplar's sparse crown, where crows and magpies shuttled back and forth among the branches, like a horde of gigantic bees, or a cloud of dismal butterflies.

"The tree's going to break!" Like tongues of flame the girl's cries were scorching his buttocks. He scooted upward even more quickly. The stinking gust stirred up by the crows and magpies as they flapped their wings blew straight onto the back of his neck, sending waves of chilliness down the furrow of his spine. The girl's cries also put him on guard: He too noticed how slender and delicate the trunk seemed, how very, very bent it was, how the icelike sky was spinning around tiltedly. One of the muscles on his leg began to throb. He lowered his head to look at the twitching muscle and saw it plain as day. At that moment he again heard the girl's cries. She was saying: "Xiaohu, come on down, the tree's falling down, it's going to fall on our house, and if it smashes the tiles, my momma will give you a whipping!" Alarmed, he stared blankly for a moment, then, hugging the trunk tightly, he looked down. All of a sudden he felt dizzy and lightheaded, shocked to see how far up he had climbed. Like a heron among hens, the white poplar towered above all the trees in the village, and he, having climbed up the poplar, felt a sense of well-being surging up from the bottom of his heart. All the houses were under his buttocks, even the sun was lower than his behind. The sun was setting very quickly, it was not round, it looked like a huge duck egg. He could see the tops of the thatch-roofed huts far and near, the rotting wheat straw flattened by the thrashing of the rains and still covered by a summer's growth of moss, the moss spotted all over by dribs and drabs of bird droppings. The road was thick with dust. A green car drove by, stirring up a cloud of gray dirt that soared into the sky and lingered there for a long time before dissipating. After the air cleared, he saw limping down the road a little brown dog whose bowels had been scrunched open by the car's tires, its intestines trailing in the dirt like a long cord. The dog did not cry at all, it just walked along calmly and even temperedly, while the warmth floating up out of its fur gradually receded, the brown dog becoming a brown hare, shrinking into a ground squirrel, finally vanishing without a trace. All around there seemed to be a noise like the resonating of an empty bottle, now close by, now far away; all the extremes of temperature, all of life's warmth and cold were smeared onto things, pieces of matter; the tree was half cold, half hot; he was quivering like a winter cicada holding on to a leaf, watching as a drop of bird dung flew straight toward a roof tile. The girl was calling to him again from below, but he did not hear her. He was looking timidly, cautiously, at the courtyard in front of the tile-roofed houses. He would never have seen this courtyard if he had not climbed up the poplar. Even though this girl with the pitch-black eyes under the tree had often invited him to come play with her, his dad and mom had told him again and again that he was not to go play at Xiaozhen's house. Was this girl Xiaozhen? he asked himself distractedly. He was always rather confused, befuddled, people in the village all said he was simpleminded. He continued to stare at the yard. Inside the yard was a wide paved footpath and a screen wall facing the gate. Next to the wall was a thorned plum bush, its petals and leaves all withered and fallen, only its long tough purplish-red stems left standing. There were also two bicycles in the yard, their nickel-plated wheel rims glinting and gleaming, pricking his eyes. A big tall fellow came out of the house and casually pissed at the foot of the wall. When the boy saw the fellow's purple-red face he was so frightened he again pressed himself right up against the trunk and hardly dared to breathe. This man had once, in front of many, many people, tweaked him by the ears and taunted him: "Xiaohu, how many legs does a dog have?" With much effort he had twisted his mouth open on one side and answered: "Three!" The crowd roared with laughter. Father and elder brother had also been among the crowd. Elder brother held himself back until his face was a bright red, father laughed sheepishly along with the crowd. For this elder brother had given him a licking, but father pulled elder brother away, saying: "If the party secretary likes to tease him, it means the man gets along with us, he's showing his regard for us." Elder brother let him go, then grabbed a shiny, black piece of sweet-potato cake and stuck it next to his lips, asking angrily: "What is this?"

"Dog shit!" he had replied through clenched teeth.

"Xiaohu, hurry up!" the girl was shouting under the tree.

Slowly he climbed upward again. By this time his legs were trembling violently. Suddenly a thick white smoke gushed out of the chimney of the tile-roofed house underneath, wisps and curls of smoke darting upward through chinks and cracks among the branches, up through the nests of the magpies and crows. Filthy feathers swirled about in the nests, while black birds tinged crimson with rays from the sun flew around him cackling and cawing. Reaching up with one hand and grasping the fist-thick bough, he gave it a vigorous tug. The whole tree shook and swayed, but the branch did not break.

"Pull it hard," the girl cried, "the tree won't fall, it was just trying to scare us, bending this way and that."

He pulled hard on the branch, which was bending, bending, just like a bow. His arm tingled with pins and needles, his fingers felt swollen. But the branch refused to break, and all of a sudden sprang away from him again. His legs began to shake even more furiously, his head sagged like a heavy load. The girl was still looking up at him. The smoke under the tree churned and billowed upward like waves. His body felt cold from head to toe. With a loud clatter two hairs on the back of his head sprang upright. Once again he became aware of how high he had climbed. The branch, so straight and smooth, still stood there arrogantly, defiantly. He crossed one leg over the other, then reached out both arms to grab the limb, and again pulled down on it with all his might. The branch hissed and swished, the tiny sprigs at its top knocking and bumping into other twigs, rasping out a noisy rat-a-tat. He put his whole weight and strength onto the branch. His legs were still clamped around the trunk, but by now he had clean forgotten about them. The more the bough bent, the more his heart filled with hate. Then, letting out a low roar, he leaped over, and the branch snapped. There was a sharp crackle when it broke. Inside his head a tendon twitched joyfully, and his whole body was immersed in a feeling of pleasure and exhilaration. Gracefully, airily, he began to fly, that very long branch flying right alongside, while up and down and all around him everything—the piercingly clear air, the white smoke from the kitchen chimney, the orange rays of the evening sun—all heaved and surged. In the midst of all this commotion he saw a woman in a brightly colored jacket running out from the tile-roofed house— now suddenly turned short and squat—while cries like a horse's neighing came out of her mouth.

The girl was still staring wide-eyed up at the tree. All of a sudden she discovered the boy hanging from the branch like a big fleshy fruit. She reckoned he must be feeling very comfortable. She was so very very envious, she wanted to hang from the branch too. But soon she noticed something different. Slowly, leisurely, the boy began to drop, the branch dropping beside him. She could see that his body had stretched itself out until it was very, very long, like an unfurling bolt of brown satin hanging straight down from the top of the tree, and the bough she had selected was whipping the satin with a swishing, rustling noise. Holding the boy's tunic in her arms, she took a step forward. Suddenly she felt a supple and sturdy branch flailing violently against her cheek, and then the bolt of brown satin falling onto her body. To her the bolt of satin felt as hard as a rock, the slightest touch and it would rumble, like a sheet of iron being hammered.

Dazed and bewildered, he picked himself up from the ground. Here and there his body felt sore and numb, though everything else was fine. But right away he saw the girl lying under the tree, her black eyes only half open, a trickle of indigo blood dribbling slowly out of the corner of her mouth. Dropping onto his knees, he stuck his hand through a chink among the branches and softly poked the girl's cheek. It was very hard, like a rubber ball pumped full of air.

The woman in the colored jacket flew around to the back of the house, shrieking: "You little bastard, you think you can fly into the sky? How did your dad and mom manage to make a bastard like you? You break one of my branches and I'll break one of your ribs with my own hands!"

Furiously she dashed up to the boy kneeling on the ground and began to kick him, but no sooner had her foot touched the boy's spine when it dropped limply back onto the ground. Eyes staring fixedly, her mouth all contorted, she threw herself on top of the girl, sobbing and screaming: "Xiaozhen, Xiaozhen, my child, what has happened to you? . . ."

Treading the dead grasses on the riverbank, a cat whose body was brindled all over with tiger stripes came to the top of the embankment, its fleshily cushioned paws padding almost noiselessly over the withered plants. Startled, it stood in front of the boy and began to growl menacingly, its eyes blazing with a green glow, its tail stiff and erect as a mast. He looked at it timidly. It did not go away, but began to sniff the thick cloying odor of blood emanating from his body. Unable to bear the intense gaze of those two phosphorescently glistening eyes, he struggled onto his feet.

The moon had risen far up in the sky, but it was still watery and not very bright. Stars in the western half of the sky gleamed with the brilliance of diamonds. The village was completely shrouded in the smoky, misty vapor. He knew, even without turning his head, that of all the trees in the village the white poplar was the only one that protruded above the mist, showing the tips of its branches like a tree in a flood. At the thought of the poplar, a sharp twinge stung his eyes and his nose. Cautiously he went around the bullying, baleful wild cat and staggered down into the river. The silvery gray shimmer between the banks turned out to be not water but soft fluffy sand. There had been three years of continuous drought, and now piles of dried grasses lay stacked on the riverbed. The cat was still growling at his back, but he no longer bothered to pay it any mind. His bare feet sank into the warm sand, leaving a trail of footprints behind him. The heat from the sand rose inch by inch from the arches of his feet up through his body, vigorously and energetically at first, at length tapering off into a wisp no thicker than a spider's thread, which then seemed to creep along his bone marrow until it bored straight into his skull. He had no idea where his body was, his whole being had turned into a blurry, shapeless mass, like an elusive shadow, tingling all over with a feverish sensation.

By the time he fell into the sand hollow, the moon was trembling incessantly, pouring its faint light—light that was like bloodied water—onto his naked back. He lay on his stomach, too weak to move, feeling the moonlight sear his back like a hot branding iron, while his nostrils were flooded with the smell of burnt pigskin.

The woman in the bright-colored jacket did not beat him, she was too busy weeping over her darling sweet baby. Her terrifying cries made his blood curdle and his hair stand on end, and he knew he was done for. He saw the big, tall fellow with the red face leaping over to him, then a noise droned in his ears, then there was peace and quiet. He felt as if he were caught under a dome-shaped glass cover while hordes of people on the other side of the glass swarmed around like bees, in a hurry, in a hubbub—to put out a fire? to charge at the enemy?—their mouths wide open and screaming, though not a sound could be heard. He saw two sturdy thickset legs in motion, a pair of scuffed-shiny suede shoes coming straight at his chest. Then he heard a frog cry out in his belly, and once again his body began to fly gracefully through the air, while a sweet putrid fluid gushed up into his throat. He uttered a single cry, and immediately thought of the little brown dog ambling slowly down the road dragging its entrails behind in the dirt. Why didn't the little dog cry at all? he kept wondering to himself. The suede shoes sent him tumbling head over heels, again and again. All of a sudden he felt as if his own guts, like the dog's, had also been dragged outside, and were now coated with a layer of golden yellow dust. The poplar bough that he had finally managed to break off after all that effort now began to fly through the air as well, its branches—pliable and tough as rawhide whips—whistling and shrieking like a hurricane, then bursting into shower after shower of splinters and twigs. A whiff of poplar sap, pure and fresh smelling, swirled gently against his lips and rippled outward. At first he was still rolling back and forth on the ground, but later, his mouth gagged with mud, he just lay there, utterly motionless.

Gradually, as the sand cooled down, the temperature of his body began to fall as well. Fine particles of grit kept being sucked into his nostrils as he lay sprawled on his face. He very much wanted to move a little, but he couldn't seem to find his body. Trying very hard to remember the whereabouts of his limbs, he finally thought of his arms. Straining, he propped himself up on his hands. His neck felt like it was broken, his neckbone popping and crackling noisily. Again he fell ponderously on his face, his mouth filled with sand

and dirt, his tongue so stiff he couldn't even curl it. At long last, after three mouthfuls of sand, he managed to turn over. And then he looked bitterly up at the night sky. By this time the moon was already due south, and, having completely lost its bloody tint, had become bright and shiny. Even the dark and gloomy sky had turned into a beautiful silvery gray. A golden sheen glittered in the river sand, a cold brilliance that surrounded him on all sides and stabbed away at him like tiny daggers. He stared beseechingly up at the solitary moon. The moon shone down on him, its face wan and pale, the shadows in the moon extraordinarily sharp and clear. He had never looked so carefully at it before, and now the shadows in the moon really astounded him. The moon seemed so very strange and unfamiliar, he would forget how it looked as soon as he closed his eyes. While he was thinking hard about the moon, the face of his father emerged out of the pale white orb.

It wasn't until today that he came to know father's looks. Father had two puffy eyes, his eyeballs were like water chestnuts that have been soaked in brine. Even when father was kneeling on the ground he was quite tall. Perhaps Suede Shoes had kicked father too, perhaps not. Down on his knees, father had begged pitifully: "Mr. Party Secretary, please forgive your worthless servant, sir, this son of a bitch, I'm sure going to beat the daylights out of him. Even ten of his dog lives aren't worth one of Xiaozhen's, I'll do anything to make her safe and well again, I'll even cut off a hunk of my flesh. . . ." The party secretary looked at father and laughed, his eyes puffing out ring after ring of blue smoke.

Elder brother headed for home dragging him in tow. His heels scraped against the rock-hard ground. They walked for a long time, but still they had not walked beyond the white poplar's shadow. Magpies and crows flitted by overhead, their shadows brushing against his cheeks like down.

Elder brother threw him on the ground in the courtyard and gave him a hard kick right in the buttocks, screaming: "Stand up! You're always getting the whole family in trouble!" He lay on the ground, refusing to move. Elder brother repeatedly kicked his buttocks, hard, saying: "Get up, dammit! What is this, you think you've done a great deed instead of something terrible?"

Miraculously he got on his feet and retreated step by step until he had backed into a corner of the wall, where he stood, looking with terror at elder brother's lanky figure.

Furiously, elder brother said to mother: "Let's just thrash him and finish him off, otherwise he'll only bring us more trouble. I had a chance to get into the army this year, but now it's all over for me."

He looked sorrowfully at mother. She had never once hit him. Mother walked over to him, tears streaming from her eyes. Grievously he cried out to her—"Ma!"—and began to sob and sniffle.

But mother yelled at him ferociously: "Bastard! You dare cry? You feel wronged? I could kill you and still I'd curse you!"

Mother's thimbled hand slapped savagely at his ears. He let out a dry, hollow wail. For an instant she was taken aback by this cry, which sounded like nothing a human being could have produced. Then she bent down and picked out from among a pile of hay a dried stick of cottonwood, and with a blind frenzy began to rain blows all over his body, the stick clattering and jangling so fearsomely that the sparrows perched on top of the wall all shot into the gathering dusk like bullets from a gun. Straining to lean back against the wall, he watched as the stick of cottonwood traced one red arc after another right before his eyes.

The thin, weak crowing of a rooster in the village stirred him out of his stupor. His belly felt as if it had frozen into a chunk of ice, his body was chilled through and through. The moon was already leaning to the west, and the river of stars in the sky was filled with waves piled one on top of the other like roof tiles. Trying to flip over, he managed to turn easily, much to his surprise, his body rolling and rolling like a piece of roundwood. Little did he know that he was tumbling down a small slope, at the bottom of which was a wretched little patch of sweet-potato vines. A faint bitter taste emanated from the purplish vines, while droves of fireflies the size of jujube pits swarmed all over the tendrils and flitted in his eyes and ears.

Swaying from side to side, father walked over to him while mother stepped back, still holding the stick of cottonwood, now stripped bare from the beating.

"Get on your feet!" father roared angrily. He shrank back with all his might.

He shrank back with all his might. The sweet-potato vines rustled and hissed. Moonlight covered the earth, and a layer of ice was congealing in the river. The piles of hay looked like blockhouses scattered chaotically all over the riverbed. Once again the sweetish putrid fluid surged up into his throat, and, seized with an uncontrollable urge, he opened his mouth wide and threw up clot after clot of something that felt like lumpy boiled dough. The coagulated clots lay next to his lips, looking like some cat shit he had once seen. He was terrified, and a vague premonition began to take shape.

There was this young married woman with fine long eyebrows, lying on a reed mat, her face like purple flower petals. Next to her were several people weeping as though they were singing a song. This young woman was so very pretty, she had looked like a flower when she was alive, and now that she was dead she looked even more like one. He had squeezed inside with a crowd of people to watch all the excitement. It was an empty house, a red trouser sash still hanging from the beam. The dead woman's face was calm and serene, she thought nothing of anyone there. The commune party secretary with the red face came to view the body, all teary eyed, and the crowd quickly made way for him. Suddenly, as the party secretary stood in front of the corpse, his eyes brimming with tears, a beautiful and radiant smile blossomed on the face of the young woman and her eyebrows fluttered like swallows' tails. In an instant the party secretary had dissolved onto the floor, a clear, colorless liquid gushing out from all over his body. Everyone said what a pity it was that the young woman had died. But when a person who was nobody when alive could attract so much attention when dead that even the party secretary came to pay his last respects—well, it was clear that death wasn't such a bad thing after all. That's what he had thought at the time—that death was something quite alluring. Soon after, however, as he walked out of the empty house with the pell-mell crowd, he had quickly forgotten all about the young married woman, and about death. But now the woman, death, and vaguely the little brown dog as well, all were coming toward him, without any anger or reproachfulness, along the river bottom that was awash in a silvery glow. Already he could hear the patter of their footsteps, he could see their immense black wings.

After he saw those wings, he all of a sudden understood whence he had come and where he was going. He saw himself stepping on the icy frost-work and walking to and fro in the river, while droves of eels slithered back and forth in the water like noodles. Vigorously he pushed the eels aside, and dropped into a house gleaming with black lacquer. A little north wind came roaring in unceremoniously, down the chimney and through the ratholes and chinks in the walls. He looked angrily at this golden world, as the sunlight of deep winter came streaming through the window paper and shone on a pile of fine-grained sand on top of the kang. He dropped wetly onto this sand, which coated his body from head to toe. With might and main he cried, cried for the world's coldness. Father said to him: "Go on, howl, howl, as soon as you were born you were howling like mad!" When he heard those words, he felt even more bitterly the cold that was chilling him to the bone, and his body, shriveling like a silkworm that was spinning silk, shrank smaller and smaller and became covered with wrinkles.

Yesterday afternoon at that moment, he was leaning against the mudwall of his own home, trembling as he watched father coming over to him step by step. The setting sun illuminated father's hefty body, as well his anguished face. He saw father walking unevenly, one foot bare, the other shoed. Carrying a shoe in the left hand, father with the right hand picked him up easily by the scruff of the neck and gave him a mighty toss. For the third time he felt himself flying through the air. When he got back onto his feet, confused and disoriented, he found that father's body had grown even bigger, its long, long shadow spread out over the entire courtyard. Mother and elder brother were like dolls cut from a paper bag, fluttering in the blood-red sunset. The first blow from father's thick-soled old shoe landed on his head, and almost hammered his neck right into his chest. But more often than not the old shoe landed on his back, now fast and furious, now more slowly, the sole becoming thinner and thinner, while flakes of mud and dirt spattered everywhere.

"I could kill you and still I'd curse you! You mongrel! What cruel fate brought us together as father and son!" father said woefully, all the while continuing to thrash him, the sole that had by now been worn thin smacking ever more loudly each time it made contact with his gluey back. He became filled with an unbearable rage, his heart turning rigid and hard like one of those iron weights on a steelyard. A desire to speak began to grow inside him, a desire that became more and more urgent with every blow father struck, until he finally heard himself squawking hoarsely at the top of his lungs: "Dog shit!"

Father was stunned, his shoe dropping silently onto the ground. He saw the green tears overflowing from father's eyes and the veins on father's neck squirming like green worms. Gnashing his teeth, he screamed again at father: "Stinking dog shit!" With a low, rumbling snort, father pulled down a stiff hemp rope hanging from the eaves and plunged it into a pickling vat, then picked it up carefully and held it away from his body as drops of muddy brine pitter-pattered from the rope. "Strip off his pants!" father said to elder brother. Quivering from head to toe, elder brother swam over from a big shaft of pale yellow sunlight and came to a standstill in front of him. Not daring to look into his eyes, elder brother gazed at father's eyes instead as he mumbled: "Dad, let's just leave them on. . . ." With a resolute wave of his hands father said: "Strip them off, I don't want to wear out the pants." Elder brother's glance flitted swiftly across his frozen face and his scrawny chest with the ribs that looked like fishbones. Then, staring blankly at his pants, elder brother bent down. He felt an icy chill between his thighs as his pants wafted down like a cloud and lay at his feet. Grabbing his left ankle, elder brother pulled off one pant leg, then, grabbing his right ankle, pulled off the other. He felt as if a layer of his own skin had been peeled away. Watching as elder brother's figure retreated coweringly, he again cried out: "Stinking dog shit!"

Father began to swing the rope. It danced and fluttered in the air, meanderingly at first, until it drew near his buttocks, when all of a sudden it straightened and rang out at the same time with a crisp, clear crackle. He groaned, and the now-familiar curse again squeezed out between his clenched teeth. Forty lashes father gave him with the rope, forty times he uttered the curse. On the last

stroke, the rope did not straighten but landed on his bottom meanderingly, flabbily; his cry also sounded meandering and feeble, like
a moan of pain. Father flung the discolored rope on the ground and,
panting heavily, went into the house. Mother and elder brother also
went inside. Angrily mother said to father: "Why don't you kill me
too? I don't want to go on living either. Just kill us both, me and
my son, it's better to be dead anyway. It's all your dad's fault, that
muddle-headed old fool, he knew very well the Communists were
coming, but still he went and bought those twenty acres of soggy
swampland that not even rabbits would shit on. So then they decided he was an upper-middle peasant, and now, one, two, three
generations later we're still living like outcasts, not quite demons
but not quite human either." Elder brother said: "Then why did
you marry into this family in the first place? All those poor and
lower-middle peasants, why didn't you marry one of them instead?" Mother burst into tears and began to bawl and wail, even
father broke down and sobbed, gasping and blubbering. Amidst
the sounds of their weeping, the rope began to twitch and squirm
like an earthworm, now wrapping itself into a fried dough twist,
now twirling into a spiral ring. Abruptly he cocked up all the hairs
on his body as his muscles tightened into bundles and bands, and
by dint of this energy, he got onto his feet, ruminated for a few
moments in the dusk-darkened courtyard, then ran leaping and
bounding to the wooden door and crept out through the opening.

Before daybreak, he once again came to, but he no longer had
the strength to lift his head for another look at the pale white moon
or at the pale gray watercourse. From the top of the riverbank came
mother's piteous cries: "Xiaohuuuu—huuuu—huuuu—huuuuer-a-
la-la-la, my poor, poor child ai-ya-ya-ya . . ." The cries stung him
until those parts of his body still left with any feeling began to ache
and tingle, and his heart was filled with the joy of revenge. With

every last ounce of strength he cried out—whereupon a burning sensation seized his chest and a sound like that of dust-dry paper ripping and tearing reverberated in his senses, and immediately afterward came the onslaught of an unbearable coldness. He even heard the sound of his own body falling through a hole in the ice, the half-frozen water swiftly embedding him after it sent seven or eight slivers of ice—no more than that—splashing up into the air.

At the very instant when the bright red sun was about to rise, he was awakened by a chorus of an oppressive and barbarous song. This singing was like a furious gale shrieking through a primeval forest, sweeping along all manner of dead branches and rotten leaves and slimy muck and filthy water as it surged down the dried-out river course. After the tempest passed, a strange, tense silence prevailed. Amidst this silence, the sun emerged slowly from the ground, and all of a sudden burst into warm and tender music, and the music caressed those buttocks striped with gashes and scars and kindled the fires in his head, and at length those tongues of yellowish and reddish flames turned green, grew smaller, flickered fitfully, and died.

By the time people found him he was already dead. His parents stared blankly, their eyes like those of fishes. . . . Folks with faces as bleak as the desert gazed upon his sun-drenched buttocks . . . as if looking at a beautiful and radiant face, as if looking at me myself. . . .

FIRST PUBLISHED IN AUGUST 1985 IN *BEIJING WENXUE (BEIJING LITERATURE)*

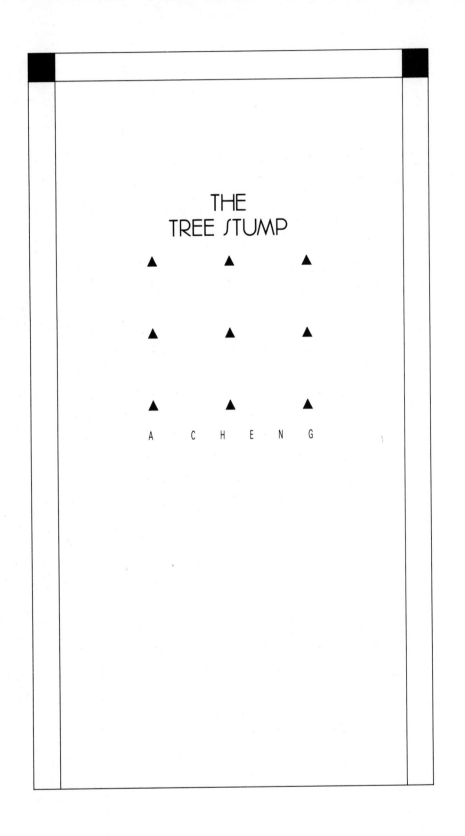

▲   ▲   ▲

▲   ▲   ▲

▲   ▲   As soon as sunlight appears at the east
end of the street, a short, squat stump of a tree crops up. Youngsters
passing by pay it hardly any mind, laughing and chattering as they
bustle along. Hill folks come trudging in under towering bundles
of twigs, all held together by swaths of burlap tied around their
foreheads. Thus constrained from looking around, they too rush by
without a glance. A plume of smoke wafts up out of the stump. An
old man sees it, and, standing with his hands behind his back, asks
hoarsely: "Hello, have you eaten yet?" Smiling faintly, the tree
stump nods once or twice, answers the question by asking it in turn,
and then, falling silent again, watches slowly as passersby hurry on
their way.

The tree stump had no name, neither first nor last, people just
called him Granddad—what did they call him when he was young?
—no one seemed to know. And how many years had the tree stump
seen? Nobody knew that either. Young and old, everyone on the
street called him Granddad, from tiny tots to their elders to their
elders' elders—no one could even tell which generation he be-

longed to, all they knew was he was old. So old, that he would smile slowly, smoke his pipe slowly, and when he lifted his hand slowly to wipe his face slowly, even his muscles—shriveled and near to transparent—would fall slowly, slowly back into place.

Once in a while folks from the big city would walk down this street, entering from the west and going east, peering left and right, looking up and down, poking around asking this and that and enjoying themselves no end—but just as they were about to turn back, they would catch sight of Granddad, and then their hearts would shudder, and for a good part of the day they would feel ill at ease. If by chance they started at the eastern end, the whole street would seem lifeless and gloomy from first to last, and though they may admire it for its antiquarian air, in the end they would feel a heaviness of the spirit and, sighing now and again, depart. Granddad was rather like an uninscribed stone marker, timeworn and weather-beaten, on which passersby could read the street.

The street was very old, very worn. The shopfronts were wide but not deep, room enough for no more than a shallow little stand, displaying packs of inexpensive cigarettes with brand names like Golden Sand River and Red Tassels, though here and there a few packs of Spring City would lie about, their foil wrappings covered with a layer of dust since customers for this costlier brand were few and far between. There were also shops that sold notions and dry goods, whose fresh bright colors stood out all the more sharply against the stores' battered wooden shutters. It is said that the look of the street can be traced all the way back to the Song dynasty— hard to believe, but, on the other hand, what's not to believe? On either side of the street was a row of blackish tile roofs, with tufts of fragrant thoroughworts springing up among the cracks. When the thoroughworts were in bloom, the entire street would be filled with the scent of this favorite herb of the kings. Visitors from the city would then marvel and sigh, envious that their own plants in their ceramic pots back home—specially inscribed with the legend "Fragrance for the Study"—never grew with quite the same luxuriance and vigor. The street was also very narrow, so narrow that if a peddler were to try to shift his shoulder pole crosswise from one shoulder to the other, the pole would thump against the stores' shutters on either side. Rows of cobblestones ran down the center of the street, while on each side was a foot-wide shallow ditch in which the street's sewage was drained away, the water running clear when it rained, and muddy when the skies were clear. Laden with kindling, wild game and medicinal herbs, men from the mountain villages would come down to the street to sell their wares. Afterward, the money burning a hole in their pockets, they would burrow into some tiny wineshop to drink until, many rounds later and thoroughly soused, they tumbled into the foot-wide ditch where they would sleep off their drunken stupor, after which they would drink again, until they found they had no money left, and then, all muddy and wet, they would stumble home.

The street lay at the center of a ring of mountains, in the valley plains that people in Yunnan call *bazi*. In fact, all the major towns in that province are situated on such bottomlands, and even the largest of them—cities like Kunming, Dali and Chuxiong—are to be found in bazis encircled by countless mountains, the only difference being that in their case the plains are broad and wide. This particular bazi, though, was very small—so small that when you stood at one end of the street, you could see the mountains towering over it on all sides just as if you were standing in a little alleyway in a crowded city, looking up at the tall buildings all around. But small as it was, this bazi was still the flatland at the bottom of a valley, which meant it was at the confluence of several rivers and streams, which meant it was a center, however small, of commerce and culture. The commerce consisted of not much more than the buying and selling of firewood, rice, local products, dry goods and sundries. As for the cultural part, well, that's a very long story.

Legend has it that in the time of the Three Kingdoms, the brilliant statesman and strategist Zhu Geliang came all the way to Yunnan in hot pursuit after the renegade Meng Hu. Late one night, Zhu and his exhausted troops were passing by this street when, through the murky darkness, his eye was caught by an inscription pasted to a door. Intrigued, he stopped his carriage and got out for a closer look. Much to his surprise he found that it was a couplet written on two vertical strips, the first line of which read: "Where the ruler transforms himself, his subjects put on a new face." The second, and complementing, line was: "Where the common man uses brawn, the gentleman uses guile." What's more, across the top between the two vertical strips was a horizontal inscription that read: "If you perceive, ask not." Zhu was astounded to find evidence of such an extraordinary intelligence in a region long considered to be primitive and uncivilized. The couplet—with its allusions to the divinations in the *I Ching* on change and on power, and finely balanced between the ominous and the auspicious—was actually about the art of governing, and, moreover, articulated perfectly Zhu's own strategy for subjugating the border tribes. Zhu was just about to look for the owner of the house in order to take his counsel when he realized that he and his troops were in a valley surrounded by tall mountains, and, fearing that the whole thing would turn out to be a trap, decided to press on instead. Later, after his expedition was over, he sent an emissary back to the street, only to learn that no trace of either the couplet or its author could be found. Well, a legend is just a legend, but perhaps this one was not without some basis in fact. For example, at every celebration of the lunar new year, the street would be festooned with propitious couplets, many of which would contain some unusual expression or a peculiar turn of phrase, which a person of erudition would recognize immediately as a quote from some ancient and venerable source. But if one were to ask the head of the house about it, he would most likely answer that he had no idea what it meant, it was just something he had seen his elders write, and they in turn had learned it from their elders, and that in carrying on this tradition each generation was merely hoping to bring good fortune to the family. Another local custom—a quaint and charming one—was to ink the bottom of a rice bowl and stamp it onto a couplet, to signify the wish: "May every mouth in this house be safe and sound, may the porkers in the sty be fat and round."

There was only one elementary school here, but many of its graduates did well enough to be accepted by the middle school in the county seat, and some even went on to the university in the provincial capital. After that they would find many opportunities to put their talents to use in distant places, and often it would be a good eight or ten years before they came home. Whenever a local kid won some honor or made good in that outside world, the news would somehow find its way back to the street and in no time at all would be on everyone's lips, and then pity the poor passerby who, when asked whether he had ever heard of So-and-so from these parts who had done such-and-such, should so much as hesitate at all, because he would thereupon be branded an ill-informed ignoramus, while the folks on the street would continue to bask blithely in their native son's reflected glory.

But what filled the residents of the street with the most pride was the fact that so many famous songsters came from within their midst. In the many mountains of Yunnan, people can often walk almost shoulder to shoulder and yet not be able to grasp each other by the hand, because between them would be a deep canyon, and it would take them at least a half day's journey up hill and down dale in order to meet face to face. Bored with trekking along in the mountains all by themselves, the solitary travelers naturally welcomed any encounter with another person and, with it, the chance to talk. But to raise their voices and shout at each other across the chasm? Well, one couldn't keep that up for very long, and besides, it would sound too much like a shouting match, and that would be no fun. So instead they would carry on their conversation in song—a way of communicating that was as entertaining as it was effective. And if the travelers who met across the canyon happened to be a man and a woman, it was only to be expected that they would tease and flirt with each other, letting fly all manner of suggestive puns that city folks would find too raunchy but that were so clever and witty one couldn't help but be tickled by them. Fortunately, while the verbal salvos could be as off-color as one pleased, any attempt to go beyond mere wordplay was a strict no-no. After the joking and the bantering were over, the two people would go their separate ways in the mountains, and that would be the end of that. The story is told of the fellow who was once outsung by a woman: As she went on her way singing gleefully about her triumph, the news of his defeat was spread for miles and miles around, and after that he could not get any woman to marry him. He was so upset that he went to pieces, singing and squawking to himself incoherently, incessantly, until one day when he took a bad fall and ended up crippled. When the woman found out about this, she was so stricken with remorse that she decided to marry him, and they lived out their days singing to each other. And that, so the story goes, was the origin of many of the best and most popular songs in these parts. Then, in modern times, someone who made his living writing movie tunes came and collected these songs, and that was how they came to be sung across the length and breadth of China.

In spite of its small size, the street used to play host every March to a grand and festive event, when songsters from all the nearby settlements would gather on the surrounding slopes to take part in round after round of singing, until in the end a winner emerged—the one who had outsung them all. Afterward this champion singer would be treated like a conquering hero and invited to sing at each village in turn, where everyone would sit around a bonfire and listen, enraptured, to their honored guest until the wee hours of the morning and even beyond. From then on he would be recognized wherever he went in the mountains and accommodated in whatever he desired, including, of course, affairs of the heart.

So it was that whether young or old, male or female, any resident of the street who could not sing would be considered deficient somehow, like a mute almost, and not only would this hapless person be left out of all the fun, he would find himself left out of most other things in life as well.

Sad to say, this singing came to a sudden end when it was branded as one of the "Four Olds."* In its place, the only songs heard in the street were those sung everywhere else in the country. People who overheard the schoolchildren at their music lessons would sigh and wonder how these new songs, so insipid and monotonous, could even be considered songs at all. The music teacher came to be regarded as the number one nincompoop of the street. But as the days wore on, the street lost its own music. Once in a while, in

*The "Four Olds": old ideas, old culture, old customs and old habits—all condemned during the Cultural Revolution.

an unguarded moment someone would burst into one of the old songs, but after one or two lines he would catch himself and then, his mouth agape, would freeze on the spot until he was quite sure that no one had heard him, whereupon he would quickly and furtively lick his lips in relief.

But while the street may have lost its voice, the songs lived on in the mountains, where you could sing freely and openly without being recognized. And so what if you were? Even if they went after you, how would they ever find you? Whenever someone in authority denounced this behavior at a meeting, people would pretend not to hear or act dumb, as if this were a story from the edge of beyond, and of course nothing ever came of it.

But with the demise of the songfests, the title of champion singer also went unclaimed for years.

Then suddenly, out of the blue came the news that people were beginning to sing again in Kunming, not just one or two here and there but thousands upon thousands of them all gathered together, and not just singing but competing again in one of those lively singing meets. There had been no explicit directive lifting the ban on singing, but as other activities became permitted one by one, people came to realize that they would also be allowed to sing their old songs again.

For more than a fortnight the street was abuzz with talk about the revival of the singing meet on its customary date in March. Residents of the street, determined to revive not only the songfest but also the special stature of the street itself, had gone to great lengths to organize the event and to publicize it among the neighboring villages. The news spread so quickly along the grapevine that soon everyone within a hundred miles knew about the meet. When the big day finally arrived, a huge throng almost ten thousand strong converged on the bazi and took their places on the slopes of the surrounding hills, their excitement rumbling in the air like distant thunder. Even officials from the county and the special administrative district were there: At one end of the street several tables had been set up for them, complete with a row of chairs behind and a row of tea mugs on top. It was an honest-to-goodness big event.

The first to sing was someone from the street, but no sooner had he finished when the response wafted down from somewhere up on the slopes, and thousands of heads turned in the direction of that sound. Undaunted, the first singer piped out his rejoinder, and again a retort came right back. So it was with each new verse, the sea of heads turning first one way and then the other, and the competition began to heat up.

But soon the audience noticed something rather peculiar about the singers: They were all middle-aged, in their forties at least, while the young folks just sat there, listening and laughing and clapping and calling out encouragement from time to time, but taking no part in the singing. There were probably some among them who could sing a little, but they knew that their repertoire was limited at best and insipid to boot, and so decided to stay out of the contest rather than embarrass themselves in front of all those people. An old cadre from the special administrative district who was in charge of cultural activities sighed as he reminisced about the time, oh, thirty or forty years ago, when he came here for the same event and heard a fellow who could sing circles around everyone else and who, after a fortnight of competing against all the best songsters in the area, won the title of champion singer. When the cadre asked about the name of this singer, he was greeted with an indignant glare and the scornful reply: "What! You mean you haven't even heard of Li Er?" Sighing again, the old cadre wondered if anyone knew whether this Li Er was still around. One of the officials from the street who was playing host to the visiting dignitaries mulled this over and finally, after racking his brains, said: "I wonder if that's Granddad?"

The word was put out, and, what do you know, the answer came back that Granddad was indeed Li Er and none other. The young folks, stunned to find out the old tree stump had had such a colorful past, were all kicking themselves for having paid such little attention to Granddad when they walked by him every day, and now they all rushed to join in the search for Granddad.

Actually Granddad was sitting right there in the throng on the hills, listening to the singing with a hand cupped behind one ear, all the while smoking his pipe and smiling slowly, as was his habit. Someone with a sharp eye spotted him and led the search team up the hill and through the crowd to Granddad. Not knowing what was going on, the audience saw there was a commotion on one of the slopes with a bunch of people standing around an old man, and they began to fear that after all the effort that had gone into reviving this singing meet some hooligans had come to disrupt everything. Even the singing stopped. But when word began to spread that a champion singer of long ago by the name of Li Er had been found, the news created a furor in the crowd. Most surprising of all, at least to the young folks, was the spectacle of all those elderly grandmothers weeping softly as they pushed their way down the slopes to see the fellow they once knew, to ask him whether he still remembered the words of his songs and the girl he sang them to on such and such a date once upon a time?

The young folks, tactless and insensitive as the young are wont to be, naturally began to snicker and make fun of what they considered the unseemly behavior of these old women. Imagine their surprise when Granddad not only remembered but chatted amiably with all these grandmothers, each of whom had been a well-known songster in her own right back in the old days. The cadres hurriedly got up from their chairs and offered them to the old folks. Someone stood up and, singing, told all the people on the slopes about what had just happened. The applause that swept all over the hillsides startled a flock of birds flying by overhead and threw them into disarray, but, finding no place to land on the slopes, the birds flapped their wings and went on their own way.

Naturally everyone clamored for Granddad to sing. A smile spread across Granddad's face, and with the laughlines still in place, he said slowly: "I will need a partner." Then, turning around, he asked one of the old women to join him. Blushing pink as a peach blossom, the grandmother walked up to him daintily and, brushing away a tear, asked Granddad to begin.

Closing his eyes, Granddad let out a long note. Right away a hush fell over the audience, and even the sky seemed to recede. Though his voice was somewhat hoarse and uneven from years of disuse, Granddad had lost none of his easy charm and mischievous wit:

> *On yonder hill there stands a* pipa,*
> *Whose it is I do not know.*
> *I'll carve and shape it into a pipa,*
> *From my arms it will not go.*

Before Granddad had quite finished, a thunderous round of cheers and applause broke out all over the hills. But this old woman was no ordinary grandmother either, and straightaway she was ready

---

*pipa: homophones for (1) a kind of tree with yellow edible fruit and (2) a plucked string instrument with a fretted fingerboard.

with her reply. Her voice still clear and bright, she also started off
with a long note that immediately got a big hand:

> *Oh—I am the pipa on yonder hillside,*
> *My roots are buried deep and strong.*
> *Awake, oh fool from your pipa dreaming,*
> *All you're clutching is your own little prong.*

Once again the hills resounded with a roar of cheers and applause.
The youngsters were all dumbfounded: Who would have thought
these old folks had once been so bawdy and full of life! They may
be old now, but they were still flirting and teasing, and the old
songs—like fine wines—had aged gracefully, growing in richness
and charm yet maintaining their zest and humor. And, in a trice,
some smart young folks had learned the songs by heart.

Not concerned with winning or outdoing anyone, Granddad
went on to sing a few more verses against some of the other grandmothers, all of whom beamed with pride and joy at the honor they
were being given in front of all these thousands of people. Even
their children and grandchildren were surrounded by admiring
throngs, and, giddy with all this attention, began to hold forth as
if they knew everything under the sun.

Someone from the street brought out some wine and proposed
a toast to the old folks. As Granddad took a few sips, veins began
to pop out all over his forehead. He was just about to sing again
when he suddenly stiffened and fell backward, a trickle of saliva
seeping out between his clenched lips. They rushed up to help him,
only to realize that Granddad had suffered a stroke. He died as they
were carrying him home.

From then on this street and these mountains once again resounded with their own songs. The name Li Er was etched in the minds of the young folks, who never tired of telling every out-lander about this Li Er. Everyone felt that Granddad had erected a monument for this street, for these hills.

FIRST PUBLISHED IN OCTOBER 1984 IN *RENMIN WENXUE (PEOPLE'S LITERATURE)*

THE
NINE PALACES

ZHANG CHENGZHI

▲　　　▲　　　　▲

▲　　　▲　　　　▲

▲　　　▲　　　　Han Thirty-eight ran into that shaggy-
haired fellow from the city right when the sun was burning up the
desert with its blinding glare. After he got off the tractor, the young
fellow had seemed like he wasn't sure where to put his feet, stopping and starting as he walked slowly along. Han Thirty-eight took
one look at him and figured that he was planning to find an inn or
a guest house among the handful of adobe huts in this tiny hamlet.
Without stopping to exchange any greetings with Shaggy Hair,
Han Thirty-eight went directly into the fields where he tended to
his stand of corn, right there under the harsh, scorching rays of the
sun.

That was about three or four days ago.

Today Han Thirty-eight was again working in his cornfield. The
time had come, and the drought was so bad, he couldn't wait any
longer to water the crops. For some time now he had been worrying about how he'd be able to repair the irrigation ditch. With his
gimpy leg he could manage ordinary chores all right, but a big
project like this was more than he could handle. While he was

working in the field on the edge of the desert, he noticed that the shaggy-haired stranger was also wandering around nearby. Reckon he's found a place to stay, Han Thirty-eight thought to himself, I wonder who he is.

Between the highway to the north and the desert to the south, this was the only settlement for hundreds of kilometers around. Back when he was a lad Han Thirty-eight had once traveled to the next village, a whole day's journey by tractor. If his father hadn't given him a little plot of land so he could find a woman in that village to marry, he probably would have never even set foot outside this patch of red clayey soil. Ever since that trip he had spent all these years right here, standing watch over this field of red earth and looking out on the pale sands of the vast endless desert, day after day after day.

It wasn't just his leg that was lousy but his whole body—scrawny arms, with hardly any muscle on them, that tired after just a little work, joints that would grow stiff and crackle loudly when he tried to straighten up. Holding on to the sturdy cornstalks for support, Han Thirty-eight looked up for a moment and saw that shaggy-haired fellow again. I wonder what he does, he thought to himself. Just then the fellow looked in his direction and gave him a sheepish grin. Han Thirty-eight hurriedly cracked a smile in return, then went back to his chores.

The fiery sun continued to beat down on the tiny patch of silted ground at the northern edge of the desert. The clayey soil was so scorched it began to give off a reddish powder that wafted up into the brilliant blue sky. The desert lay all around, empty, arid— nothing but glittering yellow sands as far as the eye could see. With the rocky wasteland on one side and the endless desert on the other, the highway threaded through the landscape like a go-between, though no one quite knew where it led in either direction.

Rubbing his sore and watery eyes, Han Thirty-eight turned away from the scorching desert and resumed the task of leveling clumps of red clay with a shovel, and slowly, slowly, a rectangular plot began to take shape, its sides as straight as a ruler. Ever since he became lame from that childhood illness, he had had to do his chores in this fashion—slowly, unhurriedly. People in the hamlet were always teasing him, especially the tractor operator, Ma Zhuang'er, who would tell him that when he worked in the fields he looked like one of those actors singing a female part in Shaanxi opera. Actually he and Ma Zhuang'er had been friends since they were children, and he knew it was none other than Ma who had the greatest respect for him. Their fields lay right next to each other's on the alluvial plains of red clay, and every autumn Han's tall stands of corn would cut Ma Zhuang'er down to size. Whenever Han Thirty-eight thought about this his heart would be filled with a delicious tingle. Thick and sturdy, his cornstalks would flutter in the breeze like a grove of trees, their big fat leaves rustling loudly in the clouds of sand stirred up by the wind, and when the wind died down the leaves would again be a deep emerald green, almost the color of ink. The sight of it would so cow Ma Zhuang'er that far into the winter he would still be listless and droopy eyed, and he would spend all his time tinkering with his walking tractor until he looked like a regular grease monkey.

It was time to rest for a spell. Reaching for the earthen jug full of water that he had set down on the edge of the field, Han suddenly remembered the shaggy-haired fellow and turned around to look for him. Where did he go? He turned to look at the dirt road leading into the village, but that was empty too, and the only things he saw were the adobe huts and the mud walls around the vegetable patches, all coated with a thin layer of dust, squatting there in a rosy blur under the sun. Where did Shaggy Hair disappear to? Han

Thirty-eight felt rather puzzled. In the shade of the cornstalks, he picked up the earthen jar and drank a mouthful, and as the cool water slowly moistened his insides he began to feel refreshed—even his burning eyes felt soothed.

The thing that really worried him was this eye disease of his. It had got to the point where if he so much as opened his eyes and looked around a field that was baking in the sun, drops of salty, bitter tears would run from his eyes in an endless stream. Sometimes all he had to do was glance at the parched red soil and his eyeballs would smart as if from the stings of a needle. Nobody paid any attention to an eye disease, it was not like a gimpy leg that was there for all to see. Actually nobody cared about a gimp either. There was a lame old man in the hamlet who made his living as a trader, leading his camels on foot from village to village in the outland. His woman was left to take care of the crops with the children hanging all over her, and whenever she was upset she would curse that good-for-nothing gimp of hers for not walking any faster to get home. She had every right to curse, Han Thirty-eight thought, having to drag around five or six kids while trying to farm thirty hectares of land, her hard life turning her coarse and dark like a lump of iron.

Picking up the pot again, he drank some more water, and that was when he saw Shaggy Hair. That fellow was going into the desert! He was so astounded that he set the jar down. No doubt about it, the young man was really walking away from him and onto the gleaming white dunes, dragging his dark shadow behind as he trudged along, his feet sinking into the sand with every other step.

How strange, Han Thirty-eight thought to himself as he caressed the clay pot. In this quiet and remote little village they never saw anybody from the outside. To the north, on the other side of the huge and ominous-looking expanse of wasteland, there was a string of Uighur settlements, all connected by the highway. But this was an isolated hamlet, far from the hustle and bustle of caravan traffic. And yet, somehow, for some reason, that stranger not only came here, but was now heading into the desert for a walk. Watching the tiny figure receding in the distance, Han Thirty-eight shook his head disapprovingly. That's an ocean over there, a big ocean, its waves of sand go on and on forever, what are you doing wandering around in there? But he decided to stop worrying about what the stranger was up to, and, setting the water pitcher down on the ground, went back to smoothing out the soil in his rectangular plot.

On the edge of the gritty, lead-gray wasteland sat a reddish-brown hill of sand and gravel, and it was from this hill that the muddy red water ran down into the desert, ran and ran until, after so many years, it had managed to build up a fan-shaped delta of red clay between the barren gravelly flats and the desert to the south. Han's village was built right on this patch of red earth. Generations ago people began to bring in the clay by the river's edge to build their mud dugouts. As the adobe dried in the sun, it would turn a wretched shade of red that stung the eyes.

But Han Thirty-eight didn't mind this patch of poor, sourish red earth. Working on his little plot, he would wield his shovel evenly, accurately, breaking up the clods of sticky mud until they were spread out in a smooth powdery layer. For as long as anyone could remember, the Hans had made their living off of this patch of red clay and the two precious crops it produced—cornmeal that was white as snow, and big, luscious, golden-yellow apricots. Anyone who wanted to live comfortably in his old age would also have to look to this red earth for a little extra pocket money. In autumn, even old women in their seventies and eighties would hobble into the fields to help snap off the fat and sturdy ears of corn. At times like that, there was not a soul who did not feel happy and content, no one who thought this soil too parched, too sour, who found its burnt-red color irritating to their eyes.

And so Han Thirty-eight always worked diligently and conscientiously. When the fields were being irrigated he would never sneak home to sleep like the others; instead, he would squat in the fields all night long, keeping his crops company as they quenched their thirst. With his shovel he would dam and stop up the ditch here and there, diverting the water smoothly and evenly so that all his crops would get their fill. Right now it was an idle time in the fields, and all around not a soul was to be seen—except for Han, who was already working away quietly and steadily, leveling the ground and straightening the pathways between the fields, trying to get a head start because of his handicap. He was afraid of losing heart, afraid that, with his gimpy leg and his eye disease, he would fall apart while still a young man.

Squinting to avoid the brilliant glare of the merciless sun, Han Thirty-eight looked over at the desert. Beyond the haze of red dust hovering over the fields, he could see a shimmering vapor rising from the flat horizon far in the distance. That shaggy-haired fellow has disappeared, he's really gone into the desert, Han thought. Dragging his crippled leg into place and steadying himself, he began to prod the ground deftly with his shovel. The soil was so sticky it had to be crumbled up into tiny pieces, and each field had to be laid out in a broad rectangular plot. He harbored a secret plan: Next year he wanted to switch all his fields over to wheat. The size of his plots was best for planting wheat, he figured; he would plant twelve rows in each, and there would be room enough to use a walking tractor for the seeding. How long can Shaggy Hair stay in there before he has to turn back? No matter what that fellow was up to, Han was rather curious about how long he would last in the desert. Have you ever seen an ocean? he asked that fellow silently.

Whether or not you have, that's an ocean in front of you. Having lived all his life on this patch of red earth, Han Thirty-eight had never seen an ocean himself. But he did walk into the great desert once upon a time—for three days, on the strength of his whole heart and soul, he had wandered around inside. Three days of walking in the endless waves of sand, and ever since then he'd felt as if he had seen the ocean.

A hot, dry wind began to stir, and the leaves of the cornstalks rustled in reply. Smoldering in the fiery sun, the desert to the south lay stretched out in an unbroken line all the way to the horizon, where, just above the rim, a dazzling bright light shone and glittered.

Shaggy Hair finally collapsed next to a stand of red willows. It wasn't so much that he couldn't as that he didn't dare to go on anymore. Everything seemed calm and quiet, but that was only the feeling one had when nightfall first came upon the desert. That feeling belongs to a newborn calf who doesn't know any better, he thought to himself, it is the feeling of an arrogant, mad fool. So quiet—pulling his knapsack over, he laid his head down on it—so quiet that it really makes you feel as though you've left the world behind. But at the moment waves of terror were washing over him, and every single strand of hair ached—they were all standing on end as if they would never ever lie down again. The night hung black and low over the desert. Forget about the ruins, even these trees might be the only stand around. You're lost, he thought, you don't even know whether you're still walking south. You can't wander around like this, if you want to find the ancient city you've got to know your bearings first of all. You didn't come here to fool around, you came to look for Toghuz Serai.

Actually there had been so many topics to choose from, including quite a few where the fieldwork would have been a snap. And then there were those topics that bore no relation to the real world, no more than a child's game of building something out of toy blocks. More than half of the dissertations in the journals were like that. So what if he found Toghuz Serai?—Shaggy Hair thought, knitting his brows—even that wouldn't be anything really creative. Perhaps it was because the pitch-black night hung so oppressively, because there was no moon or a single star shining through the darkness— whatever the reason, he found himself in a foul mood. There was a famous ancient city mentioned in the history books, and in the geography texts there was the name of a site. That name was Toghuz Serai, and he had had a hunch that it was none other than the ancient city. But right now there was not even a flicker of phosphorescence in the desert at night—though there should have been, and not only phosphorescence but also huge forests of dead trees, dried-out waterways after the seasonal rivers had changed course and wooden beams sticking out of the sand dunes under which the ancient ruins were buried. Sure, and buried in the sand there should also be a lovely two-thousand-year-old maiden whose beauty would be unblemished after all these centuries—he began to laugh at himself—her cheeks soft and rosy, her body swathed in silk and satin, she would be buried right next to this stand of red willows, and as soon as you arrive she would spring to her feet and begin to dance. What would be so significant about finding Toghuz Serai? That so-called historical geographic method—what an out-dated, useless crock.

He was exhausted. When he passed by that patch of red earth on the edge of the desert earlier in the day, he should have asked for some water from that young fellow working away silently in the field. He shook his water bottle gently, then ran his fingers through his tousled hair. Half a canteen left, he'd better save it for tomorrow. Just yesterday he had been barely able to contain his impatience. After three or four days of being holed up in that tiny village of the Han clan his frustration had reached the boiling point. There were only about twenty-odd families in the hamlet, all of them living in those red adobe huts that were dug halfway into the ground. From the map it appeared he had made the right decision to get off at this place: Going south from the village one should run right into the fabled Toghuz Serai. But the villagers all seemed to be in a daze, never managing to say anything without first going "aw-aw-aw" for what seemed like forever—perhaps the fierce sun had gone to their heads. There was neither a village chief nor a headman, and the women, all flustered and jittery, would scamper to shut their doors as soon as they saw him. When he finally got around to asking about Toghuz Serai it was even more ludicrous. The villagers looked him up and down through squinting eyes, their gaze finally settling on the hair on top of his head. They must be sunstruck, he again concluded, just think, their brains must have been fried by that hot sun, the same fireball that has been roasting the earth until it gives off plumes of dust even on an absolutely windless day.

He turned over, and a stream of sand swished down his collar while another rivulet flowed into his shoes. With a start, Shaggy Hair admonished himself: Don't forget you're in the desert, a huge desert that's like a dead sea, so stop woolgathering and watch out for sandstorms. If the wind rises the sand will cover you, layer by layer, until it has fashioned a nice round tomb over you. Then you wouldn't be able to gripe about the Hans' village anymore, then you would have no choice but to look underground for that two-thousand-year-old sleeping beauty. On his guard now, Shaggy Hair did his best to stay awake, keeping watch in the deathlike silence that covered the desert.

But the desert was fast asleep in the deep, dark night. Not a breeze stirred, and the sand dunes stayed where they were, not moving an inch. After midnight a few stars appeared in the sky.

This was the first time since Shaggy Hair took up his present occupation that he felt he was going to fail. Before he joined the museum as a researcher he had been a furnace attendant in the neighborhood factory for quite a few years. Back then he liked to work the night shift, and even when he didn't feel like reading he could always stare at the warm glow from the furnace, where the dense yellow flames would dance brightly in front of his eyes. He was never able to make one of those translucent, pale blue fires—his were always like a wood fire, hot, dry and intense. Anyway there was plenty of coal, and he loved to toss big shovelfuls of coal chips into the furnace and watch his own gigantic shadow flicker in the vast emptiness of the boiler room. What an enormous shadow that was, he thought, lost in a reverie. Back then, when he used to sit in front of the furnace watching that huge shadow dance on the wall, he would always fall into a brown study too. Now those days of living by the sweat of his brow are gone forever—but in the last few years there has not been a single place, a silent, empty spot all to himself, where he could be lost in his own thoughts. Gone, too, are the mysterious flickering shadow and the incandescent flames that had seared his heart—instead all he has now is this life of running around with the aid of a compass and a map. He didn't want to think about those lovely furnace fires with such wistful longing. When he opened his eyes, however, and looked around at this corner of the great Taklimakhan Desert in which he was almost buried, it seemed to him full of hidden dangers and a secret restlessness—not something that would evoke any fond memories.

Hitching a ride on the walking tractor with that fellow named Ma Zhuang'er didn't turn out to be such an auspicious beginning after all. The village of Han was a genuinely godforsaken little hamlet. It didn't even have a travelers' tavern, though in the end he was allowed to lodge at the elementary school, and he spent the next three or four days trying to find out about Toghuz Serai. But all he learned was there were no camels, no donkeys, no cars or trucks, no means of transportation whatsoever. This village is at the edge of the world, the villagers would say to him. The desert? No one can go in there! As for camels, there are only two, and they've been gone almost a year. . . . At times like this all the hairs on his head would stand on end. How he came by this trait he had no idea, but whenever he made up his mind to go all out for something his hair would stand up in a tousled, shaggy mess. Back home in the city people often laughed at him because of this. His friends nicknamed him "Exploding Hair." Once, when he was still working in the boiler room, he was chatting with a girl he had just begun to date when she asked, very casually, how come he didn't know a single word of a foreign language, and right then and there his hair exploded. Later, when he ambitiously took the examination to become a researcher at the museum, his hair exploded again. The last time before this that it had exploded was when he tried for a promotion in the museum. But this time, this time it's not working, he ruminated morosely, this time the smartest thing to do would be to turn back. This is an ocean—he thought to himself as he stared at the dark, foreboding sand hills lurking all around him—a dead ocean. And I don't even have a donkey, let alone a camel or a car. Nothing but a map and a canteen of water—a profound sense of grief came over him—and now the canteen is only half full, while the map, well, it turns out that the real function of a map is to lure you into a dead sea.

The young fellow who drove the walking tractor had told him that a long time ago everyone in the hamlet had been surnamed Han, but that later they began to take as brides young women from the clan of Ma, also ethnic Moslems, and so eventually there came to be two family names in the village—Han and Ma. Actually the roots of the Han clan were different: They were once the Salars of Qinghai province. The Salars? he thought to himself, why did they come all the way here to the edge of the great Taklimakhan Desert? Surely not because of the crops one can grow on this red clay. He could tell just by looking at the fan delta at the mouth of the muddy red stream that the soil was quite acidic. What a shocking shade of bright red, he thought, it's a miracle they can get any crops to grow here at all. Right on the desert's edge, far away from any traffic and other human habitation, yet standing watch over the entrance to Toghuz Serai—what a strange place this is, this village of the Han clan with its red adobe huts. Why do the maps show it guarding the route to the legendary Toghuz Serai? he wondered. One thing is for sure, though: This blazing, pitiless sun can definitely wreak havoc with a person's nervous system—perhaps he's already been out in it too long. For the last few days he had been feeling rather sick, as if that dazzling sun had scorched him until he too had fallen ill. Smoothing his tangled hair, he tried his utmost to think calmly, dispassionately, to not let himself be upset by those dark sand dunes crouching menacingly nearby. Maybe he's not sick—after all, that fire raging in the furnace had been damned hot, too. "But those days are over and done with," he heard himself saying out loud.

Just then another star appeared in the sky. Shaking his flask, Shaggy Hair listened to the water sloshing around inside and again thought, I should have asked for some water from that young peasant working away so silently on his plot of land. He seemed to remember seeing an earthen jug on the ground next to the fellow, its gray color standing out bright and sharp against the field of red clay. Even under the fierce sun the young peasant had seemed so calm, so good-natured that he had left a profound impression. Watching him wield his shovel steadily, evenly, Shaggy Hair sensed that here was an honest and solid fellow, someone so accustomed to working under the burning sun that not only did he not find it torturous and wearisome, he seemed to actually take a certain pleasure in it—perhaps he was even humming a little tune to himself. If only I had asked him for some water then, Shaggy Hair thought. He had charged into the desert on a burst of energy and enthusiasm, completely forgetting what anyone—even a schoolgirl in the city whose favorite pastime was munching melon seeds at the movies—could have told him: Water is the essence of life in a desert. Well, it's too late now. If he were to press on into the desert with only half a canteen of water he might as well commit suicide right then and there. With the most vicious words he could think of he cursed himself roundly before finally calming down. Then, as he lay peacefully in the sand, he began to feel that, improbable as it seemed, the tension and restlessness were fading from the desert night. He continued to lie there motionlessly, waiting for himself to figure it out.

A corner of the sky began to stir, and as the commotion continued the intense pitch-blackness began to lighten little by little. Then a smooth crack appeared in the darkness, and, almost imperceptibly, a faint white streak emerged.

Straightaway he found his bearings. North, the direction he was facing, was also the way back. Some time during the night his tousled, unruly hair had calmed down somewhat. He smiled ruefully to himself. Actually you knew this would happen when you started out, that's why you only brought one container of water. You knew all along that with the likes of you, any attempt to find the ancient city of Toghuz Serai in the vast desert was doomed to failure.

He got up and started on the road back, his head hanging low, his feet trudging through the soft, loosely-packed sand. To his right, the ribbon of early morning light was beginning to spread.

Han Thirty-eight came to the fields again, leaning on his spade as he walked slowly along. The next task was repairing the irrigation ditch—it was really in terrible shape. When he went to examine the trench that twisted and turned as it snaked from the river to his fields, he had found it overgrown with weeds and so full of gaps that water leaked from it all along the way, turning the clayey soil on both sides a sickening shade of bright red. I've got to dig it out again, Han Thirty-eight mused as he leaned on his spade. He'd heard tell that this old ditch was dug by their ancestors many generations ago, but now it just looked like a long, long worm with blood trickling out from all over its body. Not like the big trench, the one that had just been dug and was lined with gray-green cement, where the water gushing in from the river would swirl around and splash up in the air in a crystal-clear spray—what a beautiful sight, enough to make anyone feel all refreshed and cool inside.

But it's only the old gully that comes close to my land, Han Thirty-eight thought to himself as he knitted his brows. The big cement ditch was too far away to irrigate his fields. That Ma Zhuang'er is something else, so slick it's like he has slathered himself from head to toe with rapeseed oil soap. At the thought of Ma

Zhuang'er he began to feel irritated and anxious. Today at lunch he had wolfed down his food without enjoying it one bit and then had rushed right back to the fields. Now, slowly sitting down on an embankment between two plots, he stared blankly at his beautiful strips of cropland and the battered old ditch, so dilapidated and cracked it was like a muddy rut. Han Thirty-eight turned his face away abruptly, he couldn't bear to look at it any longer. It seemed to him that the sun was purposely beating down on that old ditch to make it even more dried out and cracked, just to spite him. Those stinging drops of tears began to ooze out of his eyes again.

Scouring and splashing against its muddy banks, the river flowed in a southerly direction until it seeped into the dry, hazy desert. Though its channel was narrow the long-running stream had never once dried up. Year after year it would trickle through the fields and quench the thirst of the parched corn seedlings, pushing before it the silt it brought down from the mountain until, at the edge of the desert, it ran right up against the line of gleaming yellow dunes, which stopped the advance of the moist red clay and forced it to spread out like a fan. Sitting on the raised border of his field, Han Thirty-eight looked into the distance at this red fan made from layer upon layer of silt. Reckon it was thanks to this piece of land that our hamlet had come to be in the first place, he thought, and then had managed, by hanging on to this bit of earth, to get a firm foothold on the edge of the desert. He glanced back at his tiny village. The adobe huts baking under the sun were all dusted with a layer of dull red ocher. This most certainly is not that place called The Nine Palaces, the city of glazed blue tiles inlaid with emerald and jade that the old folk were always talking about. Nothing here but barren flats of gravel and a huge desert, except for Allah's little patch of red clay and stream of muddy water. Our forefathers sure had gumption, he marveled to himself, they took root here on this

poor barren soil in spite of everything. Picking up his spade, he got
onto his feet and walked over to the ditch. In the distance, barely
visible through a shimmering vapor rising from the ground, the
entire village appeared to have taken on a pale reddish tint, while
a blurrily incandescent sun hung motionless above the desert, sending down wave upon wave of infernal heat onto this mortal earth.

Before he began digging, Han Thirty-eight cast his eyes over the
lay of the ditch and then drove the sharp edge of his spade into the
roots underneath a clump of weeds. Hoisting his good leg, he
planted it on the shoulder of the spade and carefully balanced
himself so that when he pushed down on the spade, his gimpy leg
would be barely touching the ground. Then he gave a low grunt
as he scooped up a big lump of clay with the roots still sticking out
of it, and, making use of the momentum, swung the burnished
spade handle up across his knees and dumped the heavy clod of
mud onto a gap in the side of the ditch. Immediately, as the moisture evaporated rapidly from the damp clay, the deep red color
began to fade from its exterior, and a whitish crust spread over the
beveled gouge marks left by the spade. Without a pause Han
Thirty-eight heaped another spadeful next to the first and watched
as the two lumps of soft mud settled into each other. Taking care
to nurse his gimpy leg, he tossed pile after pile of heavy wet clay
onto the clefts in the ditch, panting heavily as he worked, his arms
straining until every muscle was stretched taut. Little by little, a
length of ditch that had been an eyesore began to improve in
appearance as the gaps in its sides, which had looked like missing
teeth, became filled and smoothed out with clay.

Pretty soon the beads of perspiration on his brow turned into
salty rivulets that washed over his sore and swollen eyes. His damp
cheeks felt feverish and tight, as if a fieriness within were being

suppressed and sealed in by his skin. But Han Thirty-eight paid no attention to any of this and continued to wield his spade evenly, serenely. Chunk after chunk of red mud squeaked as it was uprooted, then lay meekly on the embankment above the ditch. He could feel his sweat-soaked cotton tunic being dried by the sun, then becoming drenched again with the perspiration that welled up continuously. But he didn't mind the wear and tear on his clothes —besides, for a peasant a worn tunic was mostly a means of warding off the sun. The important thing was to repair this old ditch. Every other family in the village would be able to irrigate their crops with water from the new cement ditch except for him and Ma Zhuang'er —their fields were too far away. Trying to get out of his share of the work, Ma Zhuang'er had told him that he had to drive his tractor to Hotan tomorrow, and even took the tractor apart right then and there and began to work on its grimy, oily parts like a grease monkey. Han Thirty-eight couldn't help laughing at this— ever since they were kids he'd been wise to Ma Zhuang'er's tricks. His cornfields were behind Ma Zhuang'er's, and were the last to be reached by the old ditch. Ma Zhuang'er knew very well that whoever was at the end of the line would have to make sure that the sections of the ditch before his were also in good repair, other- wise he wouldn't get any water at all. That lazy rat, Han Thirty- eight thought diffidently, as soon as I finish repairing the ditch all by myself and bring in the water he'll show up again, and then all he'd have to do is scratch an opening somewhere and there'd be water for his crops.

It was getting late. Hanging low in the western sky, the sun cast its slanting rays over the wide open desert, and the contours of the undulating dunes were etched in stark outlines of light and shadow. The village, a long stretch of dullish red, was still enveloped within the shimmering vapor rising from the ground. Squinting a little through his sore and swollen eyes, Han Thirty-eight continued to dig away at the ditch, steadily, single-mindedly, stopping only to grab the earthen jar for a drink of water. Turns out it's no big deal that Ma Zhuang'er has sneaked off to Hotan, he thought to himself. When he went to talk things over with Ma Zhuang'er last night he had been quite upset. Actually you were worried that with your gimpy leg you wouldn't be able to do the job alone, and you were hoping Ma Zhuang'er would lend you a hand. At the thought of this, Han Thirty-eight chuckled out loud. How ridiculous he had been the night before! The important thing was not to lose heart.

He finished filling in another gap, and began to walk slowly along the bottom of the ditch. Even if you're in a hopeless situation, as long as you don't lose heart you'll find a way out. You're still a young man, no need to worrying yet about the eye infection and the bad leg.

According to the stories told by the old folk, the Han clan hadn't always been part of the Hui Moslems. They were originally Salars from the twelve villages of Xunhua, in Qinghai province. Then, in one of the many persecutions during those times, troops sent by the Manchu emperor swept through the villages killing everyone in sight. A few families managed to escape this massacre, and, gritting their teeth, crawled out of the piles of dead bodies and fled along the edge of the Great Desert until—thousands of miles later—they arrived here. Eventually they became assimilated into the Huis, but at least those few families did not die out. You can't lose heart, that's all, Han Thirty-eight thought to himself as each motion of the spade became more and more vigorous. It's no easy thing trying to make a living: Digging a ditch, building a house, finding a woman —none of it is easy. But just hold steady, one step at a time, first switch your cornfields over to wheat, then you can send for the woman, and when you've got some money, maybe you can even build some brick houses with tile roofs right here on this red earth.

Lost in his solitary reverie, Han Thirty-eight continued to work evenly, rhythmically, digging up clod after clod of the sticky mud at the bottom of the ditch until twilight began to settle in all around him and smoke was beginning to rise from those blurry huts far in the distance. Above the desert, the setting sun—having turned a dusky red—seemed much more gentle now, and the dark green leaves on the cornstalks were glistening with a golden yellow light.

Just as Han Thirty-eight picked up the jar for another drink of water, he was again stunned by what he saw: There in the twilight, on the undulating, dark brown horizon of the desert was a human figure. It was only after he had searched his brains for some time that he remembered the shaggy-haired stranger who had walked into the desert around noon yesterday, all by himself. Under the setting sun, the desert lay stretched out to the south in gentle crests of soft round curves, and the slopes that were still in the light appeared smooth and clean, with not a single speck of impurity in sight. Squiggling along on the sand dune directly facing him, the diminutive figure stood out in sharp relief, looking like a tiny insect.

It's him! Han Thirty-eight thought in surprise. Yesterday that fellow walked into the desert without a word to anyone, and by now he's been in there almost two days and one night. It's time he came back, he must be so thirsty even his skin is burnt. What are you looking for in there? That's an ocean, I tell you, one that neither god nor man can go across. Han Thirty-eight gave the earthen jar a little shake: It was still half full with clear, cool water. That time I was even more hotheaded than you—three whole days and three whole nights I stayed in there. He began to reminisce about something that had happened far in the past, something that now seemed as vague and hazy as if it had taken place in another life. He had no idea what that shaggy-haired fellow from the city did for a living, but he reckoned that the guy must have a lot of gumption. Well, you can't let that gumption get out of hand though. In silence he rubbed his fingers back and forth over the earthen jar, then set it down again in the shade of the cornstalks before going back to the ditch to work some more in the cool of the evening dragging his gimpy leg as he went. A soft warm breeze wafted slowly by, brushing lightly against his cheeks and giving him a pleasant feeling inside. Bracing himself on his good leg, Han Thirty-eight bent forward from the waist and pressed the weight of his whole torso onto the sharp edge of the spade, his hands tightly gripping the slippery handle. With a squishing noise the spade sliced through the roots of the weeds and thrust straight down into the sticky mud. The faint but unmistakable sensations of wet earth sticking to the back of the spade and of roots being chopped by the blade traveled up to him through the smooth wooden handle. Han Thirty-eight continued to work silently, the evening breeze penetrating his tattered, sweat-stained tunic to caress the muscles on his chest. I'll save that half jar of water for that stranger, he thought to himself, he must be all dried out and burnt. Again a remote feeling of blistering thirst wandered through his memory. What people are capable of if they have that strength of heart, that gumption, he mused as he panted for breath. Legend had it that when their forefathers escaped from Qinghai they suffered untold miseries and hardships along the way, but they kept their minds on Allah and on a place called the Nine Palaces. He remembered listening to his grandfather tell of the place: an unsullied land, with green grass that covered it like a carpet, and nine palaces of glazed blue tile standing in a row. Vigorously tossing the last spadeful of red clay onto the side of the ditch, Han Thirty-eight turned around for a look. Before his eyes was a trim and tidy length of ditch, the newly-dug channel deep and even, the spine arrow-straight, the walls filled and sealed tightly with mud. Just a half day's worth of work and I've already covered so much ground, he thought with satisfaction as he panted heavily. Another three or four days and I can irrigate my crops, and Ma Zhuang'er—well, he could almost see Ma Zhuang'er chortling as he comes up and scrapes an opening in the ditch to water his own land. Han Thirty-eight chuckled and shook his head. That was the way Ma Zhuang'er was; he'd known him well ever since they played together as kids, and by now he was completely used to it.

He looked over at the desert, where the perfectly round disk of the sun was now nestled against the horizon. Below it the earth was a dark expanse through which a layer of deep red was still visible. The waves of sand holding up the setting sun seemed to have solidified, looking like an ocean that had gone to sleep. The tiny figure was still wiggling along, and now Han Thirty-eight could see that the fellow was walking stiffly right in his direction.

He sat down in the shade and felt around with his fingers for the water jar. I'll wait till that shaggy-haired fellow has had a drink of this cool water before I go. It doesn't matter if I get home a little late. He must be dying of thirst, Han thought, he was too hot-headed, too carried away with his heart's desire. Even our ancestors, those staunch and unyielding folk, in the end even they couldn't find those nine palaces of glazed blue tile and green jade, even they had to endure their grief and the injustices against them in silence and settle down on this bank of red clay. He let out a sigh as he tore off a leaf from a cornstalk and began to wipe off the mud sticking to his spade. The figure shambling out of the desert was drawing closer and closer.

Kicking the sand that challenged him at every step, Shaggy Hair gritted his teeth and stumbled along as his feet kept sinking into the soft sand. There was no way he could walk any faster. He had tried vigorously running a few steps, but he ended up wallowing in sand up to his knees. So he went back to the "camel step": lifting up the rear foot gingerly and taking as big a step as you can. And the desert went back to that lazy, monotonous rustling noise, as if it had all the time in the world to torment him. He scratched his head and glared balefully at this yellowish, hazy, endless trap. Right away the desert became silent and still, as if it were sneering maliciously at him. At first, perhaps helped along by the cool of the early morning, Shaggy Hair had walked in a straight line, plowing through dunes and hollows alike, forging ahead in long, swift strides, and in the semidarkness the desert had seemed to step aside and retreat before him, hurriedly opening itself up to expose its wide flat underbelly. And Shaggy Hair had seemed to hear the desert swishing and whispering tauntingly under his feet: So you think you won, so you think you're some hero! When he took out his canteen for a drink of water, the desert had snickered behind his back, and when he screwed the cap back onto the bottle a gust of wind toyed with the flowing sand and hissed: Have some more, drink it all up! And again he heard the sand screeching and laughing shrilly at him. But once the sun was high up in the sky, the desert gradually erased the insidious look on its face and, abandoning all restraint, began to torment him openly, ruthlessly. Within the first hour after the sun became broiling hot, he was already feeling as if every last drop of moisture in his body had been sucked dry by those shiny golden needle-like rays of the sun. His skin felt like a parched and charred sack, drawn so tightly and painfully over his face and hands that he thought it would crack open at any minute. In that same hour he began to lick his blistering lips strenuously and repeatedly, but the desert, turning violent and wild under the fierce sun, was absolutely merciless as it seared his lips and left them encrusted with a layer of dried blood. Then, at about ten o'clock in the morning, a dry wind arose and swirled around him, leaving his mouth and throat so parched he couldn't even make a sound. When he fell headlong into the sand, he clutched his water bottle for dear life. No, I can't drink any now, I've got to save some for the afternoon, he told himself. He knew that in the afternoon it would be even more unbearable, but the desert was so delighted it began to shriek with joy, violently hurling sand and grit all over his body while screaming at the top of its voice: Drink it, drink it all up!

But Shaggy Hair knew very well that this was just an ordeal he had to go through. The desert could not make him lose his bearings: Each time the sun rose a little in the sky he would anxiously check his directions again. Using his watch, his compass and the sun, he was absolutely sure that he was walking step by step toward a green oasis, or perhaps he should say a red oasis, thinking about that peaceful patch of red clay. He had merely penetrated the outskirts of the desert, and even from this periphery he was now beating a retreat. With cool detachment he trudged on, stubbornly saving the half bottle of water for the afternoon. Against the swirling yellow sands that obliterated heaven and earth as they assaulted him head on, against the blistering sun that burned him with its cruel flames—he fought back with all his strength, all the while laughing coldly at himself. He felt an indescribable sorrow. First the retreat, then this life and death struggle even after his defeat —all this filled him with a deep sadness. Actually there's no real danger, he told himself, I'm sure I can get out of the desert and back to that red adobe village before it grows dark. Stumbling with almost every step, he trudged wearily through the sand, ignoring his cracked lips and his burning eyes, oblivious to the incandescent disk above his head. Toghuz Serai, Toghuz Serai, he thought to himself despairingly, I will never be able to find you now. After the two days he had just spent in it he was finally beginning to understand the desert, even as his eyes, burnt by the glare from the glittering yellow sands, had lost all feeling in them. I will never be able to reach Toghuz Serai, he repeated over and over to himself as he walked slowly along, mechanically moving his legs one in front of the other.

He remembered a magazine that he had once come across. In it was an elegantly written article, amply illustrated with photographs and charts, about the French scientist Teilhard de Chardin's expeditions in China. The photographs showed several strange-looking vehicles, specially built for archaeological fieldwork, crawling across a mountain pass in Xinjiang province and lumbering beneath Dongsipailou, one of the decorated archways in old Beijing. The mountain pass was full of jagged, grotesque-looking rocks; the antique archway was ornate and refined looking. Angrily, Shaggy Hair bit his still-bleeding lips. What a first-rate vehicle that was! It had nonskid tires in front, caterpillar treads over its double wheels in the rear, and hanging from its front bumper there was even a metal pulverizer. It was a tank, an iron bear with a steamroller between its teeth, it was a monster. What was there to be afraid of if you were equipped with that? As for me, in this modern day and age almost a hundred years after Teilhard de Chardin, I can't even find a little donkey! Clenching his teeth furiously, he continued to plod along, occasionally falling into deep sandpits, leaving behind him a zigzagging pathway amid the sands. The clumsy shapes of those strange field vehicles lingered for a long time in his mind: He could see them rumbling past with their road rollers lifted high up in the air, while in the background was the archway at Dongsipailou in turn-of-the-century Beijing.

He had shown the magazine to the grayhairs at the museum, enthusiastically suggesting that the museum should also have a few of these vehicles specially made for their research. He would never forget the look the grayhairs gave him as they took in his shaggy hair, a look that even seemed to warn him not to forget his past as a furnace attendant. That's right—he told himself, wearily lifting his sand-filled shoes, his heart filled with a heavy sadness—you made a mistake, you're asking for the impossible. By the time the sun began its descent in the west and the air had turned a little cooler, he was feeling as though he would soon collapse under the weight of this profound pessimism. Several times he wondered whether he had become sick from the relentless torture by the cruel desert and the harsh sun. Retreat, just beat a thorough, clear-cut retreat. The more expert, the more knowledgeable one was about maps and fieldwork, the more clearly one would see that this was the only way. In the last few years, ever since he started working at the museum, he had spent a lot of time doing research in the field, and underneath that thatch of exploding hair there was actually a cool head. He knew the way only too well. Under these circumstances—he thought to himself, angrily, bitterly—the only person who wouldn't know when to quit would be one of those silly girls who let their fantasies run wild, imagining herself to be the damsel in some romantic novel, inspiring her knight in shining armor to ever more daring feats. All of a sudden he thought of his girlfriend. What would she say? he wondered. Most likely she'll send me a telegram of encouragement. Actually this savage and hideous desert may well turn out to be the one who really understands me. It's true—he smiled to himself, forcing his lips apart with great difficulty—the desert is the only one that really understands everything.

The long unbroken line of dunes glimmered in the twilight as deep shadows spread across the dark side of the slopes. Suddenly Shaggy Hair had a feeling that these dunes were the last ones he would have to cross. See how the ridge stands there like a thin, flimsy screen, he thought, its every undulation making it seem not only frail but—he knitted his brows as he tried to fathom the sandy ridge straight ahead—gentle as well. See how its color has also turned weak and flabby, no longer dazzling and irritating to the eye, see how it's looking at me quietly, thoughtfully. Oh, hell, this must be a genuine case of desert sickness, he thought. He just couldn't stand it any more, all these crazy, absurd ideas of his, one after another: now finding fault with his girlfriend, now looking upon this evil desert as his closest friend, the only one who truly understood and appreciated him. I must be sick, he thought. All this has been such a blow, it must have been too much for me, and now I am sick.

When Shaggy Hair reached the crest of that line of dunes lying across his path, he breathed a sigh of relief. It was just as he expected. See, the patch of red soil was right there in front of him. The distant hills straight ahead were already enshrouded in the evening haze, but he could still make out a gash that came zigzagging down from the mist and ended in a little motley patch of red and brown soil shaped like a fan. That's the river, those are the croplands, and over there is the hamlet of the clan of Han, he whispered to himself, identifying each in turn. In the fading light of day he struggled to bestir himself, and then began to walk toward the settlement. The ground, suddenly turned hard and rough, rubbed painfully against his heels. He had no wish to turn his head, no wish to take another look at the desert.

Han Thirty-eight felt rather pleased as he watched Shaggy Hair gulp down the water. The two of them had not exchanged a single word, not even after the fellow had finished drinking all the water in the earthen jar, not even after his breathing had returned to normal and he had had plenty of time to stare into space, lost in his own thoughts. By now exhaustion had crept over every part of Han Thirty-eight's body—even his eyeballs ached and throbbed. He had only been waiting here for Shaggy Hair, and now that he had given him the jug of water, there was nothing else Han wanted to say.

Shaggy Hair sat in a corner of the cornfield and stared rather ruefully at the jar, almost as if he were in a trance. His face looked like it had been smeared with greasepaint—it was shiny and red, and the skin over his cheekbones was burnt and peeling. Without a word this peasant had given him some cool water to drink, which took him a little by surprise. Han Thirty-eight was waiting quietly for this stranger to begin talking. Around the villagers he was known for keeping to himself, for never being the one to strike up a conversation. It was getting dark now. This was such a small village that he felt obliged to invite this young fellow to come home with him for dinner and to spend the night. The dull red sun was barely peeping above the rim of the sand dunes, and the Taklimakhan Desert, after having glittered brightly the whole day long, was already a dark shadowy expanse. The corn leaves began to rustle noisily as the first cool breeze of evening fluttered by. Some grains of sand flew against Han Thirty-eight's iron spade and struck with a few soft, metallic notes. It was time to go home, Han Thirty-eight decided.

Just then Shaggy Hair spoke: "Mister, are you going back to the village?"

"Uh-huh, just about. And you, sir?" Han Thirty-eight asked.

Staggering a little, Shaggy Hair got onto his feet. "Let's go," he said, as, with some effort, he hoisted his knapsack to make it hang more comfortably from his back. Exhausted as he was, he was all the more touched by the friendly manner of this peasant, and rather hoped he could stay in his company for a little while. "Don't call me sir," he said. "You saw me coming out of that desert?"

"I saw you when you went in yesterday," Han Thirty-eight answered. "You've had a hard time these last two days," he said, looking sympathetically at Shaggy Hair's swollen eyes and blood-encrusted lips. "It's not easy to be out on the road. Come home with me, have some soup and noodles with us."

Shaggy Hair looked gratefully at the peasant's simple and honest face. He made an effort to fight off his weariness. "That over there," he said, pointing at the desert with his chin, "have you ever been inside?"

To his surprise, the peasant nodded in reply. "Went in there once for three days. But then I couldn't take it anymore, I had to come back out. It's wicked in there, just an ocean of sand, a dead ocean—" he paused, "and so I had to turn back."

Stopping in his tracks, Shaggy Hair stared intently at Han Thirty-eight as he asked: "In the desert, is there a place called Toghuz Serai?"

Han Thirty-eight looked at him blankly. "Never heard of it."

"In this village here, can I find a—a camel or a donkey?"

"No."

"A car? A tractor? Anything that can go in the desert?"

"No. Why do you want to go into the desert?" Han Thirty-eight asked innocently, gesturing with his upturned palms.

Becoming more and more agitated, Shaggy Hair almost shouted: "Then do you have any bus service? Any kind of transportation? How do people get around?"

His guileless eyes wide open, Han Thirty-eight answered: "No, no transportation." Then, after some thought, he added: "There's only Ma Zhuang'er's walking tractor. He got that year before last. But he has to take it on a long trip, he told me that yesterday, said he has to take his tractor to Hotan tomorrow. He's home today cleaning and oiling the parts, most likely he's really going to Hotan tomorrow. Once he goes, there won't be any transportation in the village at all." Han Thirty-eight gave Shaggy Hair the whole story. Then all of a sudden he remembered something: "Wait, we have camels. Old Gimpy Leg has camels."

Shaggy Hair grabbed him by the arm: "Camels?!"

"Two of them," Han Thirty-eight answered. "Old Gimpy Leg took them with him last year when he left, we haven't seen any of them since. They've gone to Ningxia, I hear, Old Gimpy's kinfolk are in Ningxia."

Shaggy Hair walked along in silence, his head hanging low. By now the sun had already been swallowed up by the vast desert lying dimly to one side of them, and on the horizon nothing was left but a swath of fiery red clouds. The desert seems to be saying goodbye to me, he thought, or maybe it's just taunting me. Well, there's nothing more I can do. Didn't you hear this peasant say, I have to turn back. The village was drawing nearer. The low-hanging rooftops of reddish clay hugged the ground solidly, while wisps of white smoke from cooking fires floated among the dark green trees. What an interesting village, he thought to himself— hiding in the middle of nowhere, far away from any traffic route, hanging on for dear life to this patch of red earth firmly rooted at the desert's edge. Well, it may be humiliating to turn back, but even that's not easy, they don't have any transportation at all in this village.

Han Thirty-eight walked alongside the fellow from the city, his spade hoisted over one shoulder. Somehow he began thinking back to his own journey into the desert. He was only a teenager then, brash and high-spirited. The legend told by the old folk was like a flame that scorched and licked at his heart. How terrible had been the atrocity his ancestors suffered, how deep their sorrow! It was said that in the prefecture of Xunhua the blood of the dead flowed like a river. The emperor had decreed that the Han clan was to be wiped out completely, and there was no one left to turn to, no place on earth where they could pour out their troubles and hope to find justice. So they kept their grief to themselves and kept on walking, they would go to a place called the Nine Palaces, an unsullied paradise where, on a carpet of green grass, they would find nine palaces of blue glazed tiles and green jade, standing all in a row. But, the old folk said, when their ancestors reached this patch of red earth they found this ocean of sand lying across their path. Again and again they charged at it, but each time they failed, and no one who went into the dead ocean came back alive. Finally their ancestors plowed up the red clay and sowed their seeds in the furrows, built their holes in the ground of red adobe bricks, and, burying their heart's desire, squatted here on the edge of the desert. As time went on they forgot their native dialect, and then, as they began marrying girls from the clan of Ma, they gradually became part of the Hui nationality. In the end the clan called the Salars disappeared, and in its place was the village of the Hans. He was just a teenager, Han Thirty-eight remembered, when, his heart burning from this story he had been hearing ever since he was a kid, he walked right into the desert carrying nothing more than a leather sack full of water. That was many years ago now, he thought to himself—back then the old ditch was still wide and deep, back then it didn't need any repairing at all.

They had arrived at the door to his house. Putting down the spade, Han Thirty-eight pushed the door open for his guest and said, "Go in, have some hot noodles in vinegar broth, it will really quench your thirst. Go on, and give me your knapsack." Inside, Shaggy Hair scooped some water into a basin and washed his face while Han Thirty-eight's mother and younger sister bustled about in the courtyard. Then, after Shaggy Hair had taken a seat at the adobe table in the yard and guzzled down a bowl of salted tea, Han Thirty-eight walked over to him slowly—carefully favoring his crippled leg—with a big steaming bowl in his slightly tremulous hands.

"Eat, eat, there's more when you finish this. And then you'll bed down right here. After all, you've been in the desert, you must be dead tired," he said cheerfully as he set down the bowl of noodles and vinegar soup on the table in front of Shaggy Hair. Then, folding his arms, he stood on one side as he waited on his guest, his eyes wide with attentiveness and concern.

Shaggy Hair felt rather embarrassed. What a simple, honest fellow, he thought to himself, he hasn't even asked me who I am and where I'm from. "I am an archaeological researcher at a museum, I came here to do some field work," he said, by way of self-introduction. "Sorry to have troubled you like this. Look at me, what a good-for-nothing I am, the first thing I do is sit down and eat. I didn't even accomplish what I came here for, and now all I do is sit at the table and eat," he said as he looked at the big steaming bowl in front of him.

Han Thirty-eight picked up the chopsticks and presented them to him with both hands. "You've had a hard time, now please make yourself at home. This work you talk about, do you have to go into the desert to do it?"

"I'm looking for an ancient ruin called Toghuz Serai," Shaggy Hair explained, then, pausing to gulp down some hot broth, he added: " 'Toghuz Serai,' don't you know what that means? It's Uighur for 'the nine castles.' "

"The Nine Palaces?" Han Thirty-eight cried out in surprise.

"That's right. But I wasn't up to the job, I didn't find it." Suddenly Shaggy Hair remembered that huge shadow he used to see when he tended the furnace. That shadow was very big, he thought, and I was fooled by it.

Of course you couldn't find them, Han Thirty-eight thought, even our ancestors didn't, and there were none so brave as they. I carried a sheepskin pouch full of water, went into in the desert for three whole days, and I didn't find anything either. Well, well —he thought to himself as he looked closely at this shaggy-haired stranger covered with the dust of his travels—so this young fellow came here to look for the Nine Palaces. Shaggy Hair was busily wolfing down his food. This fellow is one of us, Han Thirty-eight thought as he stared at the head of tousled hair. No doubt about it, anyone who remembers the Nine Palaces must be one of us.

"Cheer up. Take your time, don't eat so fast. Want some hot peppers?" Han Thirty-eight pushed the jar of hot pepper oil toward his guest. "That place, Allah has hidden it, and we can't find it anymore. Here, have some peppers."

Sweating profusely, Shaggy Hair put away bowl after bowl of noodles until, so full he couldn't stuff another morsel into his belly, he waved his hands wearily and mumbled: "Can't find it, that's right, nothing I can do. Why don't I go back, tomorrow I'll go back."

Han Thirty-eight hastened to remind him: "The only way you can do that is to hitch a ride on Ma Zhuang'er's tractor. He's going to Hotan tomorrow on his tractor." As he said this, Han became a little worried. "Let me go talk to him, he'll do what I say. Otherwise, once Ma Zhuang'er leaves on his tractor tomorrow, there'll be no way to get out of here."

Shaggy Hair was silent for a long while. Finally he said: "Let's go find Ma Zhuang'er."

Night had already fallen when the two of them walked out of the courtyard behind the low adobe wall. The sky above the little village was perfectly clear, as if nothing—no clouds, no water vapor, nothing—separated the village below from the brilliant black sky studded with clusters of sparkling silvery stars. Sloping this way and that, the adobe huts squatted silently as here and there an oil lamp cast a flickering orange-yellow light. To the south was a dark, shadowy expanse where nothing at all could be seen, though one could feel the desert's deep breathing on the night wind. Han Thirty-eight limped along as he led Shaggy Hair past one compound after another, going ever deeper into the village. Now and then a few grains of fine sand caught up in the breeze flicked against them as they walked.

FIRST PUBLISHED IN APRIL 1985 IN RENMIN WENXUE *(PEOPLE'S LITERATURE)*

A CHENG was born in 1949 in Beijing. In 1968, like so many other youths during the Cultural Revolution, he was sent to work in the countryside, first at a commune in Shanxi province, then to Inner Mongolia, and finally to a remote part of Yunnan province. He returned to Beijing in 1979 and found work as an art editor for a small magazine while pursuing his interests in painting and fiction. He was one of thirty or so young artists whose works were exhibited in Beijing in 1979 at what has come to be known as the "Stars" exhibition, the first public showing of modern art after the Cultural Revolution and at the time a controversial and celebrated event. In addition to several collections of essays and short stories, he has also published the novellas *The Chess Master* and *The King of the Children,* the latter of which was made into a movie.

CHEN JIANGONG was born in 1949 in Guangxi province and moved to Beijing with his parents in the mid-1950s. After completing his secondary education, he worked as a miner for almost ten years in the coal mines on the outskirts of Beijing. In 1978 he took the first university entrance examinations reinstituted after the end of the Cultural Revolution and was admitted to Beijing University, from which he graduated in 1982 with a degree in Chinese literature. He has published numerous collections of short stories and several novellas.

HAN SHAOGONG was born in 1952 in Hunan province and spent several years on a commune in rural Hunan during the Cultural Revolution. Upon his return to Changsha, the provincial capital, he attended and graduated from Hunan Teachers' College, after which he worked as an editor at a literary magazine before becoming a professional writer. He has published several collections of short stories and novellas.

LI TUO, a member of the Daur national minority, was born in 1939 in Hohhot, Inner Mongolia, and moved to Beijing in 1947 with his widowed mother. After graduating from middle school in 1957, he worked as a fitter in a metalworking factory in Beijing for more than twenty years. He began publishing works of fiction in the mid-1960s and resumed doing so after 1976; since 1986 he has been the executive editor of the literary journal *Beijing Literature.* In addition to several short stories, he has published numerous essays on literary and film criticism and has edited or coedited several anthologies of new Chinese fiction.

MO YAN was born in 1956 into a peasant family in a rural part of Shandong province. In 1976 he joined the People's Liberation Army and shortly thereafter was assigned to its cultural affairs department, where he began writing fiction. He has published several collections of short stories in addition to several novels and coauthored the screenplay for the film *The Red Sorghum,* adapted from two of his novels, which won the Golden Bear Award for best film at the 1988 Berlin Film Festival.

SHI TIESHENG was born in 1951 in Beijing. Upon completing his secondary education in 1969 he was sent to work on a rural commune in northern Shaanxi province. Three years later a grave illness left him permanently paralyzed from the waist down. After his return to Beijing in 1974 he worked for several years as a laborer in a neighborhood factory before becoming a professional writer. He has published several collections of short stories.

WANG ANYI was born in 1954 in Shanghai. At the age of sixteen she was sent to work on a rural commune in northern Jiangsu province. Upon her return to Shanghai after the Cultural Revolution, she worked as an editor of a children's magazine before becoming a professional writer. She has published several collections of short stories in addition to numerous novels and novellas.

ZHANG CHENGZHI, an ethnic Moslem of the Hui national minority, was born in Beijing in 1948. In 1968 he was sent to Inner Mongolia where he worked as a herdsman for four years. In 1972 he returned to Beijing to study at Beijing University, from which he graduated in 1975 with a degree in archaeology. He then worked at the Chinese National Historical Museum for several years before undertaking graduate studies at the Chinese Academy of Social Sciences, from which he obtained a master's degree in history in 1981. Among his published works are several collections of short stories, novels and novellas, as well as scholarly articles in the field of ethnography.

ZHAXI DAWA, an ethnic Tibetan, was born in 1959 in Sichuan province. After spending his childhood in various parts of Tibet and Sichuan, including Lhasa and Chongqing, he and his family returned to Lhasa in the early 1970's. Upon completing lower middle school in 1974, he began working at the Tibetan National Theater in Lhasa, first as an apprentice scenery designer and later as a playwright, before becoming a professional writer. He has published several collections of short stories and coauthored the script for a television program adapted from one of his stories, "Basang and Her Brothers and Sisters," in which he appeared as the narrator.

ZHENG WANLONG was born in 1944 in a rural part of Heilongjiang province but was sent to live with relatives in Beijing after his mother's death in the early 1950s. Upon completing his secondary education in 1966, he was assigned to a pharmaceutical factory, where he worked as a laborer for eight years. In 1974 he began working at the Beijing Publishing House in various clerical and editorial capacities; since 1986 he has been the executive editor of the literary journal *October*. He has published several collections of short stories.

ABOUT THE TRANSLATOR

JEANNE TAI was born in 1951 in Hong Kong and immigrated with her family to the United States in 1969. She obtained a bachelor of arts degree in anthropology and Oriental studies from Barnard College in 1973 and a juris doctor degree from the University of Michigan Law School in 1984. In 1985 and 1986, she spent eighteen months in various parts of China on a legal education and research fellowship, during which she became interested in the new fiction then being published in literary journals all over the country. Eventually, in the course of her travels in China, she met and interviewed nine out of the ten writers whose works are included in this collection.